The Caterpillar Man

Text copyright ©

Cover art by Carl Greaves Extendedimagery.com

A big thank you to my brother James for his support.

Contact
cameronbellauthor@gmail.com

Also by Cameron Bell

The Dead & The Drowning

When The Night Is Dark

**"The shadows
betray you because
they serve me."**

Unknown

CHAPTER 1

The phone call was vague, and Olivia Holland wanted to keep it that way. She asked if I would come and see her. I queried the reason, and her reply was to give her address and a time. If my circumstances had been different I might have pressed harder for some detail, but a bank account on life support was all the incentive needed to defer my curiosity.

It is a quarter to seven when I leave the house and the sun is already dropping behind the rooftops. It is mid-September and the leaves on the Sycamore trees lining the estate where I live are dying, curling crisp at the edges, and drying to a rusty tan.

I take my work car, an eight-year-old dull-blue Mazda 2 hatchback, and drive across town to Pen-Y-Cae Road to meet Miss Holland. I park in the street and look for the house number. It is on the elevated side of the road, the posher side with a better view of the town and the sea.

The house is an imposing turn of the last century red brick with big bay windows and an attic room above the second floor. At one time it would have belonged to a Captain of hard industry: shipping, coal, iron and steel, - dirty industries where the workers hacked up their lungs, bled and died lining the pockets of the town's elite.

The front garden is a well-maintained lawn and long enough to play a decent game of five-a-side football on. I walk up the tarmacked driveway and parked near the front door is a midnight-blue Honda CRV. Reliable and understated, it is a sensible and mature car. A safe bet that the description applies to the owner too - in my experience Hondas and hellraisers do not tend to mix.

The door is opened before I get to it. The man standing on the doormat appears older than he really is. He is snake thin, bald on the top like a monk and has a neat white beard. Passive brown eyes look over a pair of wire-rimmed glasses resting on a drooping nose. He is dressed in a beige cardigan, checked shirt and the kind of sensible green trousers you would find in Mark's & Spencer. One day his creaseless white face would catch up to the clothes and hair.

'Mr Cutter, I presume,' his voice is reedy and educated.

'You presume right,' I say.

'Enter, please … and I will show you to Miss Holland,' he says.

The hallway is spacious and laid with polished wood block flooring. This is complemented by a wrought-iron hat and umbrella rack that is not merely decorative. The retro theme is continued by old fashioned puce flock wallpaper divided by a dado rail to a white artex upper wall and ceiling.

A dog's deep, resonant bark comes from a room at the back of the ground floor. Not the yapping of some toy dog, a proper dog's bark, guttural, and foreboding, belonging I make a guess to a guard breed such as a rottweiler, mastiff or Rhodesian ridgeback.

I am led into a large lounge with a high ceiling. I suspect that blackout curtains must be drawn across the bay window because the left side of the room is a murky black. Against the opposite wall to the window is a bureau with a tortoiseshell lamp. It shines a meek light, faint illumination giving way to dimness and soon after to solid darkness. The man points to a stiff, wingback leather reading chair crafted to have dimples and buttons.

'Take a seat,' he says.

I sit down in the gloom wondering why he has not put a light on and where my prospective client is. He stands at the doorway, and I keep my eyes on him and my ears attuned to what I cannot see. Seconds seem to stretch in the quiet.

'That will be all father.'

I whip my head away from the doorway much quicker than needed to the source of the voice. It belongs to a young woman and is emanating from a corner of the room's cave-like darkness. It succeeds at being eerie and irritating in equal measure.

'A dramatic entrance … or you can't pay your electricity bill.

To be honest, I haven't the time nor patience for either. What is going on here?' And I hear the tetchiness come out in my voice.

'I apologise for the … cloak and dagger theatrics, Mr Cutter, but my reasons will become clear soon enough; and you can be assured I have the funds to pay you.'

Then a searing-red lava screensaver burns a bubble of light into the corner revealing a rough form. A figure smudged by shade and obscured by the plump chair seating her.

She is slim and has her legs tucked underneath her. A slender right hand is resting on her knees while the forefinger and thumb do battle with each other like two rutting stags. I hear the hard flicks and see the rubbing and spiking of the nails into her skin. The light reaches the folds of a baggy grey jumper, though Olivia Holland remains headless.

'It did cross my mind, Miss Holland; now, what can I do for you?'

'We've met before, although I would have left less of an impression on you than you made on me. It was at my friend Amy Oswald's house on Victoria Road. It must be … four years ago now. I was having a drink with her when her ex-partner turned up roaring drunk and got nasty. He smashed the house up and busted her lip open. I phoned 999 and you and a female officer came to help. I remember you bouncing him off the walls and dragging him down the stairs in handcuffs,' and there is a dollop of relish added to the final sentence.

'I can't say I recognize you,' I say dryly.

'You probably wouldn't, even if you could see me,' she replies ruefully.

'So … why am I here?'

'You are very direct,' she says.

'I don't like going around the houses. I prefer to go through the front door. Right now, I'm taking a tour of the estate.'

She gives her warring fingers a break and sparks a cigarette. The tip burns brightly from a strong pull and strands of smoke hang in the air like mist over a dawn lake. Her hand returns to her knee where the thumb fidgets with the filter of the cigarette. The room is unaired and musty, stale smoke-stained air and a smell of unhealthy confinement fuse with the fresh smoke, and something else in the canon of bad human experience.

'Very well Mr Cutter. I will get to the point. The attacks began before you went to Ibiza to find Hannah Morgan. They continued while you were in prison. There have been five that we know of, four in Port Talbot and one in Neath. Same man, same method … night-time break-ins targeting lone women in their homes. He binds, rapes, and disfigures his victims. The last attack was sixteen months ago. He hasn't been caught; he is still out there somewhere.'

Her words crack, stall and waver from emotion; more importantly, she has not just randomly plucked my name from the spewing of a search engine - she has done some homework on me which has gone beyond reading a couple of reviews, which begs the question why? And why again after what she has found out?

'I am one of his victims. It is fashionable these days to use the term survivor, to announce proudly that you are a survivor of abuse or rape or whatever. The thing is Mr Cutter … I don't feel much like one and I resent the expectation that I must be resilient and rise above it. It diminishes what I went through and what it took from me. It took everything.'

I get the drift of where the conversation is going and begin thinking of how I will turn her down.

'The leads have dried up and the trail has gone cold. The police have moved on to other investigations. The case remains open, though despite what the police say I know it has been scaled down significantly. I want to hire you to work the case, Mr Cutter … I want you to catch the bastard.'

With an elbow propped up on the armrest, I bend my head into a lifted hand and stroke my brow with the tips of my fingers. I see my finances flatlining, and under the shield of my hand I grin grimly and suck it up.

'Miss Holland … I'm really sorry for what has happened to you, but I am not going to be able to do anything more than the police have already done. In fact, it will be less and done less well. I won't accept money for a job I have no hope of delivering on. And if another private investigator tells you otherwise ... he or she is stringing you along. Save your money and put your trust in the police. They are not going to give up on a serial rapist. He'll slip up and they will get him.'

I lean forward and press my hand against the arm of the chair. 'Wait! You found Hannah Morgan. You found her in three days. You took on a dangerous biker gang, ruthless sex traffickers and widespread police corruption and sleaze ... and you rescued her. You didn't let anything stand in your way.'

Her flattery feels like a kid pulling on your arm and making a sad face for you to stay when you have to go - the guilt outweighed the good. 'Yes, and I lost a best friend and three years of my life. Her dad and I were like brothers ... Hannah is almost like another daughter to me. I bent and broke laws and crossed moral lines. I made an exception and I paid for it. I don't regret it because they mattered to me, but I don't intend to repeat it. Miss Holland, only prosecution cock-ups, a top-notch defence and a sympathetic jury prevented me from being sent down for murder,' I explain, remembering the appalled faces of the jurors as they listened to the harrowing testimony of Hannah, Amelia, Elena and the other victims of the island's international sex ring.

'It is my money and there isn't anything more in this bloody-awful world that I want to spend it on. I don't care if you don't get anywhere and turn up zero. All I want Mr Cutter is for you to try,' she insists, her thumbnail now bayoneting the pad of her forefinger.

I sit back in the chair defeated; usually, when you tell someone that you are not up to the job, that they would be pouring their money down a drain sponsoring a fool's errand, it is dissuasion enough, heap on top of that an admission of having been tried for murder, and it should have capped it off. Not here though, not with this lady - my time behind bars seems to be an added credential.

'Still, I don't feel comfortable taking your money for

something I have a snowball's chance in hell of getting done. This is police work, needle in the haystack stuff that a Major Crime Team with all the investigatory arsenal at their disposal haven't yet been able to crack. Miss Holland ... my area of work is catching out cheating partners and dishonest employees. It is shining a spotlight on fraudulent insurance claims, it is finding missing persons ... missing dogs even, that's the level I'm operating at,' I say, opening out my hands and then letting them fall and clap on my thighs.

I rock forward and stand up. I hear a click and light from a table lamp sweeps the darkness from her face. I lean back without thinking, an automatic reaction to a truly shocking sight. The poor woman's face is a road map of scars. Deep long ruts arcing across the cheeks from jawline to hairline. A chunk of the left cheek sliced off like a piece of apple, the sides of the mouth cut into a Glaswegian grin, the right side of the nostril split and the scar bending left over the bridge of the nose. Gouges too, the point of the blade dug in, and the flesh picked out leaving craters like the surface of the moon.

The worst disfigurement is a fat red squiggle of scar tissue meandering from the top right lobe of her forehead and dropping off the side of her jaw. It reminds me of a snake tattoo winding from one part of the body to another. It had healed the least because maybe two blades had been used. A convict trick is to melt a toothbrush head and solder a razor blade on each side - the makeshift weapon creates wide, awkward wounds that prove difficult to stitch. It may not be that, but some thought had been put into it, the wrong kind of thought.

I try to look beyond the hateful handiwork and see her and what she was before a madman carved her with a knife into what she is now. She was pretty in a mousey way. Where not scarred the skin from a lack of sun is a pallid light brown. She has neck-length curly dark hair with a suggestion of red, and it is worn in a fringe reaching over the eyebrows and pushed around her cheeks. The hair doesn't conceal her wounds as she intends it to.

Her features are small and frugal, like whoever was dishing them out didn't have quite enough after making the eyes. She has sad cow eyes, heavy and bagged. I bet those eyes hardly close unless forced to by a doctor's prescription. I picture four o'clock terrors and those restless, twitchy eyes and destructive fingers, Olivia feeding herself cigarettes, wrapped in her seat, or pacing the room, her own horror film playing on a loop in her head.

Olivia Holland locks her eyes onto mine and says, 'Rape and this to five women. Five lives ruined. The third victim, Kelly Thomas, killed herself. His second victim, Jodie Green, is a catatonic shell on a psych ward at the Caswell Clinic; the rest of us aren't doing too well either. I need to undergo several surgeries to have something remotely resembling a normal face. And inside … well no surgeon can fix that. Somewhere in this town or one nearby is another woman who is going to go through this. Take the job Mr Cutter … please.'

I put my hand out in submission to stop the mauling I am getting from a six-hundred-pound emotional tiger. I say to her, 'All right, you win, I will take the job. It is twenty-five pounds an hour or a flat two hundred a day plus any expenses I incur, and some of those expenses you won't get receipts for.'

'That will be fine; can you start right away?'

'No, I have another job that I am halfway through. I should have it finished in a day or two and then I'll devote my time trying to track this monster down,' and as I say the words they ring hollow to me and sound insincere.

'I see on your website that you accept PayPal. Phone me when you are ready, and I'll send you a two-week advance.'

She reaches over to an oak Hatcher side table. Below the reveal lamp is a shelf with an A4 sized manilla envelope. She fishes the bulging package through the gap and hands it to me, the light and shade playing with her scars as she moves. 'In the meantime, you can familiarise yourself with the case. I've typed every painful detail I can remember and all the facts that the police have told me. If you have questions after reading it, I'll do my best to answer them.'

It is dusk when I walk back down the drive and the warmth of the day has left. I drop into the car and puffing hard through my lips finish in an exasperated frown. Way to go, Will, you played that well, as patient and tactful as a barbarian at the gate.

Her striped face visits me on the drive home, one of a dozen returning thoughts and images twirling in my head like a carousel. I don't want this case. For some, it would be money for old rope. Go through the motions for a month, kick the arse out of it for two - tap into that hot streak of revenge and take the messed-up girl's money.

I shake my head and screw my lips, 'Nah,' I say quietly to my own audience, I don't want to do that. I don't want to profit or exploit, not even passively, not even with her full, eyes-wide-open consent. It is fraudulent and I would become something I don't like. Sure, I lie, when I need to, when it is for the greater good - If you swim with sharks you must learn to smile like one. There is a difference though, and you must know it, or you'll slide into dishonesty, and you won't be able to tell which of the two faces is truly yours. I'll tell her tomorrow. I'll tell Olivia that I could do no good for her. I'd be chasing a phantom. The case is a white whale, and I had no desire to be Ahab or a shyster.

I pop the cap on a bottle of chilled Birra Moretti and sit in front of the computer. The tower whirrs to life. It is ten years old which must be the equivalent in dog years for a computer and the screen loads slowly. I suppose I should remove some more programs and defrag the hard drive again. I swig down some beer and wait because rushing to get online only slows it down more. I check my watch and log onto Chess.com. Xavier is already in our game.

I met Xavier Juan Rojas whilst incarcerated at Ibiza's Centro Penitenciario awaiting trial, and he rekindled a childhood enjoyment of chess. After my convictions for obstruction of justice, possession of firearms and endangering the public, I was shipped off to Algeciras Prison on the mainland, whereas luck would have it Xavier was transferred three months later.

Xavier was serving five years for beating his wife's lover into a three-month stay in hospital. He was a financial advisor, lived a square life, and never put a foot wrong until finding his wife in bed with the gardener. Then a different Xavier emerged, one he had no idea was there until the release button was pushed.

I video call him on WhatsApp and his picture appears. He is a trim fifty-five with thick black soap opera style hair greying at the sides. His eyebrows are wide and wayward, and he sports a walrus moustache below a bulbous nose.

I say to him, 'Hey, hermano, how have you been doing?'

'Good, I've been looking forward to destroying you all day.'

'To be fair Xavier, you're only beating me four out of five times now. Soon it will be only three out of five. I'm improving more than you are improving, so watch out.'

'I don't think I need to worry; the time I don't win you only manage a draw. It is true that you've got better because you couldn't have been any worse, but that mind of yours Guillermo, it is full of abstraction and distraction,' he says, breaking into a laugh.

We play and I lose decisively. He boxes me in tight and slowly strangles my position until it is hopeless, and I concede the game but three moves from a checkmate that even I can see coming.

We schedule a time for a game later in the week and finish our call. I drain my second beer and leave it at that. I now open the door to the thoughts that had sneaked in and trespassed during the game. The manilla envelope is on the dining room table. I think about opening it and reading the gruesome facts of the case. There is no point other than a prurient interest to do so. I leave it on the table and go into the kitchen.

I select a frozen chicken Biryani from the freezer and fry it for twelve minutes in a wok. I eat it at the dining room table while reading *The War of the Roses: The Fall of the Plantagenets and the Rise of the Tudors* by Dan Jones. I go to bed early and take the book with me. Reading for an hour does not make me drowsy, and impatient for sleep to come I go back downstairs.

In the drawer of the sideboard is my lockpicking wallet, my

collection of locks and a Yost portable vice to hold them in place. I became interested in lockpicking about ten years ago after seeing a locksmith swiftly access a property with minimal disturbance.

An energy company suspected that a customer had tampered with the meter and was abstracting electricity. They obtained a warrant to examine the meter and repair any cack-handed system of diversion. They hired a locksmith to gain entry and asked the police to attend in case there was anything more than verbal opposition.

After the shift, I looked into it online and found that it is a hobby with competitions and dedicated Youtube channels. I ordered a basic lockpicking set from Amazon, played around with it, and soon got the bug. From there I progressed onto tougher, complex locks and a more advanced toolset.

I select a grade two standard security padlock and a five-lever mortice cylinder door lock and carry them along with the vice over to the dining room table. From the wallet, I take out a tension wrench and insert the short flat ninety-degree end into the bottom of the padlock's keyway. Holding the handle, which is the same as a nail file, I quarter turn the tool until the right amount of torque is applied to the lock plug. I tease out a three-peak raking tool from the holder and inserting it above the wrench vigorously scrub the lock until each of its pins hit the shear line and sit on the ledge. This happens in under fifteen seconds, and then with pins set the tension turns the lock all the way, and the shackle springs open.

I repeat this a dozen or so times, then moving on to the mortice I change over to a longer-headed tension wrench. I then use a short hook to single pin pick the lock. The short hook has the same nail file handle and slim neck but with a head like a golf putter set to sixty degrees.

This technique is far more involved and the attention to the process empties my head of extraneous thought. Edging the tip of the hook along the line of five pins I press upward listening for a quiet click of the pin being set on its ledge. The order of manipulation for this lock is four, two, three, one and then finally five, and after two minutes of probing and listening to find the correct combination, the lock gives way.

For over an hour I fiddle with these locks and others in the drawer for fun, relaxation and for getting into places I have no right to be.

CHAPTER 2

The alarm from my phone wakes me at half-past six. I put on a pair of training shorts, an old t-shirt that shouldn't be allowed out of the house and lace on a pair of Lonsdale boxing boots. In the kitchen, I neck a pint of water, eat a banana, and make a strong coffee. I listen to the news, drink the coffee, and walk myself awake by doing laps of the kitchen.

By quarter-past-seven I am in the garage for a morning communion with the heavy bag. I stretch a sweatband around my forehead, slip the left hand into a fourteen-ounce glove and on my phone play a Spotify playlist called *'Punch'*. I set the timer for thirty minutes and ten seconds and start it, then rush to wriggle on the right glove and fasten the velcro strap with my teeth.

The heavy bag is hit and miss. Of all training modalities, it is the harshest and most unforgiving of weakness. If a little off, I can still slog through a run or grind out reps with a kettlebell - not so on the bag. The bag requires pep, needs zing and pop. Feel flat, a little listless and it will push your tiredness back on you twofold.

The first few minutes are the tell and today my fists snap into the tarnished brown bag with satisfying thuds. My heavy hooks dig deep into the one-hundred-sixty-pound hunk of leather and cloth, and it jigs on the chain like a man dropped through the trapdoor of a gallows.

Over and over, I pour myself into it and throw my soul into its destruction. If you mistreat it correctly it will break in three to four years - and I have owned several. Today is a good day and I stay strong sending forth thunderous volleys until the alarm signals the end of the session.

Drenched in perspiration, I return to the house and shower. I have the water tepid, then cold to stop the sweat. After drying off, I dress in khaki chinos, a navy-blue polo shirt, a fitted brown, V-neck woollen jumper and brown Altberg boots.

I pull down the loft ladder and climb up. I open a fire-proof case that I keep important documents in and extract the keys for my firearms cabinet. I unlock the cabinet and a pang of loss sinks through me. I know it is empty, nonetheless, I feel it like the first time - when the day I returned home the police confiscated my guns.

I am a convicted criminal and criminals cannot own guns, not even legal-limit air rifles. All I have left is my Titan Hunter catapult and the nine, ten and twelve-millimetre lead ball bearings that I let fly with it. I grab the padded delivery envelope lying on the floor. It is fat with twenty-pound notes - four and a half grand fat. I take it to the kitchen and toss it on the table. I make myself a strawberry protein shake.

I sit down to drink it and consider the two envelopes in front of me. One a solution to a problem, the other? Well, just a problem. The cash - a long hand to pull a man named Lloyd Jenkins out of a big bloody hole. The file, I find myself staring at it for longer than you should when you've already made a decision.

I take the car keys off the hook and realise this will be one of the last times that I drive the Toyota Hilux. No guns, no hunting, no off-road farms, no money, no need.

I can now add broke to my résumé. It will sit nicely between ex-cop and ex-con. A sometimes employed, small-town P.I. eking a living sticking his snout in other people's dirty laundry. The Hilux belongs to someone faring better than I am.

It is currently on Autotrader, and I have already had a nibble. In the forty-eight hours since the ad had gone live, I have had two time wasters call and a car dealer from Newport showing genuine interest.

The car dealer knows what he can sell and will probably take it off my hands. The issue with the dealer is going to be the asking price and how much he is going to want to chisel that down. It is one of those situations where you want to have the excuse of having tried but would be happy if no one bought.

Outside drizzle falls from a dirty-white sky. In Port Talbot, it is difficult to discern whether a dirt-smudged sky is rain cloud, smoke, or some other pollutant. I drive into an area of town known colloquially as Little Warren - a dozen streets curling into each other like a confusing connection of rabbit burrows – I never saw it myself.

The area is clearly defined by the river Afan to the east, the beach to the south, Newbridge Road to the north and Victoria Road to the west. Near the beach there are some attractive and expensive houses, but most streets are a result of a mass building project from the 1960s and are named after famous writers.

I park in Dickens Avenue and pull up the hood of my green Trespass windbreaker. The rain is busy pattering rings in the puddles, and they form in the gutter and in the basins of an uneven pavement. I walk a short distance to Darwin Road and search for number eight.

Number eight is a semi-detached house with a double extension on the side backing onto the Green Stars Playing fields. It is coated in sand-coloured pebbledash and has brown window frames and a matching door. The front garden is covered in concrete and patterned with an imprint of slate-grey paving stones fanning out in concentric circles. It functions as an extended driveway and a pearlescent-white BMW X5 SUV bearing the registration plate SN87OKNG is parked there. A red-brick wall mounted on the end pillar by a Stallion's head statue partially encloses the driveway.

What I know about Sean King I could write on the back of a business card. He is originally from Aberdare, has a much younger partner called Kaylee and an adult son named Jayden from another relationship. He works the doors, is an avid bodybuilder and enthusiastic fisherman.

He also lends money to people to who no one else will lend money to. I found out most of this information from reading his Facebook profile. I learned that he is an unscrupulous loan shark from speaking to my client.

I ring the doorbell and stand back from the door. A bald man, early forties, reddish tanned and built like a brick shithouse, answers.

Sean King fills the doorway. He is a fraction broader than me, then again maybe not, but does have about an inch of height, which would put him at five feet ten inches tall. The real difference between us is mass - King has the thickness of a rodeo bull and must weigh around seventeen stone.

He wears red trainers with graphite-grey joggers and a matching long-sleeved top, that is as thin and tight over his muscles as a surgeon's glove.

'Mr King, my name is William Cutter and I work for Gerald Jenkins. I am here to settle the debt of his son Lloyd Jenkins.'

King says nothing. He looks at me, then over my shoulder, then casts his eyes over the street. I begin to think they are shrewd eyes.

King cups the knuckles of his right hand in the palm of his left and the two thumbs tap out a Morse code that only he has knowledge of. He ought to have hands like a gorilla, but he has average-sized hands, and they look like those of a watchmaker when compared to the rest of him. His feet, also, are only about a size six or seven and his head has the delicacy of a man much lighter - he is not a naturally big man.

King moves his mouth into a straight-lipped smile, and it manages to convey the warmth of a dead fish. 'You said you worked for Gerald Jenkins … what as?' asks King in a deep, even voice.

'A delivery boy,' I reply, flashing a smile.

'You don't look much like a delivery boy to me … more like a copper.'

And it is true, that twenty-five years of policing with all that it entails will leave an indelible stamp on your face.

I sigh and say, 'It has been said. Look, I understand your suspicion but I am just here to pay off a bad debt. My client doesn't get out much. He has advanced COPD and is hooked up to a tank of oxygen for most of the day. Lloyd, as you know, is an inveterate gambler and cannot be trusted with money. Giving it to him to pay you will only give the bookies a profitable day. So, that is where I come in.'

King nods slowly, although does not seem convinced.
'Listen, I'm not Police or Trading Standards. If I were, there'd be a bunch of us with a warrant and a big red key to bash your door down with. This is what it is.'

I hold the package out and say, 'Here is four and a half grand, consider the loan and interest paid in full.'
I receive that winning smile again and he takes the envelope. He rips the top open and flicks through the ninety notes. 'This is a good start, but they are twelve hundred light. I am now owed five-seven. Go back to your boss and deliver that message.' And the order is issued with a slow, get-right-under-your-skin condescension.

It is neither my money nor my grief. I could go back and tell Gerald to cough up more money, even though I know he is broke. I don't think I want to have that conversation. I roll aching shoulders and the motion reminds me of my old mucker Jay. He would tell this inflated bag of meat to piss off.

'The loan was eight hundred. Five and a half times the return is enough. I couldn't give a tiny rat's arse about your forty per cent compound interest … it's all made up bollocks and illegal. That's your lot sunshine, accept it and close the account.'

'Or what! What are you going to do to stop me collecting,' and he punctuates the reply with a pointed finger.
'That is a good question. I wanted to appeal to your better nature, but it appears you don't have one. You've taken a great big bloody chunk out of a dying man, whose only wish is to save his useless son from broken kneecaps. I say to you, don't be greedy, save the old man a lot of grief and leave it there.'

The skin around his eyes creases and the tongue flicks the bottom lip. Then the flatline smile, if that is what it is. His voice now has an edge to it when he says, 'I don't give a fuck for hard-luck stories or you telling me my business. Lloyd knew what he was getting into. So, I'm going to collect what's owed … and you,

you can fuck off!'

He laces his fingers together and they are turned over and clicked. I think it is meant to intimidate me - it doesn't, and I wonder what the next tactic will be in the doorman's repertoire. I don't have to wait to find out; King steps forward and I step back. Taking the backward step I test the grip of my boots on the rain-slicked concrete, and it holds.

He ambles forward a couple of paces into my reactionary gap - a three-yard radius of safety I like to keep so I can see surprises coming. After retreating two steps I drop the right leg back and load the hip.

'As I thought, you're all noise and no bottle. Stick your tail between your legs and tell Gerald he has ten days to get my twelve hundred. After that, it'll be seventeen hundred.'

I smile as King mops his driveway with my pride. His words prick at me and riled, I bite, 'You shouldn't underestimate me. I can make your life difficult. You're thinking violence but that is only one strand of the rope I could put around your neck.'

I can taste the salt in my words and the eagerness of my mouth to get the rest of me in trouble. At fifty knocking on fifty-one years old, I know myself well enough for this not to be a surprise - I'm a dumb dog that will never learn.

'You're an old cunt past his sell-by-date if you ever had one at all. Now, get the fuck off my drive!'

His shoulders flexing give me a warning. I skip back from the push and only his fingertips make contact with my chest. With the eyes widening and the lips pursing, a greater effort is made to shove me. I cuff his right hand away with my left and slide away in that direction.

Before he knows he's in a fight I pop him in the nose with a scorchingly-quick straight-right hand, thrown with a loose arm and no show. King makes a sneezing face as the punch stings him. His hands flinch to the place of attack as I want them to, swatting for a fist that is no longer there.

I shift all my weight onto the left foot and stab a vicious left hook into his liver - it feels like hitting a side of beef. The involuntary grunt supplies the feedback that the shot has hit where it should and hurt. I pivot out. King's face is suddenly strained. The arms come down and hug his sides and a split-second later he folds like a deckchair.

Kneeling and doubled over, it appears as if he is in the act of committing Seppuku. He lifts his head, helpless and unable to move, his body shut down by cramping pain. A bead of blood rolls out of his nose.

'Pushing is for pussies, Sean. I've closed the account. If you call on them, I'll call on you.'

I walk out into a rainy overcast street. I look back because I am careful instead of cool. Still suffering, King gets up and goes back inside the house. I run to the car because dented pride can make a man reach for something to restore it.

CHAPTER 3

On the way home I stop at Olive Street to see Gerald Jenkins. Gerald lives in an Edwardian mid-terrace house between a settled Irish Traveller family and a young single mother with two kids.

For most of the day, Gerald sits alone in his living room. A solitude only interrupted by the carers that call twice a day. Lloyd comes and goes depending on who he has upset. At the moment valuing his kneecaps he is elsewhere.

I stand on the pavement outside the door and think how I will explain the change of plan - that his four and a half grand may not have bought him peace of mind after all. I realise I'm not a guarantee of that. Sure, I had humbled King a little and given him something to think about. But it was far from absolute, not a drubbing, not abject humiliation, not compliant fear - just an initial skirmish if the man has the mind, the heart and resentment to feud.

Whether King is a plastic gangster who is easily discouraged or a serious player who is not going to let this lie remains to be seen. I had given Gerald Jenkins better service than he had asked for and saved him money that he didn't have. That is the positive spin on it. Of course, I may not have done either of those things and only succeeded in making matters worse. I go about persuading myself that what I did was right and my reasons noble. It is a con I fail to pull off. Mixed in with the right reasons are a couple of wrong reasons and my conscience sees where I'm trying to hide them.

I am still staring at the front door when a flatbed lorry jammed with junk rattles into the street and squeezes into a space between two cars. An irregular pile of scrap metal composed of radiators, washing machines, children's pedal cycles, old boilers, copper piping and garden gates threaten to spill onto the road.

A criss-cross of tie-down straps holds it together, though I am sceptical of the load being safe.

The driver climbs out of the cab. He is a heavyset man with a well-fed belly and wild, wavy black hair. He has on a blue and red checked padded work shirt, faded-black sweatpants marked with a streak of white paint and a pair of brown rigger work boots. A lively-faced boy, aged about fourteen, jumps out the other side smacking the pavement hard in his scuffed, oversized rigger boots. Settled or not, scrap came before school.

I knock on the door and allow plenty of time for Gerald to answer. There are roses etched in the small glass panel inset into the white UPVC door. Hunched over, Gerald wobbles in the haze of the dimpled glass.

'Mr Jenkins, it's William Cutter.'

Gerald opens the door and holds onto it. Gerald is short, small, and round-shouldered like a jockey. He has a good head of ivory-white hair combed neatly from a side parting. The skin of a gaunt face is marred by spider veins and the drawn-out process of dying. At a guess he is a shade over seventy, though he could be several years younger - people have a habit of ageing badly in this town. The shirt he wears hangs loose around the collar and the belt around his trousers is pulled in tight. He is underweight and it passed the point of it becoming a problem fourteen pounds ago.

He struggles silently for breath as if he is sucking on a straw clogged with cotton wool. The face sags with exhaustion and a purply-blue tincture to his thin lips denotes a man starving of oxygen.

I give Gerald my arm and help him to his chair in the living room. I watch frail, liver-spotted hands desperately work an oxygen mask over his mouth. I know better not to fuss; he chided me the first time we had met when I offered more help than he needed.

I take a seat on a sofa covered by a traditional Welsh blanket. The room is quaint and of another time. It is clean and ordered. Hanging on a white painted wall are four Welsh love spoons intricately hand-carved out of limewood. Next to them, is a painting of black-faced miners leaving a colliery after a shift underground. On the mantelpiece are a brass Davy lamp and an iron fireplace set which includes a poker, tongs, shovel, pan, and brush suspended on a stand. The hearth is an old coal fire still in use. I got rid of a crappy convection heater with its fake log fire facade, and like many other homeowners replaced it with a multi-burner. Gerald never changed anything, and the trend had circled to him.

'I've paid Sean King the money, the trouble is it wasn't enough. The interest had hiked the debt to five thousand seven hundred. Four days sooner and it would have been wiped.'

'I haven't … got anymore … money,' he wheezes, and I lean forward on the edge of the sofa to hear him better.

'I know, I know this has cleaned you out. So, we had words and I leaned on him a little, and it might be all right.'

'It's now … five-thousand seven hundred?' says Gerald.

'Yes, but I told him four-five was all he was getting.'

I see confusion elide with illness and both weighing heavily on his face. Then it strikes me I have only my word that the transaction went the way it did. What would be my angle? - skimming twelve hundred off the top, short-changing King and leaving part of the bill unpaid. I would hate it if he is thinking that of me, although my mind is performing the same cynical calculation. Pleasingly, such a scam runs aground pretty quick. King would say the number and explain the math and Gerald would know I played straight. Unless King lies and tells Gerald I only gave him three-three. I'm exposed and I don't like it. I should have covered my arse better and worn the buttonhole camera and recorded the pay-off.

'Will, you said it might be all right … what do you mean?'

'I mean he may back off or he might still try and collect. If he does, you call me. He has no right to demand that level of interest; loan sharking is illegal, and you've already paid him more than you should.'

'Right, Will … now what do I owe you?'

It was a simple job until I chose to make it complicated. I had interviewed Lloyd, browsed a few social media pages, and ran Sean King through an investigative database that I pay a subscription to. It was where I found his address listed as the company address of Centurion Security Solutions. From there I only had to pick up and drop off the money. In all, probably four hours of work.

'In hours, the job took half a day ... so, that'll be a hundred ... no eighty pounds will cover it,' I say.
Gerald picks up an old brown leather wallet from an occasional table at the side of his chair. He fingers through the dividers and shakily tweezes out some twenties and a single five-pound note.

'I'm ashamed to say I've only got sixty-five ... but I'll be able to pay you the rest ... when my pension is paid this Thursday,' he struggles to explain.
It is Tuesday. Two days to have bugger all in his wallet. 'It's all right Gerald, just give me forty and forget the rest.'
'No ... I want to pay you ... call by Saturday and ... I'll have it for you.'
'No, really, it's fine. I get to decide what I charge for my time ... and today it's forty per cent Tuesday.'
I walk over to him and pluck two twenties from his hand. 'Any grief from meathead and you give me a call, okay. Don't get up, I'll see myself out.'

I'd made forty quid and an enemy, Gerald had sacrificed his savings, and King had multiplied his money. There is no doubting Gerald and I are holding the shit end of the stick. It rankles, it really does. I might have to do something about it.

Loansharking is largely an invisible crime. The victims are complicit. They willingly get in bed with their lender, and though they won't like how much they are screwed - they agreed to it and direct the blame to themselves. Loan Sharks also tend to be nasty individuals with reputations for violence, and fear is an effective zip for loose lips. Perhaps I could build a case for the police?

It is still miserable outside and the old terraced streets -

enclosed, impoverished, treeless make it more so. A smack rat I used to know rides past on a mountain bike, hood on, fag in mouth, hands off the handlebars. The bike could be his, was someone else's, could still be someone else's - nothing is a given. Beg, borrow, steal, sell, barter, and buy, street commerce where brown is gold and money is fleeting - out of the hand and into the arm.

On the way home I continue to ponder the iniquity of the world. First on the big stage and then how it featured in an obscure little sideshow in a dirty Welsh town. King had bled a dying man dry, and someone got off on ripping apart young women's faces. I put the radio on and try to think of something pleasant - I don't.

From the time I stop the car I am in motion. I make a flask of coffee, grab the Titan Hunter and a bag of shot from the loft and chuck them and a pair of binoculars in a rucksack. I rummage around in the garden shed for my rodent target. It is a sitting red rat fashioned out of a steel plate, attached to a thick spring middle and a spade-shaped strip at the end to plunge into soil. It goes into the rucksack too and hooking it over my shoulder I head back out.

I walk to Pentwyn Road and to the West End Service Garage - an MOT testing station shared for the last ten years with a Kurdish hand car wash. I cross the road and climb the winding lane leading to a row of houses nestled into the foot of the mountain called Fernfield. But before reaching Fernfield I divert left, into a steep, narrow lane just shy a few feet from being better described as a track.

I hike up, passing a lone house patrolled by four noisy Border Collies who bark themselves into a tizz. From there I enter a flat firebreak separating two swathes of fir trees. After eighty yards I emerge onto a burnt mountain of charred tree stumps, blackened grass, and balding earth. The consequence of summer fires ignited by an arsonist's match.

I plant the eighteen-inch target on the high side of the path, so it is roughly level with my height. I estimate twenty-five yards and set the rucksack down. I load the catty reminding myself to pinch the pouch in front of the ball. I push the paracord wrapped frame out sideways with the left hand while drawing the band with the right. Anchoring my thumb to the corner of my mouth I use the dimple in the top fork as a point of reference. I place it over the three-inch rat and release the shot. The twelve-millimetre lead ball clanks into the rat's chest. The spring absorbs some of the impact from the twenty-foot pounds of energy that the band and ball produce and the rat nods furiously.

On an elemental level I connect with loading, aiming, and shooting, be it a shotgun, rifle or slingshot. And over the next hundred shots or so, I clear out my head and achieve an almost zen-like state through the simple repetition. I don't record an overall score, but out of every ten times, it is never more than three and never less than one that the rat's ears don't get rung.

CHAPTER 4

Hungry from the mountain, I am at my table eating a roast chicken and spinach ciabatta toastie garnished with a chilli chutney. I am also pretending to read a book. It is no fault of the book, it is interesting and sharply written, nevertheless, my eyes stray over its pages to the file on the table. I hadn't phoned Olivia Holland yet. An earlier rehearsal was awkward and weaselly. It seemed whichever ethical explanation I chose, or however I phrased it, I could not escape sounding like a reneging piece-of-shit. I hadn't stuck to my guns and now respect is lost either way.

I pick up my mobile phone and stare at the screen as if it is an oracle that will eventually reveal an answer. The phone rings. It is an unknown landline number. I answer it.

'You are fucking dead. I'm going to break every bone in your body for that cheap shot.'

'There was nothing cheap about that left hook Sean, years of practice paid for it. That punch dropped a future world champion, so a no-skill chump like you …'

King interrupts, 'You've got a smart mouth Cutter. You only caught me because you sucker punched me …'

'You said it, Sean,' I counter, cutting him off as he did me.

He is livid now, absolutely hopping mad and ineloquent in rage as he spits into the phone, 'You, you … fucking prick! … I'm, I'm going to knock all your teeth out and smash your jaw in seven places.'

'Is that before or after you break every bone in my body,' I taunt, bitch-slapping him down the line with a carefree insolence.

'You wait, you wait … you fucking slag, you'll be sorry when I get hold of you. I'm going to burn you, then bury you in a forest.'

'Well, thanks for the warning dumbo, perhaps I'll see you before you see me.'

I cut the call. The forgive and forget box is left blank and a big bloody cross struck through the option for a feud and a funeral in the forest. King seeing the error of his ways was always an outside chance.

Pacing the kitchen, I backhand an empty plastic milk jug off the counter, and it pinballs off two kitchen cupboards and onto the floor. Not satisfied, I convert it over the table and into the bowl of fruit on the sideboard. Not even a month out of prison and I'm up to my neck in it again.

If he can find me, let him, take it as it comes, roll with the punches then counter. At least that way if he got hurt I could claim self-defence, and avoid a further stint behind bars. However, the problem with waiting and reacting is you've got to get the chance to react. If King got the drop on me, it could be over before I got wise to it. If he turned up in numbers, it wouldn't matter anyhow. Sitting back and waiting is like allowing a crocodile onto a boat and then asking it to leave.

I could always go to the police, but that is a can of worms waiting to be opened. King would probably hit back with a counter-complaint of assault, and if he is devious, he'll get his Mrs, or his son or a lackey to back his story. There is an alternative - stamp it out, kill it before it can get off the ground. Set up an ambush and put him in traction. Inflict a diminishing and debilitating injury to discourage any further ideas. From a tactical standpoint it is the sensible course of action to take, but the way out is also the way back inside. If I go down that road, I'll need to cover my tracks.

The phone rings. It is a mobile number. I answer like a fizzing rocket about to screech into the sky.
'Mr Cutter, it's Olivia Holland, are you free to speak?'
I disarm my tongue and reload it with a friendly reply, '... Hello, Miss Holland, yes, I can speak and please call me Will,' and inside I'm squirming.
'I know I'm impatient ... calling you when you said you would call me. I'm afraid it's a symptom of an overactive mind fixed to a bad use. Much like a washing machine on an endless cycle churning, churning, churning ... no rinse though ... ha. My

therapist talks about talking, about processing, about closure … she likes the washing machine analogy by the way. What do I want to say? … oh yes, you are taking this case, aren't you? You see I doubt myself, mistrust what I hear, see, and believe … another treasure from the changing of me. I'm prattling on, aren't I? But you haven't changed your mind? … have you completed your other case yet?'

She sounds fuzzy and scattered, her words being led astray by her prescription and an unknown accomplice - booze, weed, more meds. I am on the verge of telling her, yet I am unable to pull the trigger and say it - I lack the heart.

'Will, you are not saying anything … are you annoyed at me?'

'No, not at all,' I say, as my conscience and compassion duke it out.

Despite deciding against aiding false hope, it feels crueller right now to crush it and walk away. Turning my back on a messed-up woman with a split face.

'I'm ready to work on it. I'll read up tonight and make a start tomorrow.'

'Good, it makes me happier to know you'll be looking for him, hunting him … watching over me … Will …'

'Yes.'

'Never mind … no, I'm curious to know, how many bad men did Jason, and you kill in Ibiza?'

'I prefer not to say.'

'I'm sorry, I shouldn't have asked … sorry. But you are starting tomorrow?' she slurs.

'It's okay, it's fine. And yes, as of now Olivia, I'm working for you,' I say, slowing down my words and handing them out with kid gloves.

'This morning, I baked a chocolate orange cake, it's rather wonderful, I can save you a slice if you like?'

'Thank you, that'll be nice. Olivia, have a good evening, I'll speak to you tomorrow.'

I spend the first part of the evening fortifying my home in

readiness for an attack. The good news is the basics are already in place. Both front and back doors are made of a tough composite plastic and have Ultion multi-point locks. Motion activated security cameras are fixed high on the front and back of the house. Inside the integrity is protected by a burglar alarm and a fire bag behind the letterbox.

My home is a semi-detached three-bedroomed house situated at the end of a close. It has a short front garden which I converted to an open drive and can accommodate two cars. A path at the side of the adjoined garage leads to a wrought-iron gate secured by a padlock. A six-and-a-half-foot high wall encloses the back garden. Regrettably, the top of the wall is flat brick. A little uncomfortable for the bare hand, though nothing to cry about. A reasonably athletic man could haul himself over without any bother. Accomplishing this led to the weakest point in the defence - the conservatory. Easily breached by a simple builder's brick - going through the patio door would take a twentieth of the time as either one of the reinforced doors.

I needed to turn a good idea into a bad one and an obscure police memory provides a solution. I remember a wall backing onto a lane in old Aberavon. As a deterrent to climbing his wall the owner had thought to cement broken glass bottles along the top. I spotted it in time and chose another wall to scale, finding vantage, to survey the rows of terraced gardens for a disturbed burglar going to ground. Tomorrow, I crown the top with jagged shards of Birra Moretti; it'll make the wall look like something out of a Siberian Stalag - it is the type of thing only a single man or a widower could do.

The ballpeen hammer hadn't moved from where I had left it over three years ago. Tucked in a nook between the bookcase and the archway from the dining room to kitchen. For a man in the habit of acquiring enemies - it is more useful there than in the shed.

Upstairs should have an equivalent, especially for the mean hours, where under the hood of night bad blood flows and twisted plans unfold. I choose to sleep with a garden spade behind my bedroom door and the Titan on the bedside table. For me the spade is a talisman - a totem of action.

I pour an unhealthy measure of Bulleit bourbon into a tumbler, put my reading glasses on and settle down in the recliner to read the file. It begins with her account. There is pain in the pages. A harrowing depiction of depravity typed in an ink of nerve endings and tears. It makes an uncomfortable read.

The crime was committed at sixteen Ash Grove on the westside of Baglan in Port Talbot. It is a semi-detached house situated in a quiet, spacious close of thirty houses circling a wide green, which would have a further six houses built on it if the close had been constructed today. There are established trees along the pavement and on the green, and the backdrop is a wooded side of Baglan Mountain. The residents are mostly blue collar, shop floor and junior clerical - bosses live higher on the hill or out of town altogether.

Olivia was working a weekday nine-to-five job at the Tata Steel plant in Port Talbot as a Human Resources Officer; she was twenty-eight at the time and living with her boyfriend Jack Westbourne. Jack is an engineer in the Royal Navy and was at sea serving with HMS Montrose in the Gulf. He was four weeks through a twelve-week deployment.

In the nascent hours of Wednesday 5th May 2021 Olivia Holland was at home, alone and asleep in her bed. She was awakened by a latex-gloved hand pressed over her mouth and a knife threatening her throat. The attacker straddled her, pinning the quilt over her arms. He told her that if she didn't do what he commanded her to do he would slice her throat from ear to ear. The attacker hissed his words, masking an accent. His breath smelled of mouthwash.

The attacker stuffed a thick, rolled-up sock in Olivia's mouth, then gripped a clump of her hair and dragged her downstairs to the living room. The attacker was about five feet eight inches tall, heavyset, and felt immensely strong - effortlessly moving her as if she were a malnourished child. The attacker's features were squashed and distorted underneath a black nylon stocking, his ethnicity probably white, his age uncertain, but no boy or old man.

A dining room chair from Olivia's table was placed tipped over in the middle of the living room floor. It had been tipped forward so that the edge of the back rested on the carpet and the legs pointed upwards at an angle. Positioned behind it was a video camera held in a stand, the white light of the flash and the red recording light already on.

The attacker pulled Olivia through the legs of the chair onto the back. A cable tie had already been looped through the slats waiting like a snare for her wrists. Arms outstretched and bound, waist wedged between the chair legs, mouth gagged, eyes assaulted by the pinpoint light of the camera.

He cut off her pyjamas leaving them draped over her calves, then zipped her ankles together with another cable tie. He then raped her from behind. It went on for goodness knows how long - such an ordeal warps a person's measurement of time - in her own words it felt like eternity.

When he had finished, he knelt next to her face and whispered maliciously into her ear, 'You're a stuck-up bitch like all women are, but you won't be when I'm done with you. I'm going to transform you, turn a beautiful, aloof butterfly into an ugly, crawling caterpillar. That is power. You will feel my power every miserable day of your fucking life.'

Then he calmly took a box cutter to her face.

A cocktail of disgust, anger, and pity well, rise and flush through me. I fight it with the remainder of the bourbon and go for another to help me on. He left her like that, exposed, her face hanging off and bleeding onto the carpet. Olivia was trapped in that position for thirty-six hours, until her father, not being able to get an answer phoned the police and insisted they force entry into the house.

The rest of the contents are a jumble of pictures, screenshots, print outs and both typed and handwritten notes. There are scraps of information picked up from the police, cut-out newspaper articles, rambling thoughts and summaries of conversations scribbled down. There are also psychological profiles of serial killers and rapists printed from forensic studies. This fattened further by ill-informed social media posts peddling theory, rumour, and occasional fact, while all the time piling wood onto a bonfire of fear.

The monster has a moniker, terror will earn you one and his is 'The Port Talbot Slasher' or just 'The Slasher.' Port Talbot's own ripper has the town in his grip - although this ripper raped and disfigured instead of killing - I'm in two minds which is worse.

I sift through the disordered pile and extract what is useful. I look for what the police have told Olivia and add it to her account to construct the modus operandi of the crime. The point of entry was either through the front door or the back door and was unforced. The backdoor key was kept in the lock. The front door key was kept on Olivia's car keys, and these were hung on a hook in the kitchen.

Olivia was ninety-five percent certain that she had locked both doors. It was habitual for her to do so after use, rather than locking them before bed. The trouble was five percent could be ten percent could even be fifteen percent - it happened all the time with regular cash driven creeper burglars playing the percentages.

A criminal I knew named Craig Ferry was a nut for it. Rolling on counterfeit Diazepam otherwise known as MSGs or Dog Valium, he'd try every door in a street for an insecure one. The only thing he'd have in his pockets when you stopped and searched him was a handkerchief, duster, or rag for the door handle.

The car keys were found in the front garden, indicating that the attacker had used them to lock the front door after exiting. The back door key was where it should have been, and the door was also locked. The rear garden was easily accessible through a waist height lift-latch side gate and directly backed onto a rear garden in Thorney Road. It would be simpler and incur less risk to approach the house from the front. In addition to the road access from Greenwood Road there is a footpath from Thorney

Road and one from the rear of Acorn Place.

The police believed that the attacker wore a condom because there was no ejaculate. He had also taken precautions to prevent the transference of pubic hair. The medical examination at the SARC found only the presence of a water-based lubricant.

The intruder left a clean forensic sheet. He wore the stocking which stopped him shedding any hair. He wore surgical gloves so did not create any fingerprints. The sock was new and unworn and almost certainly only handled with gloves. He did not lick, drink or spit to leave saliva. He was careful not to cut himself and be caught by his blood. There were no footprints to be found in or outside the house. House to house enquiries produced no witnesses.

The only piece of evidence the police had was footage from a neighbour's CCTV camera. It showed the profile of a thickset, hooded man in dark clothing walking deliberately with his head down past number eighteen. The time was nine minutes past three. A dead time. Too late for those with work in the morning to be up and generally too early a start for shift workers. The same camera captured his return at fourteen minutes to four.

The attacks were spread across Port Talbot with one also in Neath. It meant he drove or rode to a location nearby, much like I had done this morning visiting King. The police had trawled the surrounding streets searching for more CCTV. Hours were viewed and no other trace of him found.

The fifth victim of the serial rapist, Olivia had only a tenuous connection with one of the other victims. At Afan College she was in the same sociology A-level class as Kelly Thomas, and for two years, until going to different universities they were acquainted with one another. They were as close as you could be without being called standalone friends - a relationship existing beyond a situation that two people share.

News of Kelly Thomas' rape and mutilation leaked and spread through the town. Through the digital grapevine Olivia became aware of it and had thought of reaching out to her. She didn't. It felt awkward, an intrusion, a trespass into a prohibited area far beyond the boundary of a bygone relationship.

A month later Kelly Thomas drove to Southerndown Cliffs and threw herself two hundred feet to her death. These are Olivia's words scrawled angrily with strokes of regret on a piece of lined A5 note paper. Paper clipped behind it is a photograph of Kelly Thomas' Face printed from a Facebook post dated the 21st of February 2020.

Cruel havoc had been wreaked on that face. Four tears across the left cheek are equally spaced like the swipe of a tiger's paw. A hashtag was carved into her forehead. The tip of the nose was amputated. The lips split in several places and left in tatters, sewn back into form and now angry red exclamations. A railway line of prominent scar tissue wending like a lazy river from ear to chin to forehead - jeez, he hated women. Underneath, the caption:

'My rapist murdered me; the fall will just be finishing the job. I need you to understand that I am not committing suicide, he's pushed me off this cliff. Sorry, it's better I let him kill me than go on with this prolonged suffering.'

I finish the second bourbon with some idea of where to begin, no idea how to I'd make any headway and a firm idea of how it ends. It ends like a boat whose rudder is jammed, fated to turn in circles until its sputtering engine stalls.

CHAPTER 5

I awake at seven o'clock with a metallic taste in my mouth and my heart beating quicker than it ought to. I drink a strong tip-the-jar into the mug coffee and rustle up some breakfast. I crack open four eggs and eat them scrambled on toast with some black pepper and tomato ketchup. I drink another coffee with it and check my PayPal account, and as I expected my fee is there plus an additional three hundred for expenses. I transfer the money into my ailing account; then put some clothes on - practical ones, loose and hard-wearing.

I peek through the blinds of the landing window at the long street outside the close. Nothing unusual. I look through the window of the front bedroom and there is a guy from the neighbourhood walking his dog. Nothing out of place.

I unlock the Hilux from inside and cautiously leave the house with my bookcase hammer in hand. I stop at an ATM outside the Baglan Spar and withdraw two hundred pounds, then drive to Ash Grove.

I'd been here twice before. Once for a suspicious sudden death that quickly climbed down from a potential murder to an explanation of chronic alcoholic abuse, untied shoelaces, and both those factors descending a flight of stairs. The other time was delivering a death message to a mother after her son was killed in an industrial accident - happy memories.

The close is a little different than I remember it. A belt of tall deciduous trees stands amongst a brook on the right side which I can hear babbling from recent rainfall. The trees extend from Thorney Road down to Chestnut Road and overlook the rear gardens of the lowest numbered houses. A coarse, muddy footpath runs through its middle. It affords an excellent peep spot to hang out and perv, however, Olivia lived on the opposite side where there is no vantage to be had from here.

Using my phone, I check the weather for the 5th of May 2021 and for the three days preceding the date there was rain, which meant muddy shoes and footprints from the tread or dirt transfer from the rims. The house had neither and so it is probable that the rapist used a different route to his target.

I walk into the close from the road entrance off Greenwood Road. At the side of number twenty-two there is a cut-through to a shared lane of garages. On one side garages for Acorn Place and the other Ash Grove. The lane can be accessed by car from Acorn Place and Thorney Road. Walking along the line of garages there isn't a CCTV camera on any; this explained by a couple no-no's: focusing on a public place and being too easy to vandalise.

Near the top of the lane is a curved path flanked by hedges leading back into Ash Grove. I walk its narrow confines and it could just about fit two people side-by-side. During the night the attacker would be invisible in the close height of the hedges.

Coming out of the path I sidestep the attentions of a frisky spaniel. The tall, outdoorsy woman walking him reels the dog in from a long lead and apologises. Smiling, I wave it off and note that the entrance is between number eighteen and nineteen. He got picked up on eighteen's camera marching to number sixteen.

I double back and come out of the lane onto Thorney Road, and standing at their nexus, alternatively survey each. Although the garages and high walls attached to them provide a prowler with adequate cover there is decent street lighting in the lane and a better alternative in the path. Thorney Road also has something in its favour in reducing a criminal's exposure, it is mostly one-sided. The houses are similar to those in Ash Grove but stepped lower than the road. The other side is woodland save for a pair of cottages and a couple of large individual houses set into the foot of the mountain. These are raised above the road, oblique in their facing and each reached by a driveway.

The belt of trees begins here and offers a discreet place to park a car or perhaps a motorbike, particularly as the house opposite it has its privacy guarded by tall Conifer trees - if you can't see in you can't see out. No, not a bike, a car I think, a bike's engine growls and whines and disturbs sleeping ears.

Another advantage is Thorney Road went into Maple Avenue which is a dead end - it isn't a throughway, meaning there would be very limited traffic passing by. In the other direction Acorn Place overlooked Baglan Rugby Club and its pitch. Next to the clubhouse there was a small car park which I know is monitored by CCTV - he didn't park there.

I return to Ash Grove by the route I think he has taken. It is the route I would have chosen to minimise contact and to avoid association with the vehicle used to drive there. He parked at the belt of trees, walked quickly down the mountain side of Thorney Road, turned into the lane, and took the closeted path into the close.

The house has received a modern facelift and stands out from the dowdy and dated facades of its neighbours - the expression I suppose of twenty-something drive and aspiration - to imprint young love's dream.

Olivia had moved in with her father and sold the house to a graphic designer named Rhys Dixon. The file states that Dixon works from home. I ring the doorbell and hear a carillon playing a melody that I recognize but cannot name. There is no answer, so I set the bells to their tune again. When there is still no answer, I resist the urge to employ my policeman's knock. It worked when I was law, though it does not endear you to people and is often counterproductive to polite civilian enquiry.

Eventually, after a third play, a tired-looking man with a serious case of bed hair opens the door. He wears an open plaid dressing gown over a *Foo Fighters* t-shirt and blue bed shorts. The man is encroaching on forty, has two-day old stubble and the bleary eyes of someone doing double-digit hours in front of a computer screen.

'Mr. Dixon, I'm William Cutter, a private investigator working for the former owner of this house Olivia Holland. When she lived here, she was the subject of a horrific crime perpetrated in this house. She has hired me to conduct a follow up investigation to support the one the police are pursuing. Here is my card.'

I hand him a business card, which would normally be backed up by a licence issued from the Association of Private Investigators. With the industry still being unregulated it is not a legal requirement, still, being a member of a trade association adds a degree of authenticity and respectability to a profession that suffers from a sleazy reputation. On account of my stay at Algeciras Prison I was disbarred from the association - the card and a good helping of blag would have to do.

He rubs worn, sleepy eyes and yawns. 'Excuse me,' he says, battling the yawn.

'Not at all, sorry to have got you up but I wanted to catch you before you left for work.'

'I work from home,' he replies, stifling another yawn.

Convenient,' I chuckle amiably.

'Yeah, well, so … you're investigating The Port Talbot Slasher?'

'Yes, I am,' I say nodding earnestly.

'It was dreadful what happened here. I was in two minds about buying the house, but it became such a bargain that it would have been daft not to snap it up; she even left the furniture, which with my divorce came in very handy.'

'I can relate to that, my ex didn't leave me with a pot to piss in,' I add, telling another lie.

'Yeah, it's rough … so how can I help you?'

'It would be of great help if I could come in and examine the crime scene.'

'Oh … I'm not sure … what do you want to look at?' he asks.

'The layout, what the intruder would have seen. I want to try and recreate his movements and thought processes.'

Dixon wags the tip of his tongue along the inside of his bottom lip in an idiosyncrasy of doubt. 'Look, I'm not comfortable with you coming in. I mean you could be anyone.'

I smile affably and try my best to appear harmless when I say, 'Fair point, though I am who I say I am, and my intentions are honest. Still, you're not to know that … and I suppose me looking like a bruiser who bangs heads for a living is not helping my case.'

Dixon flexes his mouth briefly in a facsimile of a smile and I infer apprehension. Like a person who lost a trust of dogs after he got bitten by one, and now has a rottweiler on his doorstep asking to be patted.

'I didn't like to say, but yes ... so I'm sorry but I'd rather not. Now if you'll excuse me, I have stuff to do.'
I need to get in and my brain scurries around for an idea, a key to make it happen. One appears and it feels like magic. 'I was a police officer for twenty-five-years, a Police Sergeant and a decorated one. Here, take a look.'

I slip out my phone and show him a photograph from my Google Drive. In it I'm dressed in number ones: a silver-buttoned police tunic, razor-seamed trousers, and mirror-polished parade boots, and I'm shaking hands with the now former Chief Constable of South Wales Police Sir Richard Seagrove. It is 2014 and I'm being presented with my third and last commendation for bravery.
'Your right to be cautious, but I'm one of the good guys and you can be one too; and on top of that I'll give you fifty quid out of my expenses for the inconvenience.'
'Uhm ... well I ...'

As he is fumbling for an answer, I pluck out two twenties and a ten and push them towards him. 'Twenty minutes tops and I'm out of your hair. If you want more insurance, take a photo of me and send it to your friends.'
The money stops the bumbling and taking his silence as consent, I cross over the threshold into the hallway and set the camera on my phone to record.

The front door is made from UPVC with a white oak veneer and a sliver of frosted glass running the entire length. It has a standard five-point mortice lock and solid steel Victorian Lever door handles.
'Have you replaced the front door?' I ask.
'No,' he replies.
The staircase and hall are covered in a light-brown Berber carpet that has yet to show the wear of trampling feet. The

staircase is on the left side of the hallway and faces the front door. There is a closed door to the right and an open door straight ahead which leads into the kitchen.

I open the door into a living room that expands without separation into a dining room. This room also has a Berber carpet and is the colour of faded lead. The room has faux wood Venetian blinds in complimentary grey and mustard painted walls for contrast. A royal-blue fabric sofa and two chairs are busy with an assortment of cushions picking up on the colour scheme. The centre of the room is bare, and I look up from the empty spot to the dining room table and chairs. It is made of solid honey lacquered rustic oak, and accommodates six chairs with black padded seats and slatted backs. I pull out the nearest one from the end and carry it into the living room.

'What are you doing?' he asks, the notes in his voice expressing a hybrid of confusion and concern.
'He tipped this chair over and tied her to it.'
'Oh!'

I recreate what I had read, and a simple piece of household furniture assumes another function, performs a new role. The legs become a clamp, the slats an anchor point and the tilt the right angle to present what a rapist would want to violate. It is sturdy on the carpet and while not a contraption designed by a fetishist - it does the job.

When he entered here did he specifically want this? Did he know what he was going to do? or did he adapt and improvise according to what was here? Did he have several contingencies worked out if the preferred option wasn't available?

Most homes of a reasonable standard had a dining table and chairs, so he could be safe in the presumption that there would be one here. Still, the bondage is important, perhaps an essential element of the crime. I will have to learn the M.O. of the other attacks to draw a comparison and to find a pattern. Then it occurs to me that Major Crime already know all of this, would have benefited from offender profiling and yet they hadn't arrested anyone. I let out a heavy sigh and feel myself sink a little into the carpet.

I replace the chair and head to the stairs. The third, fourth and eighth stairs creak loudly jeopardising a stealthy approach to the bedroom. I suppose after he had stepped on the first he could have bolted up the rest; then I remember that she didn't wake until he had her pinned on the bed. He must have crept, or was it the case that Olivia was deep in sleep and dead to the world and just didn't hear? Again, a question leading to a further question.

From the landing there are four rooms. The front bedroom is the master bedroom and is where Olivia slept. I hear a murmur of protest which I choose to ignore. I push open the door to see Dixon's unmade bed. I stare at it like it is supposed to tell me something, as if a thunderbolt of deduction is imminent. It is a charade and the bed, and the door and the chair keep their secrets.

CHAPTER 6

I sit in the Hilux rapping my fingers on the steering wheel looking out the window at a gate I'm about to go through. It belongs to an end of row bungalow in Great Western Terrace in Cwmavon.

The bungalow is small, white, and unusually has two doors next to one another like nostrils separated by a white septum wall. The door to the left is double glass panelled and has a handrail on the shallow step. The front is a cut lawn divided by a weathered-grey paving stone path and lined by potted plants. The steps from the waist-high black iron gate have another handrail.

I inspect the others in the row, and they are the same - ground living for the old or infirm. Except for the considerable stain of efflorescence oozing out of the red brick wall running the length of the row, the homes are neat and well-tended.

Stroking and tugging at my beard I sigh and scrunch my lips, then get out. I unhook the gate, trudge up the steps and call on the parents of Kelly Thomas.

A square-shaped, big-boned man just a smidge over six feet tall answers. Wisps of ash-coloured hair stretch over a bucket-sized head and his hands are like pink excavator scoops. He would have been a bull in his day and although pushing seventy years now, could still I imagine be a handful. He is dressed in a classic light-grey crew neck sweater and matching loose track pants like boxers of old would wear grinding out the early morning miles - the traditionalist in me approves.

'Good morning, are you Mr Geraint Thomas?'

'I am,' he replies.

I'm William Cutter and I am a private investigator working for Olivia Holland. Here is my card …'

'I know who you are,' he says in a rumbling voice. 'Some years ago, you worked in the village with Chris Stillman. I was good mates with Chris, God bless him.'

'That's right I did, and he was the best copper I ever worked with; not the most able mind you, nonetheless, the best when it counted and a hell of a boy … saved my skin a few times did Chris. I suppose you knew him through rugby?' I query, making an educated guess.

'Yeah, I was an assistant coach at Aberavon, then later on at Cwmavon, and as you know he played for both. And yeah, he was a hell of a boy, he was an unholy riot on tour,' and he laughs, likely recollecting some mad stunt or antic. 'Bloody shame.'

We share a moment of sadness and I get the feeling that I have probably met him before, his face lost in the foggy reaches of time, blended, and superimposed by the football stadium of people I've encountered. It happens to me more than I like.

He steps away from the doorway and turning his back beckons me to follow him saying, 'Come on in; do you know? It's nice being able to say that again this year … bloody virus made hermits of us all …. 2020, 2021 were write-offs, years for the dustbin.'

'I'd rather forget them too,' I reply, remembering a near constant apprehension of violence as a man marked for death.

I close the door and walk behind him into a dinky little living room that he is too big for. He gestures for me to sit, and I relax into a soft chair upholstered in chenille or some other fabric resembling a caterpillar's coat. The headrest is protected by a lace doily, and it is clear there is a penchant for them because they are spread like beached jellyfish over all the furniture.

On top of the mantelpiece is a gallery of lovingly framed family photographs: a bride and groom outside a church circa 1980, a portrait of a son, rugby ball in hand in a Welsh cap and jersey, another of a pretty and rather proud-looking Kelly graduating in gown and mortar holding a red-bowed degree.

A woman, blonde, glamorous, and younger than Geraint limps with a cane into the room. She is hunched over, and her nail-polished fingers are gnarled with arthritis. Expelling strain in a grunt, she collapses into a seat next to her husband.

'Linda, this is William Cutter, he used to be a copper in the village. I think he's here to ask about Kelly?' tilting his prodigious head as a cue for me to speak.

'Yes, I'm sorry to intrude and ask you to revisit painful memories ...,' and I pause at seeing Linda blench, that even the introduction of the subject is enough to twist her heart. 'Geraint, perhaps it would be better if we spoke in private, I have no wish to cause Mrs Thomas any upset.'

Geraint looks at his wife, her mouth is quivering, her eyes are forlorn and haunted. He squeezes her hand, then gets up and says, 'Right, let's go into the kitchen.'

I follow him into a narrow galley kitchen into which the two of us crowd. He fills the kettle and sets it to boil and asks, 'Tea, coffee?'

'Coffee would be good, thanks, milk and no sugar,' I answer, thinking how to delve delicately into the mutilation and rape of his daughter.

'Olivia Holland is the last victim of ... The Port Talbot Slasher,' I say, wincing inwardly at the name, a name giving power and prominence over the victims - he thought of more than they. 'She has hired me to follow up on the police investigation of the attacks,' and I stumble in the embarrassment of the statement - it sounded arrogant or absurd - perhaps both. 'I would like ... no, it is important for me to find out what happened to your daughter Kelly ... the details, the house, the method used in the attack, I need to form a picture.'

There is a moment of uncomfortable silence, stretching like an elastic band that would have to snap. Hard blue eyes scrutinise. The cauliflower ears, the bashed-about nose, the notch in the top lip - a history of warfare on the pitch. Inflicted by clothesline tackles and sharp elbows, raking boot studs in the ruck, uppercuts in the scrum and bad-tempered, full-out fights off the ball - his face a portrait of fouls from when the game was dirty. And I imagine the pictures he made of other men on those Saturday afternoons. Without doubt, those hands had crudely painted a few men red, black, and blue.

'You don't seem confident,' he says.

'I'm not, I expect to fail, to get trounced, much like a third division village team going up against *The All Blacks*, but still, you lace up your boots and play, don't you? Even though I don't like my chances I am going to try.'

Weighing what had just been said, Geraint slides a white mug of coffee across the counter; written on it in black, the Welshism, 'I'll be there now in a minute.'

'Chris, he once told me that you had the dog in you, so, all right, hopeless or not, I'll tell you what I know.'

He clears his throat and looking out of the window at nothing in particular begins, 'Kelly was living at ten Lupin Close; it's in Sandfields.'

'I know it,' I say - Sandfields, the old stomping ground.

'She was renting the house from a guy who had retired to Thailand, and she'd been there just over a year.'

'Was Kelly living alone?' I ask.

'Yes, she had yet to get over the bust-up with her last boyfriend. Kelly was living with this fella Daniel Jacques over in Swansea. It was his house, so when they split, she had to find somewhere else to live. I only wish Linda and I had a bigger home, but she was twenty-eight and wanted her own place. What could I have done?'

He grabs a piece of his face and pulls at it; blame always finds a home, invited or not it burrows its way in.

'Anyway, apart from the broken heart, which she was getting over, she was doing all right. Kelly had a tidy job as a store manager for Carphone Warehouse and ran their Port Talbot branch. She was a keen gardener, took great pride in her hanging baskets and flowerpots, always out the front tending to them, she was. She loved cats, had two, and volunteered at a local cat sanctuary. She wasn't a sad cat lady though, she liked to socialise. She had a supportive circle of friends, you know real ones, that came around for coffee and went out for wine. A crowd of them would go to Cardiff for the rugby internationals.

Things were starting to look up; Linda said she was even thinking of dating again.'
The poignancy of the last sentence pierces deep, and is hurtful and silencing - the road he is walking holding cruel ambushes and diversions.

He grits his teeth and continues, 'Sunday, February 2nd, 2020; I will never forget it. It was eleven o'clock and as long as the weather wasn't too bad, I would always pick Kelly up and we'd go to the beach for a long walk and a bite to eat at Remo's afterwards. She used to say that it blew the cobwebs away ... huh. Well, I knocked at the door and there was no answer. I knocked again, still no answer. I saw her car next to the house, and I noticed that the curtains were still drawn, bedroom and living room. I phoned her and I heard the phone ringing from inside the house. I had a key for the door, so I used it. At this stage I was still thinking she had overslept, so I stayed in the hall and called up. I heard a muffled cry ... horrible and retched-up like sick ... coming from the living room.'

Geraint's eyes well with tears and breaths bellow and tremble out from his broad chest. 'I opened the door and ... and ... there was my little girl ... in a position no father should see. I mean ... tied ... like ... a thing, you know ... like something strapped on the roof of a car. Her beautiful face ripped to shreds.'

'How was she tied?' I venture, eggshells all around the words I could say.
'Mmm,' he replies, his mind diverted to grief.
'Was she tied to anything?' I ask.
'A dining room chair had been upturned and she was bound to it with cable ties and masking tape.' There is revulsion on his lips, the memory like the taste of rotten fish in his mouth. He looks like he could vomit.

My own face is grim expectancy. 'Describe it to me?' I push, the pace of the question picking up from the last.
'Pulled through the legs, arms locked into hugging the back of the chair and masking tape used to wrap her waist to the seat.'
'The legs?'

'Bound at the ankles with a cable tie.'

'You said arms around the back; so, forced into a kneeling position, yes?'

A deep breath and then a 'Yes' in the exhale.

'The back of the chair ... solid, slats or something else?'

He peers back into his head and says, 'Black-backed, faux leather, solid.'

'Good,' I find myself saying without consideration of saying it, then onto the next question without pause, 'What time was the attack?'

'Four o'clock. Kelly could see the clock on the mantelpiece. She'd been out drinking with the girls at Bar Galois. Kelly didn't like real late nights, so would have been in bed by half twelve at the latest.'

'Taken from bed?'

'Yes.'

'Was she gagged or blindfolded?'

'She had a thick sock jammed into her mouth ... and it was spreading open the slits in her lips making them look like stubby little tentacles,' he answers wiping a tear from his eye. 'That's what it made me think of for Christ's sake.'

I shove a grotesque image out of my mind of flaps of flesh moving independently of one another.

'What type of blade did he use?'

'Kelly told the police that it had a short triangular blade with a lime-green handle; from what she said I think it was a Stanley knife.'

'Did he say anything to Kelly?'

'Yes, but I only remember that Kelly said the bastard kept calling her a stuck-up bitch, said she loved herself and she wouldn't any longer because he transformed aloof butterflies into miserable crawling caterpillars. Stuck up ... it couldn't have been further from the truth,' he laments, the grief pouring out of him like blood from several stab wounds - I won't have him for much longer.

I rush out the next question, 'What did the police say about the method of entry?'

'Nothing broken; said the front door was insecure or the keys were hitched from of the lock through the cat flap. Look no more, I've had enough for now,' he says in a worn-down voice. A voice running on the rims and faltering to a stop at having to drag out words that a father shouldn't be made to say.

I nod. 'Sorry to make you go through that, I really am.'

I place a business card next to a coffee half-drunk and make my way out the door. Geraint follows to the step and says, 'Will, if an old brute like me can be of any use to you in this, call by.'

'Sure thing,' I reply, itching from the grubbiness of it all.

The fresh drizzle is welcome, the view of the mist-scarfed mountain a relief. Scarred faces, haunted faces, shattered lives. Flowers mowed down and chewed up in the wake of a maniac's hatred. That's two entries from a possible open door. Two lone women bound to a tipped over chair and raped. Two faces sliced with a box knife. Two women told that they are beautiful, aloof butterflies. Two women told they are about to be transformed, changed into ugly, miserable, crawling caterpillars. There is a method to the madness.

Ten Lupin Close is one of two flower closes off St Helier Drive; the other is Jasmin, and the rest are named after colours. Nearby there is also Orchid, Poppy, Iris, and Daffodil Closes and many have garage compounds behind them or are joined by footpaths.

A thin tarmacked road leads in, either side of it two swathes of grass large enough to accommodate another two houses apiece. Instead, pavements offering a shortcut cut diagonally across them and a filthy-skirted red combi van with a number plate obliterated with dirt is parked on a verge. A beat-up BMW Three Series displaying a rear windshield sticker 'Boobies make me smile' is parked opposite. This lax attitude to parking is widespread throughout the estate and was referred to by an old colleague of mine as a 'Sandfields driveway.'

Sandfields used to be rough and in pockets it still is, but over the years it has undergone gentrification. Council tenants became homeowners, and the Council evicted the worst of the riffraff. The type that punched holes in their doors, let sofas rot in the back garden and were a nightmare for everyone around them. Lupin Close has keen gardeners and a couple of caravaners and overall, the houses have been improved upon rather than run-down - it is no Farmfield Avenue.

At the u-bend of the close the road diverts to the right, and I follow it into a compound and park opposite a line of garages. There are ten of them backing onto the rear gardens of Long Vue Road which runs parallel to Lupin, but as the road name suggests extends for considerably longer. To the front is a high wall separating Aster View behind - no footpath, one way in, one way out. On the left are four houses joined in a terrace. The first is number thirteen making the last house number ten.

The walls of number ten are an oat hue and the brown window frames, door and hooded porch tiles flatter one another. The front garden has been converted into a driveway and is entered from another compound. Whatever was in the flowerpots is reduced to broken and desiccated sticks.

I wind through the slalom gates of a footpath into a much larger garage compound, remembering that it is reached by car from the adjacent Jasmin Close. A six and a half feet concrete block wall surrounds the back and side of the property, and there is open access to the drive. I count sixteen garages and three cars parked here and there.

He could have left the vehicle he used in St Helier Drive, on the verges or in either compound. I discount the verges on account of mud and tyre tracks. He hadn't got caught and after five attacks that wasn't down to luck. He gave the elimination of evidence a great deal of thought. He left as much trace of himself as a ghost.

Something pulls me to here; a notion of a blacked-out vehicle, engine cut, rolling up to the side of the house. The driver's door pressed shut, a brawny man, head hooded and swallowed by nylon carrying a sling bag or rucksack skulks into the driveway and up to the front door.

He'd probably need a bag for the phone stand, Duct tape, cable ties, lubricant, sock, and blade, unless he wore a tactical jacket loaded with pockets. It didn't have to be military, I have a hunting smock that has a deep chest pocket with others on the arms, back and side, and some fisherman's coats offered the same.

Was the front door left unlocked? Increasingly it seems unlikely - too much to chance. A hot-blooded mission, yet executed with cold and callous calculation. An unstoppable urge riding a massive wave of commitment could not be denied by a locked door or any other obstacle. He must have known beforehand how he would get in - it fitted with the victims being preselected. The rapist knew that Kelly Thomas lived here alone, and he figured a silent way to invade her home. I had heard of keys being hooked out of the lock from the letterbox, so a cat flap would be a cinch.

Walking back to the car I look through the downstairs window, through an open plan living room to a table and chairs in the back. He had seen what I am seeing now. He had stood where I am standing, and knew he needed Duct tape for the solid backed chair.

CHAPTER 7

After two drive-bys of my house and overuse of the rear-view mirror, I feel it is safe to park on my driveway. I get out quickly, shooting looks in different directions before going in and re-locking the door.

At the dining table, I eat a loaded chicken salad wrap with one hand while composing a message to an old police colleague with the other. If Anthony Stanner's plan had worked out, he would have retired aged fifty-five in May of this year.

For nearly all of 2018 I had worked with Anthony, or Stan as he is more commonly called. He was the Team Four Response Sergeant at Port Talbot, and I was the Sergeant of Team Two. This meant I handed the reins over to him four shifts out of six, and in the crossovers and overlaps of the shift pattern we would talk, amongst other things learning of the roads we had each travelled to get where we were. I wanted to be there, you could cut me open and I'd bleed the street. Just prior to the Port Talbot posting I had been parked in an office because of a complaint for six months, and it starved my soul. For Stan it was a knockback - plain and simple. He knew it and so did everyone else.

He had got kicked off CID for a discrepancy between overtime hours worked and hours claimed. The brass at PSD decided that he was sloppy rather than dishonest, however, the sloppiness extended into other areas like not being where you should be. Stan had a habit of slipping off the radar and taking care of the household itinerary on work time. So, what do the bosses do when they want to punish a detective without officially reprimanding them - they send them back to uniform - and they send them to Response where the leash is tight, and the pressure is unrelenting.

To say that Stan was bitter about it would be a gross understatement - lemons were not made into lemonade and the cloud's silver lining had been ripped off and dumped at the tip. I gave a ear to his whinging and after some expletive-ridden rants he settled down. We became friendly without being friends, posts were temporary and so were friendships.

In my twenty-five years on the job, I had worked at eleven stations over three divisions and this was not uncommon - people became passing scenery. When I resigned from the job at the end of 2018 Stan was digging a tunnel to escape; mending bridges and brown-nosing DIs. It is my hope, as the message is sent that Stan had some involvement with, or knowledge of the slashings, albeit the content of the message does not give that away.

Twenty-two seconds of *The Ecstasy of Gold* plays before I reach my phone. I know that because the ringtone is about to repeat. No caller ID. Enquiry or death threat- the way things are going I'd say an equal chance of each. I answer, putting down the bottle of bleach that I was using to clean the bathroom.

'Will, it's Dave Kumar from Newport Motorpark.'

'Hello, Dave.'

'Hilux still for sale?'

'Yeah, it is.'

'How does ten o'clock tomorrow morning sound for a look and a test drive?'

'I could do that.'

'Okay, postcode and number?'

'SA12 7FF and it is number twenty-one.'

'Got that, see you tomorrow.'

Doubt knots itself in my gut and I get a taster of regret. A preview of how I will feel when the Old Girl is driven away. The door swings open and loneliness pulls up a seat, self-pity taps my shoulder and says hi. I call over anger because he's coming anyway, and he brings his friend disgust. The boys have a thirst and want me to get the drinks in.

It's just a bloody car, a hunk of metal, though it signifies more, it holds memories of a previous life - Beth had wanted me to have it. In my mind's eye I see her smiling and giving me the green light to buy it. She didn't want a chunky-tyred pickup truck sitting on our drive, but she loved me and just wanted to make me happy - damn, she was a beautiful person. As sadness envelops my thumb swipes at Annabel's number. Pick up, pick up.

'Hi dad.'

'Hi Bel, are you free to speak?'

'Not for long, I have a case conference in two minutes, everything okay?' and I can hear elevated breathing and the echo of movement in a stairwell.

'Yeah, I just wanted to catch up. Look, I'll call you after work and maybe we can meet up later this week for lunch or dinner?'

'I'd like that, I want you to meet, Henry.'

'I would like to meet him too. Well, I had better leave you go,' I say.

'Bye dad.'

'Bye.'

I must occupy myself or I'll derail. The file is spread across the dining-room table, and I immerse myself in its contents. Disorganised and yet thorough, it is sixteen months of fixation through a cracked lens. Jemma Vinson is the third victim. Olivia had deduced that from her brother Jamie Vinson ranting all over social media about killing the sicko that cut up his sister.

I had known the family and I suppose I still do, the same way the trajectory of a bullet can be predicted after it leaves a gun. It was dysfunctional then, more so now like a loopy, tumbling bullet ricocheting to where it shouldn't and dumping its energy into the wrong target.

Jemma could start an argument with a lamp post and Jamie has about as much sense and direction as a pinball. There was a third sibling named Matthew, he was the oldest until a concoction of heroin, ketamine and benzos stopped his clock at twenty-six years old. The needle, the bottle, the pipe, the prescription, theirs or otherwise blighted the Vinson family. Dad was a deadbeat drunk, mum as spaced as an astronaut - the rest of the clan half-baked, sozzled, and mean.

Jemma's attack was on Wednesday 26th August 2020 and occurred at Knox Street, Margam. The news report didn't say what house number, and it didn't have to - several years ago I'd been to the house. She had a kid named Lola or Layla, or Leila, something like that. Cute little thing, albeit grubby, aged about four with a mess of blonde hair.

A neighbour had found her wandering the road barefoot in the rain dressed only in dirty pyjamas - it wasn't the first time. Jemma was on the living room floor pie-eyed and insensible, her hair stuck to her face and cigarette burn holes through her loungewear hoodie. The house was a depository for value vodka bottles and burnt squares of foil - alcohol and heroin, a sure way to follow her brother to an early grave.

Jemma took a trip to the hospital, and I took her child into protective custody. The kid was handed over to Social Services and Jemma Vinson was subsequently prosecuted for neglect. On the positive side, I don't think she'll remember me, at least not from that day.

I had also collared her for shoplifting, or more accurately instructed a junior PC on my team that she be arrested for the offence. My team and I had dealt with her for other matters like non-appearance warrants, drugs, disturbances, anti-social behaviour, assault, concern calls, and squabbles over social media. I had encountered her enough to remember her date of birth - April 20th, 1993.

For obvious reasons, I figure that she is no longer living at twenty-six Knox Street, but if the attack had not occurred there are pretty good odds she wouldn't have remained there anyway. Whether it be due to prison, eviction or shacking up with someone else - roots are rarely laid down for long in the underclass.

A search through County Court records reveals that she had a County Court Judgement awarded against her for a non-payment of a payday loan. The date of the ruling was April 3rd, 2022, and the address provided for the loan was number one

Cound Terrace in Taibach. Taibach translates to little houses in Welsh and figuratively means outhouse or lavatory, and is certainly the toilet of the steel works. Taibach smells worse than anywhere else in Port Talbot. It is where window frames are freckled with soot and washing can get dirty on the line - the artist Banksy picked the perfect location to depict pollution.

My watch reads a quarter past four, still plenty of time to snoop about.

CHAPTER 8

Cound Terrace is seven houses squashed into a railway fence; four on one side and three on the other with cars on either side throttling the road. I don't park in it for fear of not being able to get out if I did. The houses have quarry stone fronts, and the windows are eyelined with brighter, contrasting paint.

In a series of loud whooshes and clacks, an InterCity 125 passes just beyond the green Paladin fence, followed in the opposite direction by the harsher, rhythmic noise of a freight train loaded with logs shuffling along its track.

A moon-faced woman in her thirties with a purple streak running through black, bushy hair answers the door. 'Hello, is Jemma Vinson still living here?' I ask.

She wriggles her nose and I notice it has a diamond stud piercing on the left side. She says, 'No, not any longer, she got evicted by the landlord in May.'

'She leave a forwarding address?' I ask with a sliver of hope.

'Not with me, and from what the landlord told me about Jemma, not with her either.'

'Bad tenant?'

'Oh yes!' she replies, elongating the oh. 'Understandable I suppose, given what happened to her. Are you a debt collector or something?'

'Private Investigator.'

'Really!' and her tattooed eyebrows rise in interest.

'Yep, I need to get hold of her because she's a witness in a case I'm investigating.'

'Interesting case?'

'Appalling. You could help me some more by passing me your landlord's details ... perhaps she'll know where she went.'

She gets the contact details from her phone. 'Marcella Nolan 07453981282.'

'Thank you.'

Marcella whined about rent arrears and the state Jemma left her house in but didn't know where she had moved to.

Having been out of the policing game for four years my mental map of the town's lowlife is outdated, and the memory of the old map has acquired a few holes. I can't remember the mother's first name, but I only need the surname and enter it in the electoral register. There are three households in the town bearing the name Vinson. The one listed for thirteen Trinity Court in Sandfields rings a bell and is the link my finger goes to first. The occupier is Michelle Vinson - bingo.

Trinity Court appears like it was built in a garage compound between Fairways and Acacia Close. Housing association stock built in the 80s, it is four blocks of matchbox houses split into one up and one down flats.

I get out of the Hilux and hear the jingle of metal. It is from a supermarket shopping trolley rattling over the pavement from Acacia Close. The woman pushing it has a pinched, pissed-off face and lank hair tied in a ponytail. She sees me taking notice of her and she shoots back a brazen look that says - *yeah ... and ... what?*

I stand back after knocking the door and watch the first-floor window curtains for signs of movement. They twitch, then half a minute later the door is snatched open. 'What the fuck do you want?' is how Jamie Vinson chooses to greet me.

Stepping back, I raise my hands to my chest and slowly slither them over each other like snakes, as if washing them without soap and water. I settle the motion to an absent picking of a kettlebell callus on the palm of my hand. I want him to think about my hands and I want them to be ready.

'Lost none of your charm I see, Jamie.'

'I fucking hate you Cunter, hate your fucking guts, so why would I say anything else huh?' he snarls displaying crooked, brown teeth inside a slack mouth.

He is thirty, gormless and inexplicably hard bodied considering all the junk he puts into it. Black hair is styled in a modern mullet and a five feet six frame is covered by a forest camo t-shirt, black joggers, and white Nike trainers. Visible on the inside of his left arm is a thick pink scar to remind him of the night he cut his wrist open in a coked-up rage. He bled over four streets, he bled so much he could be tracked. It was the police that saved him, and it did nothing to lessen the loathing for us.

'I am after Jemma, I need to speak to her about the attack,' I explain using a placatory tone.

'Breaking news fucktard! … you're not a cop anymore. You don't get to ask questions, you don't get to bully people and make stuff up about them, and you don't get to take their kids off them,' he berates, the loose-lipped sneer a caricature of a disaffected yob.

'Your anger is misplaced, which has always been your problem, Jamie.'

'What are you now, a fucking psych doctor? Do me a favour Cunter and fuck off.'

The door is slammed shut and the house shakes from the force. My policeman's knock gets an outing and I hammer fist the door. Three stentorian raps guaranteed to irritate and to incite a response. Touchpaper lit I stand back.

Jamie flings open the door holding a mini crowbar in his right hand, and in that sobering moment a spotlight of stupidity shines on me. It was a dull move akin to juggling nitro-glycerine and now I'm about to have a row with a jemmy-waving idiot.

'Are you fucking thick or what? Do you want to fucking go … Come on! Let's fucking go!'

I show peace hands and backpedal. 'Easy, Jamie, let's not do anything stupid here. Okay.'

'I've been stupid my whole fucking life … why should I stop now? Come on you shithouse … you're fuck all out of a uniform.'

Swaggering like a baiting hooligan he follows my retreat. I'd known him to be a thief and a burglar rather than a hardman, nonetheless, a hair-trigger temper on a senseless man swinging a crowbar is not to be taken lightly.

I inject a spurt of speed into the withdrawal and put the Hilux between us. The dopey eyes are fired alive by anger, an anger ridden by the elation of tables turned, the dog finally getting to have its day. He darts clockwise around the vehicle, and I dash a tight line to hold the distance.

I am fitter, but he could be faster over a short sprint - I have to take the wind out of his sails. He chases for two laps before switching direction. I spot it, twist, and push off in the new direction, though he does gain a yard on me. After another lap another switch. I slip on the turn and lose two yards scrambling to my feet, still, no further distance is closed. A lap and a half and I pull it back and start to gain on him.

He stops and we stare at each other over the loading bay of the Hilux. His breathing is ragged, mine within my limits. Sliding my hand into my jacket pocket I press the unlock button on my key fob and bolt for the driver's door. Frantically, I grip the handle, yank it open and reach for the ball peen hammer in the side compartment of the door. Jamie rounds the back of the Hilux as I draw the hammer and sidestep away from the truck. I hold it aloft like a blacksmith pounding iron on an anvil. Jamie hits the brakes with an expression like he's been robbed.

'A hammer beats a jemmy and I beat you ... pack it in before it gets proved,' I threaten.

He says nothing and the crowbar relaxes to his leg. Normally impervious to reason the hammer possesses an eloquence and truth above words, that no turbulent, pig-headed brain could deflect. Force always makes itself understood.

We stand across from one another in contemplation of this fact, that his skull could be caved in as well as mine, and does his hatred of me outweigh the risk. I feel a flash of sweat, the rise and fall of my chest and the thumping of the heart within, and the ever-present adrenaline - nature's electricity charging through my veins, heightening senses, and narrowing them to animal necessity.

'Jamie, no! Stop!' shouts a female from somewhere over to my left.

I steal a glance and a heavily pregnant woman cradling her bump waddles towards us from the footpath to Acacia Close.

The woman gets between us. She is irate and the pitch and volume of her voice is high, 'Jamie, don't, you're on probation, think of me and the baby,' she says rapidly. 'Who are you? Why are you fighting my Jamie?' she yaps, alternating her glare from Jamie to me.

She is barely twenty, might be younger, but definitely not older. Dyed red hair has a stripe of black roots through the centre parting. She has a gap between the two front teeth, a perky nose and a pointy chin, and presumably poor self-esteem for having anything to do with Jamie Vinson.

I lower the hammer to my side.

'He's an ex-copper, biggest arsehole in the force … thinks he can still throw his weight around and I'm not fucking having it … bell end!' spouts, Jamie.

'Jamie, went a little crazy and things got out of hand, but we're cool now aren't we Jamie?'

'No, we're not cool, you and me are never going to be cool,' he says, jabbing the crowbar to make his point. 'You had better piss off before I wreck you.'

Jamie is playing up to her because he knows he is safe. It is a paradox that he is unaware of. He hates the pigs, detests me and what I stood for, yet knows I won't hurt him unfairly, or expose his pregnant girlfriend to harm or distress.

She looks at me with partisan eyes and says, 'Stop messing with my boyfriend, he doesn't need any more shit in his life. Leave him alone and go, go on, go.'

'No bother, but I'm not turning my back on that lunatic. I'll get in my car and leave when he is inside the house.'

Jamie bridles against the girl performing the whole *Hold me back* routine like he is a big dog pegged down by a two-tonne chain. I leave him to his pantomime, and when he is near the front door I get in the car and drive away.

After giving the heavy bag a half-hour hammering, I am more at peace with myself, and the drinks cabinet loses its allure. For supper I cook a medium-rare sirloin steak along with some fat chips, fried tomatoes and peas and finish by lavishing the side of the plate with Coleman's English mustard. After eating, I play a *Goldfrapp* playlist off the Bose speaker and settle down to peruse the file.

Amongst the disarray of papers there is a psychological study on the behaviour patterns of serial rapists. Reading through the study it becomes apparent that our rapist conforms to the organised sadist archetype. Planning, preselection of victims, tools, ritual, binding, extreme violence, and prolonged suffering.

There is also more from what has been rolling around in my mind these last couple of days, the violation of the home and the denial of it as a place of abode thereafter. The facial mutilation is an exertion of power and ownership like a branding, forever deviating a young woman's life. The dead don't suffer, but the living do, and there must be a sick satisfaction, a thrill or whatever the hell you want to call it, that prefers that knowledge to the quick finality of death, because he would have no problem killing if that is what he wanted.

For the rest of the night, I dig about online reading and watching experts attempt to dissect fiends like Ted Bundy, Gary Ridgeway, and Dennis Rader. Rader scoped his victims, then stalked them intensely before invading their homes - he called them projects and gave them code names. Bundy would revisit his crime scenes and relive the kill - perhaps The Slasher has the desire to do the same. I have very little to go on and not much to offer - except hunches, time, and a hunter's patience.

CHAPTER 9

I am shocked awake by the unmistakable thump of a sledgehammer pounding at my door. The sound punches into the emptiness of the house and the force sends tremors through the walls.

I spring out of bed and rush my trainers onto my feet to the steady, ear-flinching beat of the hammer. No time for 999 and the police, it would be done and dusted by the time the call was put out. I would defend the stairs with the spade if they got in, but for now the door holds.

I grab the Titan and stuffing a handful of twelve mil shot into my pyjama pocket run out onto the landing. Below the door starts to splinter and concede. The long landing window faces out from the side of the house onto the street adjoining my close. It also leads onto the flat roof of my garage and an escape route through the back garden.

I swing the window fully open and climb out onto the roof. Apart from this pocket of violence the night is cold and starless and still. I hear the breaking of glass, the sound of metal being struck, and mens's voices savage and urging accompanying the battering of the door.

Hands tremble loading a ball into the pouch of the Titan. I draw back the band to the kiss of my lips and creep along the roof to the front of the house. As I tread towards the edge my view expands beyond the side of the house and below the raised line of the garage.

I see three burly, armed men in gym gear wearing ski masks and gloves. Two are at the door while the third, chunky and all in grey is furiously taking a baseball bat to the Hilux - he can be first.

I aim at the meat of his buttocks; the distance is about ten yards. I let the ball loose and it whacks into the back of his right leg. He shrieks in pain and a blot of blood the size of a plum appears in the light grey of his joggers. He hops, turns, and losing balance on the slight gradient of the driveway sets the injured leg down for it to fold on him like a snapped matchstick. The man falls hard onto his elbow and the bat rolls away from him into the gutter.

Hastily, I load another .47 calibre ball into Titan and stretch it out for the next target. A goon in a black short-sleeved hoodie, whose ski mask has a red-rimmed mouth and eyes, steps away from the door and looks back at his fallen comrade.

'Fucking hell! I think I've been shot,' gasps the injured thug fingering the hole in his hamstring.

The goon tilts his head to the bedroom window and is side on when I release the ball. It smashes into his right forearm with a bone-breaking crunch slapping the full-length crowbar out of his hand. He emits a guttural revulsion at a coin-sized crater erupting blood, then looks up to see a rooftop sniper preparing another shot.

'He's on the garage, shooting, run!' warns the goon as nursing his broken forearm he beats a retreat out of the drive.

'What!' pants the third still immersed in the effort to breach the door. His ski mask is army-green, and he is wearing a shiny black ribbed gilet over a barrel chest with a tight navy-blue sleeved top underneath.

I nail the brute in the gut, a second after he claps eyes on me framing him in the forks, point-blank and with half power, threading the shot below the sledgehammer held across the chest. A tuft of white quilt sprouts from a rib of the gilet, and there is a harsh expulsion of air from the brute as he cramps over.

The goon stops in the road outside the close near a car I don't recognize. He fidgets in indecision first going one way, then the other and finally going back to the wounded.

With a ball pinched between my fingers I pick who is going to get a second helping. The thug is clumsily using the baseball bat to prop himself upright. I care more for my car than for my door, so I put the fork over his good leg and shoot.

There is a satisfying crack as the ball destroys the delicate workings of his knee. The leg gives way and both knees piledrive into concrete. Now on all fours, he cries as a wildebeest does when it is stuck in mud, 'Dave! Dave ... help me.'

Hesitantly, the goon goes to the aid of the crippled thug, his eyes flitting from foe to friend. The brute bounces off the door of the Hilux and clutching his stomach staggers out onto the road. Bathed in the stark white glare of the streetlight the thug crawls like a half-squashed beetle.

The brute scoops up the arm of the thug and the goon hooks under the other. Then as an unsteady huddle, they plod left out of the close towards the unfamiliar car.

Anxious heads turn, I watch over the forks of a drawn sling, they labour onward, I let fly at the mass. The goon gets one in the back. He spasms as if a scorpion has stung him and the scrum collapses. A pile of two on the road, the third reaching for a lump of burning coal in the wing of a broad back. This disarray, a little over twenty yards from me and less than five to the car. A smile sneaks onto my lips at the rout.

The brute opens the rear offside passenger door. The goon runs around the car to the nearside front passenger door and hurriedly gets inside. The brute drags the thug to the open door and stuffs him onto the backseat.

I aim at his back and as the ball is released the brute moves and the shot shatters the window. The driver's door is flung open, and the brute throws himself inside. I load up - they can have one more for the road.

Standing like an archer on a battlement the ten-gram lead ball is unleashed at the closing door. In an instance, the shot turns the window into frosty beads of falling glass. Cursing comes from the car, urgent exclamations of fear and panic and squabbling. The hands are calm now, the nervous anticipation of brutality gone and just the coldness of the hunter remains.
'Come again,' I crow.

The brute starts the car, the right side of his ski mask

bejewelled with cheap diamonds, he throttles the engine and the car lurches forward raucously picking up speed. I wave them off from the top of the garage, and at that moment from the top of the world.

Blue lights reflect off walls and windows as two police vans in convoy enter the estate. Rough diesel engines plough the silence as they speed along the road to my house. Empty-handed I wait on the roof for them. The first stops at the side of the house while the second brakes harshly in front.

Cops eject from open doors, two from the first and three from the second, primed for a confrontation that would not be. A swarthy, wide-hipped female cop in a yellow fluorescent jacket and highlighted hair in a bun assumes the lead. I don't recognize her; I don't recognize any of their young faces.

Her eyes see the broken door gripping stubbornly onto its frame and no more than five blows from defeat. They examine the dents and fractures to the Hilux and the long, ugly gouge along the offside of the Mazda - the claw of the goon's wrecking bar the likely culprit for that. Then they take in the tools, now strewn on the drive and in the gutter, the weaponry that should make this attempted burglary an aggravated one.

'Are you Will?' she asks, her hands relaxed in the pockets of her black combat trousers.

'Yes,' I reply.

'What happened here Will?' she questions in a casual, coffee-chat way.

'Three masked men decided to come through my door at three o'clock in the morning.'

'Are you hurt at all?' she asks.

'No, I'm fine.'

'Anyone else in the house with you?'

'No, I live alone.'

I notice a red ring of light around the aperture of her body camera that is capturing my replies, and my nosy neighbour Mrs Arthur peeking around her curtains. The racket had disturbed the night's peace and several houses in the close are lit up. Across the street too, my neighbour Mike Johns is standing at his door having a nose and a fag - anyone of them could have phoned this in.

'Can you come down, so we can talk in private?' she asks nicely. 'Sure,' I reply, aware of the alternative meaning - of come down so we can safely arrest you because it is something I would have said. 'I will let you in through the back … somehow, I don't think I'm going to be able to let you in from the front.'

In less time than a Formula One pit stop I've taken a hefty belt of Bulleit Bourbon straight from the bottle, and am back on track opening the side gate for Port Talbot's finest. The female cop and a spindly male officer with protruding eyes follow me into the living room. I gesture for them to sit and wait for their questions.

She perches on the edge of the seat and clasps her hands loosely over her knees. The tall cop sits back in the chair and is reading updates and conducting checks on his police mobile phone.

'Is there a reason why three men would want to break into your house during the middle of the night?' the inflection of her voice lifting at the end of the question in expectancy of an explanation.

She is on the downside of her twenties, her hair bobble is multi-coloured, the socks purple and her long fingernails are false and French polished - the job had gone to the dogs.

Whilst waiting on the garage roof I'd weighed up the pros and cons of full disclosure and had decided for it. That is until two big factors emerged and bulldozed the others. For one I couldn't prove it was King. He wasn't one of the masked men, and although blame could be laid at his door, conclusively tying him to the attack as its instigator is a considerably harder task, especially if precautions had been taken.

Several hoops had to be jumped through to secure a conviction and any evidential snag, hole or cul-de-sac along the way could kill the case. The stake in the gamble is showing my hand and having them tied afterwards. I'd be signposting any future action against King.

Secondly, I had exceeded what could be reasonably claimed as self-defence. The truth can be contorted, and I'd bent and stretched it plenty over the years. Stuff happens, and what matters is how well it is written up afterwards. Still, those shots in the back I had savoured are a tricky tell; it is better that they remain unknown and their side unheard.

'Probably, though I don't know what it is.'

'Really! You don't,' she says, striking notes of incredulity.

The whisky backs me, its warm waves rising and lifting like a benign wind. The answer I give under its influence is flippant, 'No, I don't ... and of course there is always the possibility they have hit the wrong house.'

She slants her head and screws her lips contemplating that possibility before asking, 'What were you doing on your garage roof?'

'Defending myself.'

She smiles quizzically, 'How?'

'With a slingshot. While they were busy smashing up my cars and breaking down my door ... I shot them from a safe, elevated position.'

'Shot them with what?' queries the gaunt officer in a strong Brummie accent.

'Twelve millimetre or .47 calibre lead ball bearings. They took a couple each and didn't want to take anymore,' I say, offering a smile as I produce a ball bearing from my pocket for them to see. 'Then they sped off in an old Ford Mondeo ... about ten minutes before you guys showed up.'

'Did you see the registration plate?' the female cop asks.

'Sorry, no, too much excitement,' I reply, though in my memory it is CU10 PKY.

'I see you've got a CCTV camera covering the front, does it record?' asks the gaunt cop.

'Yes, I'll put it on?'

I put the TV on and play the footage and all is peachy until the thug on a makeshift crutch gets the second ball to the leg. The female cop sighs, then inhales deeply, holding her breath a moment before commenting, 'Was that shot necessary?'

A poke from her and maybe a preamble to an arrest, in any case, it stirs the indignant side of my character. 'If you have to ask, you don't understand … you clearly don't understand violence and the force needed to deal with it.'

Looking at me askance she fires back with, 'From where I'm sitting it looks unreasonable, he's no longer a threat to you.'

'Exactly, from where you are sitting safely on a sofa. Advantage lives in the second, seize it or the tide may turn. Can you honestly say I could expect reasonableness from those masked men … if I was lucky they'd beat me to an inch of my life. So, I didn't take any chances, I kept going until they were beaten, and he wasn't beaten yet, he was outside my house with a baseball bat.'

'Using it to try and stand I would say,' she says critically.

'Look at you with your neat, polished nails … had much blood on them, have they? If I was still in the job, I wouldn't want you at my back in a ruck, questioning my actions, doubtful of yours, the handwringing would get us both hurt.'

'I could arrest you,' she threatens.

'Then why don't you?' I snap. 'I see the headline … homeowner is arrested for defending himself against three armed thugs, thugs are unknown and remain at large. It reads well, don't you think?'

'All right, let's leave it there, shall we?' says the gaunt cop.

'I'm not putting up with this, I'll be outside,' she huffs.

The gaunt cop shrugs his eyebrows and offers a smile of sorts, one formed out of embarrassment and tacit agreement, inferred, and not said. The recording runs on and thankfully the truly gratuitous shots are out of frame.

'Mr Cutter, I want to get the ball rolling by taking a statement from you tonight and getting your CCTV downloaded. Crime Scene Investigation will be around in the morning and CID will want to speak to you as well,' explains the gaunt cop.

'I'm not making a complaint, so all that won't be necessary.'

'Are you sure, with all that damage … why not?'

'That's my prerogative.'

CHAPTER 10

The greater part of my morning is spent making phone calls and feeling tired. First on the agenda is cancelling Dave Kumar and second is finding a decent carpenter that could come out at short notice.

I dress for town in a blue checked flannel shirt, loose-fit blue jeans, Browning baseball cap, Altberg boots and a canteen-green Trespass jacket.

Before heading in I go into the garage and unscrew one of the handles of a weighted skipping rope. I tip out the cylindrical metal weight and hold it in the palm of my hand; it is four inches long and weighs a pound. I close my hand around it and my enlarged fist becomes a club; I slip it into my jacket pocket.

The little Mazda has a crooked streak of white meanness running from wing mirror to petrol cap. I stand and seethe looking at it in the overflow car park of Tesco, wishing I had nutted at least one of them. It was only judgement that had lowered my aim, not anything else - I would have gladly seen them dead on the drive.

I stroll past the mighty pillars of the M4 motorway overhead, of a road that dissects the town carrying cars over and through this smoky steel town by the sea. Through Forge Road and into Bethany Square and the top of Station Road, along the pedestrian precinct with its disused church, charity stores, pawn shops and flats. I grab a coffee from a place called Selections and lean against the facade of the shop to watch the world go by.

This little spot is a seedy nexus, a lowlife thoroughfare and marketplace, and a prime hunting ground for a loitering detective. Four streets converge in the centre of town bringing foot and pedal cycle traffic from Velindre, Pentyla, Aberavon and Taibach.

The chemist doles out Methadone, Subutex, Pregabalin and other pharmaceutical enslavers to a trickle of runny-nosed, pasty-faced unfortunates. The shops are there to pinch from, although most prolific thieves would be banned from the shopping centre itself. A shopping bag of bacon flogged in the pubs to buy a ten-pound bag of heroin from a dealer peddling in the nooks and lanes. Low-rolling gamblers fritter away money they can ill afford to lose in four betting shops a spitting distance from each other.

Across from where I stand is the job centre, for those looking for work and for those made to come in because they are not. The benches next to the phone kiosk are for the daytime street drinkers. Ruddy, puffed faces, distended bellies, and mismatched clothes. They jabber amongst each other in a lesser inebriated version of the English language, while chugging down super-strength white cider from cans and three litre plastic bottles. One is yellowing from jaundice, some have bleary bloodshot eyes, as if they've wept rivers, and all are nullified, dislocated, and rejected.

I see a wino who I know and quite like shambling empty-handed along the precinct. Right now, you could take a picture of Chris McKeown and put it on a Drink Aware poster. He'd be one of those disintegrating mugshots taken twenty years into the life. I walk into his path and say, 'Hey Chris, long time no see.'

His skin is grey and completely washed out of any vitality. Hands shake taking a nearly burnt-out rollie from his chapped, cracked lips.

'Oh, hello, Sarge,' he mutters painfully. 'I thought you retired.'

'Not really.'

He was handsome once, had a decent enough job, played bass guitar in a local rock band that for a brief time made a small splash. Chris told me once that booze always held an allure for him. It could be like that for some people - seduced from the first sip. It just took some things to go wrong for him to fall headlong into alcohol's embrace, into its grip and onto its hooks.

I have an on-off relationship with booze, sometimes I get too close, get pulled in by its comfort and deceit and I spend too much time in its company. But I've always recognized when the relationship is turning toxic, when it becomes too clingy, close, and dependent - grateful for this inner altimeter able to measure the gradual descent into alcoholism. It is easier to push away if you aren't yet stuck, albeit the push away is weak and temporary and the romance renews - I guess it has one hook in me. Chris wasn't watching the road ahead and Chris didn't have a brake, and it got him, and got him early.

'You don't look too clever, Chris.'

'I don't feel it. I badly need a drink and I haven't got any money … none,' he mumbles anxiously, the words trembling like his hands and the dark, rheumy eyes carrying an unbearable sadness.

I flick open my wallet and glance at a thirty-year-old photograph of Beth and I goofing around in a photo kiosk at Woolworths. I pluck a ten-pound note from its folds and handing it to Chris say, 'Make yourself better.'

Chris appears a little taken back by this unexpected windfall and by whom it has come from, nevertheless, his nicotine-stained fingers eagerly grasp the note.

'Thank you … you know, I don't understand why people hate you so much, you have always been all right to me.'

'Keep it to yourself, or they will think you're a snitch, and besides, I prefer the crims to have the wrong impression of me … well some of it is.'

'Thanks again,' he croaks in that broken voice of his; the sad, sagging face temporarily lifted by a passport to bottled oblivion.

'Before you go, do you know Jemma Vinson?'

Small town, small underbelly - I figure he does.

'Jemma, yeah, haven't seen her for a while though.'

'Where could I find her Chris?'

'I couldn't tell you, and I would if I could, but I reckon Mandy Jones will know.'

'Where can I find Mandy?'

'Easy, she's over there on the bench swigging from a can of White

Ace.'

'Get yourself a flagon and tell Mandy to come over and speak to me. Tell her I will make it worth her while.'

The note in his hand charges a tired shuffle into an urgent if affected walk. I place a bet with myself that Chris will return and do as I have asked - a bet not to be made with many of his ilk.

Scepticism, suspicion, and cynicism are abrasive tools to use. In stripping back lies, uncovering motives and exposing human nature for what it is your own sense of humanity is eroded. I sometimes make little wagers in the hope of winning honesty.

Four minutes later I see Chris sucking on a three-litre bottle of Frosty Jack's like he is a baby at a tit. He walks and drinks his way to the other cider-heads. He speaks to Mandy, and she toddles over wearing a drunken grin.

Mandy has a concave-shaped face, blotchy skin, and a lazy right eye. Shoulder-length brown hair is held back by a polka dot hair band and is in places tangled. The hairband makes her forehead look vast. Mandy is probably not even thirty, yet age assailed from all sides goes off-kilter and forgets normal numbering - in street years Mandy's twenty-eight is thirty-eight.

'You know Jemma Vinson?'

'I might do?' she asks, swaying gently at the waist.

'Might know her or do know her, because might doesn't interest me and won't get you any money,' I reply sharply.

'I know Jemma,' says Mandy, affirming the answer with an exaggerated nod.

'Right, where can I find her?'

'What do you want with her?' she asks teasingly.

'I want to speak to her, no hassle, I just need to ask her some things.'

'Like what?'

'That's between me and her. Do you know where she is staying?'

'Yeah.'

'Okay, I'll give you ten quid if you tell me and another ten quid if it is true.'

'Twenty, I want twenty now,' she slurs.

'All right, twenty up front, but you'd better not lie to me.'

I draw a twenty-pound note from my wallet and pinching it tightly between my thumb and forefinger offer it to her. Fingers with nails bitten to the quick tug on the note - mine clampdown.
'Where?'
'Queens Court, she's dossing with Nicky Larkin at number fifteen. Don't say I said, okay.'
Nodding, I release the note. Nicky Larkin - this will be tricky.

CHAPTER 11

Queen's Court is Skid Row. If you wind up here, you are on the bones of your arse and one move from a shop doorway - in some ways a shop doorway is preferable. It is a three-floored block of piss-yellow painted concrete with a flat roof. At the front of the building twelve single-paned windows face out onto Victoria Road, with an equal number at the rear overlooking a car park given over to nature and junk.

When a shrivelled, glum-faced guy in a dirty orange tabard dismounts off his pedal cycle, and wheels it along the path to the side entrance of the building, I follow him. He pushes open the door, gets the bike in halfway and pushes it again to allow the rest of the bike through. I pick up my heels and catch the door before it swings back shut. The guy looks over his shoulder and seeing me climb the skeletal stairs carries on to his ground floor flat.

The first-floor corridor is gloomy and the linoleum floor sticky, causing the soles of my boots to squelch as they peel away from each step. My nose twitches from funky odours of smoked weed, grime, fried food, open bin bags and spilt beer. Music rumbles from flat twelve, a heavy drum and bass pulsing against the confines of the room, a dog barks from room thirteen, and room fourteen has a section of chipboard bandaging a break in the door.

Chatter and the murmur of low volume music emanate from inside flat fifteen, then a loud laugh, joined by another, and a scoffing 'Fuck off ... you two are just as bad,' off the back of it said by a man.
'That's the last of it, you greedy, pipe-hogging fucker ... I was supposed to have a hit on that,' complains a woman.

'Weren't enough for two, now fuck up cos you're spoiling my buzz,' says the same male voice with the hardness of it sounding similar to Larkin's. 'Here's seventy … go to Barry Blobs and get four rocks and some z-bars if he has any.'

I quickly backtrack to the stairs and watch for the opening of the door. I hear it come free from stiffness and I vanish down the stairs. Lurking in the shadows below I peer through the gaps between the steps, as a woman in trainers, jeans and a baggy hooded top descends and goes out the door. She turns left for Victoria Road and after allowing her five seconds, I follow.

The woman crosses the road and walks purposefully towards the general direction of town. I get behind her, although not too close to spook, and call out her name. Jemma spins on the spot reacting as though my unexpected word is an incoming knife.

The baseball cap conceals her forehead and curtains of curly, auburn hair partially shield the cheeks and jawline. The scars have settled, ameliorated by a surgeon's skill and marzipan-make up to less angry furrows and pits. Still, there is only so much that can be done when a man and a Stanley knife set themselves to destroying an identity, and Jemma's face resembles a big-piece jigsaw. Apart from the attraction of her face, Jemma is a pear-shaped five feet five inches restlessly wriggling and ticing to an irregular rhythm.

'Jamie said you were looking for me … what do you want?' her voice is hard, yet jittery.

'To help you and the other poor four women that were attacked,' I say, cringing at what is still a pretentious sounding statement.

Her sparse lips twitch twice before she says, 'How are you going to do that … you're not a pig anymore, you got sacked for being shit and telling lies?'

'No, I resigned and the reason you lot hate me is because I was good at my job.'

'Nah, that's bollocks, you're just a horrible cunt that got off on giving people a hard time. They finally found you out and fired you for being crooked and shit,' and her crack-run mouth gurns out a mocking laugh.

I dampen down the anger that would see me lash her with her countless failings and eviscerate her with the cruellest cut of all

- that I'm glad I took her daughter and spared her from a squalid, screwed-up life with such a neglectful junkie mother. Seen your adopted daughter lately? The words are on my tongue as I watch her head wobble like a cheap nodding dog ornament for a car. I'm sick of these people, of wading through the quagmire of their irrationality and dysfunction. It is being forced to converse in a coarse nonsensical language where the meanings are whatever you want them to be. A deep breath expels the vitriol and I choose the high road over the gutter.

'I am being paid to find your rapist ... and if I find him, I am going to take him down hard, because like you say I'm a horrible bastard. I have got nothing else to do but find this sicko ... twenty-four-seven with no rules to hold me back. You must hate him more than you do me. Talk to me, give me the information to find him ... set me on him and pit two people you hate against each other.'

I hold dilated eyes that have pupils the size of pennies. My words have rooted her to the spot, found chinks in her loathing and are making her think. 'Let's go to Bar Galois and I'll buy you Grey Goose Vodka and even something to eat if you want it.'
'All right ... he's a bigger cunt than you,' she concedes.
I smile coolly, sometimes logic prevails.

The owners of Bar Galois must wish that a light aircraft would fall out of the sky and crash into Queens Court. It didn't have to be a plane, any act of God reducing it to rubble would be gratefully received, for however a swanky a pub and restaurant it is made into, the efforts are somewhat detracted by the weeping sore standing next to it.

We sit outside on dark-brown wicker chairs, situated on a patio area between a huge conservatory and a car park at the side of the pub. Jemma has a view of the seafront promenade and I keep an eye on the front of the building. The sun has separated from the clouds gifting the afternoon with warmth; in better company this is a pleasant way to round off a stroll across the beach, and Beth and I had wound up many a good walk in a pub or restaurant - this one too.

Jemma has a double-loaded White Russian and I go for a pint of full-fat coke. Before anything can be said, the glass is drained in four long gulps, and the creamy coated tumbler placed in front of me. 'Same again, Cutter,' she says grinning and scratching a scab on her chin. I order two in case she tips another straight down her throat.

'Trying to get me drunk, Cutter?'

'I would need a squad of Russians for that job,' I quip, taking a sip from my pint.

Jemma demolishes another Russian then fiddles with the empty glass, and for a moment her eyes glaze introspectively when she laments, 'I can't remember the last time I drank in a pub and had a drink that wasn't cheap.'

She then looks at the left side of my face and says, 'Your ear ... the top of it is missing ... someone bite it off?'

'No, a bullet took it.'

A barely hidden chuckle, a smile across meagre lips - it amuses her. The hostility is easing, though a new wave of it could come at any second, prompted or not - this can't be rushed. She chews the corner of her lip and says, 'What's the deal here ... who's paying you?'

'One of the other victims; these days I work as a private investigator, and she's hired me to work on the case.'

'Drinks are on her then?' she asks in a half-knowing way.

'They're expenses.'

She looks up from hooded eyes, hard, scarred eyes, eyes that see angles. 'She got money to waste, has she?' and there is envy in the voice, a hint of spite and a recognition of opportunity.

'No, she has not,' I answer firmly.

'How much could you spend today on me ... as expenses?' she says, scrounging around like an urban fox.

'We'll see, but that's not the way to look at it. There is an evil man out there who has inflicted incredible pain on you and other women and will probably do so again ... there is the greater good to think of.'

'You are making money out of it, why shouldn't I? You've

always made money out of other people's misery, that's what pigs do. You want to hear what happened to me, you are going to have to pay,' she argues, cocking her head in defiance and flashing a dead front tooth.

The truth is like a stiff jab to the kisser, and it stops me in my tracks - reason can do that to you if you abide by its code. Am I really anything more than a mercenary?

'You know I'm right ... I can see it in your face.'

My mind reaches back riffling through experiences to try and prove otherwise. Earnestly, I tell her, 'No, it was always a vocation for me ... that is why I stayed on the street and didn't seek a higher rank or a desk job. I often went further than I needed to and got hurt doing it. I admit I enjoyed what I did, and I suppose you could pull dubious reasons out of that if you wanted to. Call bullshit on it if you like ... but I mean it when I say I was proud to serve.'

'Keep telling yourself that Cutter ... I'm in this life because I have to be ... you earn from it, and what is worse you enjoy it, you've just admitted it. That is why you were the most hated copper in Port Talbot ... we knew you enjoyed hunting and harassing us. Other coppers came and went, but you stuck around all those years like a stain,' she lambasts, and the triumphant scowl, sneering tics and sewn together face make her altogether hideous to me.

An uncomfortable feeling engulfs as the ugliness derides me, reflects back at me. The urge to be mean swells behind it, rising like vomit. The urge plays on my lips until I clamp them shut. I resist the pleasure of punching something by quietly choking the arm of the chair.

'Let's get this done, I need to know the details of the attack and I will pay you fifty pounds for you to tell me ... twenty before and thirty after,' I say sourly.

Jemma drags the third Russian across the table, and I notice how swollen and discoloured her hands are. The oedema and cyanosis are symptoms of intravenous drug use: poor circulation, collapsing veins, blood clots, abscesses, gangrene, and amputation being occupational hazards of her worst vice. She quaffs half of her drink and says, 'All right, but I'm going to need another couple of these to tell you this shit.'

I stick another two White Russians on the tab which must be well over thirty quid at this point and pass her a twenty-pound note. We zigged and zagged, went up ladders and slid down snakes and Jemma had pushed my buttons - and that was only the preliminary.

Emotionally, she is the equivalent of a Moray eel - slippery and vicious. Obtaining an account without her biting chunks out of me, storming off, or me not losing the grip on my temper are slim. I remind myself to pity her - the bad life leading to an awful one. Drug damaged and emotionally untethered she is not wholly to blame for what she says and does.

'Wednesday 26th August, twenty-six Knox Street, tell me what happened?'

Jemma dismisses the third Russian and brings over a fourth before beginning, 'I was with Conrad Harris at the time … fucking idiot he is. We'd had a row a few days before and I'd kicked him out and he went and stayed with his mate. I smoked some brown and then a bit of weed and went to bed at around one o'clock, I think. It was still dark outside when he grabbed me. He was kneeling on top of me and had his hand tight around my mouth … then he hit me hard to the jaw … cunt broke it and knocked me out. I came around bent over the arm of the settee with him raping me. I tried to fight, but my hands were tied behind my back, and he was pushing my hips down on the arm, pushing so fucking hard it hurt. I tried to scream and couldn't because my mouth was taped shut.'

Jemma blows out and her eyes fill with tears. She wipes them away with a sleeve and makes a good start on the fourth drink.

'After he'd cum he pulled me onto the floor. Then I felt the knife cutting into my face. The fucker just kept cutting, I thought I was going to die … kept waiting for my body to be stabbed, throat cut, or the prick to strangle me … but it never happened. He ripped my face open, fucking dragged me into the hall and left.'

I half want to console her, and half don't - what do you say? It is going to be all right? Platitudes don't belong here. 'What did he tie you with?'

'Those plastic strip things ... you know with the teeth that they seal property bags with in the cells.'

'Cable ties?'

'If that's what they call them.'

'Hands and feet?'

'Yeah.'

'Was he wearing gloves?'

She thinks for a moment and then replies, 'Rubber ones, thin like pigs wear when they search people.'

'Did he say anything to you?'

'No, like what?'

'Well, he talked to two other victims that I know about, told them why he was cutting them, and he didn't say anything to you?'

'Not a fucking thing ... is that important?'

'It's different, just different or different for a reason.'

'What can you tell me about him?'

'Not much ... he was very strong I can tell you that. I've had fights with men, and they'd have trouble stopping me ... but he was like a brick wall. I saw blackness, a big shape of blackness over me and then I was out. He was a blocky-looking fucker like you.'

'What about when he was cutting you, what did you see then?'

'Nothing, he sat on my back, gripped my hair, and peeled my face like a fucking orange?' she says finishing off the fourth. The torment resurfacing in her eyes and her face falling from the horror of remembering.

I get a glimpse, a tiny reveal like a fragment of sun through a leafy tree, then in the span of a glint it is gone and I'm unsure of what I have seen.

'This will sound like a stupid question but it's not. Did you have a dining table or kitchen table and chairs?'

'No, never had the money, we ate in front of the tv … why?'
'He bound the others to chairs. You didn't have any, so he had to do something else. How did he get into the house?'
'CID said that he had cut through the playing fields and jumped over the back wall into the garden. They said I'd left the downstairs window open. There was a footprint left on the windowsill.'
  'Did you?'
'I must have, but I don't remember it … I feel the cold, so I wouldn't normally leave windows open, not at night. I've gone over it hundreds of times, doubted myself, but the window was found open and there was a footprint.'
  On my phone, I check the weather for the date, and it was cool with intermittent light showers. Cool is not open windows and sleep above the bedsheets weather - it is closed windows and wearing two layers outside. Then again, a zonked Jemma could have left the stove on, the bath running, or forget she was the mother to a four-year-old kid. 'The front and back doors, were they locked? And where were the keys?'
'I used to keep the front door key in my purse, and I always kept my doors locked … you can't trust druggies,' and she flicks a contemptuous smile. 'The back door key was missing. The door was locked, and Conrad had the key. I phoned him and asked for it back and he said he'd bring it back when we made up.'
  'What is Conrad like?' I ask.
'A fucking weak, lying, waste-of-space … he had to spark up a joint before he could tie his shoelaces. It wasn't him … too skinny, wrong shoe size and he was with his mate all night drinking, CID ruled him out.'
  'How long had he been living with you?'
'About four weeks. We'd been seeing each other for about four months before that. He was losing his place in Harvey Crescent and so I let him move in with me. It was a bad idea … in the same house, together all the time, he got on my nerves.'
  'Can you think of anyone that would have wanted to do that to you?'

She bites the corner of her bottom lip giving thought to her exes, her enemies, her victims. 'A few years ago, I ripped off a couple of Yardies who I agreed to carry for. If they caught me, they'd chop my hands off, but it's not them because this prick is white. Nuh, there are a few that would happily knock my teeth down my throat, mostly girls, but what that cunt did to me … no.'

'How were you found?'

'Conrad came back and he heard me crying through the door. Twelve fucking hours I lay there for, naked in a pool of my own blood, freezing to fucking death on a cold, bare floor.'

'What have the police told you about the case?'

'Basically … that they've got fuck all idea who done it, size ten footprint and nothing else … no witnesses, no DNA, no fingerprints, no fucking clue. Is that it now? I've got to be somewhere and back before someone gets pissed with me.'

'Nicky Larkin?'

Her lips curl in acknowledgement before returning to a short, mean line. I slide a business card and three ten-pound notes across the table to her and say, 'A match made in heaven; the two of you must get on like a house on fire.'

'Sarky prick.'

'One that doesn't beat women though,' I say standing up.

I recognize another brief acknowledgement of truth before she too stands and chugs down the last of the Russians. I go inside and pay the tab, then leave through the front door. Jemma is outside on the pavement being harangued by Nicky Larkin over bunking off with his money, while his two crack mates hang back watching the fireworks.

One is Ricky Lee Bosanko, a cherub-lipped, cocksure thief with black spikey hair and a nose like a kid's slide. When straight Bosanko was a sharp operator, never easy to catch, and if caught, always difficult to pin. The other guy is greasy-haired and fat for a crackhead. He has absent eyes, a flat nose and acne scars on both cheeks - his face is new to me.

Five years had passed since I last laid eyes on Larkin and those years had withered him. He is now a gangly, sharp-boned, sunken-eyed skull, shouting cocaine-fuelled abuse. Thirty years old and fifteen of them torrid. His hatchet face is even sharper, the hair now buzzcut and brown, whereas before it was highlighted and styled - addiction stripping everything down to the essentials. His clothes: distressed, low-slung jeans, an orange Adidas zip-up top and red fat-tongued trainers.

Five years ago, we butted heads, then his six foot two inch frame was prison-gym stacked and both of us wound up with lumps and bumps. On top of that Larkin got a busted knee, a face-full of CS spray and trip back over the wall for his trouble; and for mine, a complaint that indirectly cost me my job.

By my estimation, Larkin and I had had about twenty-five run-ins with half of them violent and the rest just unpleasant. What he has against him in life is also what he has going for him in certain situations, and that is recklessness - Larkin rarely thought of consequences or if he did, he didn't care about them, and that made him dangerous.

Larkin clocks me and stops shouting. Bug eyes track my movement and behind them, a crack-addled brain adds Jemma and I together for a number it doesn't like.

'Cutter!' he shouts.

Reluctantly, I stop and face Larkin. Bosanko, a long-time burgling buddy of Larkin's, stands alongside him and will probably get involved, especially if he can sneak a shot in or kick someone when they are down. Slouching with his hands in his pockets the dopey guy lazes over to the other side of Larkin; his intentions I'm unsure of.

'Tread carefully Nicky, I'm not in the mood,' I warn.

'What were you doing with Jemma? What are you fucking after, Cunter?' raves Larkin, tilting and jutting his head in thuggish challenge, his stubby, malnourished baby teeth now with a couple of gaps between them.

The fastest finger on the button is Jemma, 'Asking about you and stirring shit,' she blurts, her jigsaw face expressing a curious mixture of surprise and devilment at what she has just set in motion.

No irony here, though bitter, nonetheless. Jemma is hitting two suckers with one stone. If malice has a look I'm seeing it from Larkin now, as her words dance a jig in his deep-fried brain. After an hour of tangling with Jemma my patience is shot, and my tolerance is threadbare. I just can't be arsed explaining myself. My reputation is a stain and one I will never be rid of as long as I work in this town - you can't get clean washing in a dirty bath.

'I'm going to keep this simple and skip to where this ends, there's no crack in hospital ... and that is where you bunch of worthless maggots are heading if you don't back the fuck off.'
Instinctively, my stance becomes bladed: left in front and right in reserve with weight equally distributed between the two. I slip the little bar out of my pocket, form a fist around it and load it against the back of my right thigh.

'He's got something in his hand,' warns Bosanko.
'I do Ricky, and it's going to have you all napping on the pavement in no time.'
'The big man, always the big man ... eh Cutter,' grandstands Larkin.
'Get him, Nicky!' Jemma incites drawling out drunken words, 'Fuck him up! The cunt took my baby girl.'
I bore my serious brown eyes into his fat black pupils and coldly say, 'Go on Nicky, fuck me up ... let's see what happens when neither of us has rules to follow.'

Larkin looks down on Bosanko's five foot five inches, on a supple adolescent physique suited to shimmying up drainpipes and squeezing through half-opened windows, and then to the other dimly lit guy whose battery seemed to be running on three per cent - and the fire fades. None of them fancies it, and I allow myself a grin, a slap-on-your-own-back grin, the type I've been told winds people up - they aren't wrong.

My conceit doesn't factor in Jemma, and I don't see the clawing curveball coming my way. Seething, screaming, her arms flail for my face. I bat one hand away, though the nails of the other find their target and scrape stinging lines of skin from my forehead.

I grip the neck of her hoodie and stiffen my arm to keep her at bay. Bloated hands clutch my wrist and dropping her head Jemma bites the knuckle of my forefinger. I pull away from the pain, the right hand poised to punch, yet impotent against her. She holds on like her life depends on it and is yanked forward into a stumble as I swing her behind me.

In charges Larkin winging a wild looping punch with a crazy nine and a half stone behind it. I see his bony fist loom in from my right in its final quarter-second of flight. I've just the time to duck an inch before it crashes into my right eye. A yellow light explodes in the corner followed by an acute and refined pain scurrying in all directions like torch-lit spiders. My eyeball goes into a fit.

Jemma drags on my arm and chows on my hand. Larkin steams forward punching the side of my head. Going with the current I turn fully into Jemma and kick her in the left shin with the steel toe cap of my Altberg boot. The connection is bone-snapping brutal, and she collapses on her side howling.

Larkin wraps an arm around my neck and pulls me off balance and into the road, while a spring-footed Bosenko tries to hit me from the front with a flurry of ugly, pit-a-pat punches. Some fall short, a couple are blocked by a cross-arm defence, one gets through and fattens my top lip.

I regain my footing as Larkin is about to sink his arm into a choke. I twist away from the crook of his arm into his chest and discard the weight from my hand. Larkin moves around with me and clamps my neck in a tight headlock. Bosenko's trainer skims a sitting-duck face, and the left thumb of Larkin works towards my good eye.

I stick the side of my head into his stomach, clasp my hands together around his waist and position my left leg behind both of his. The thumbnail scratches the bridge of my nose and is a fraction from the eye. Simultaneously driving my head and dropping my weight I heave him over my outstretched leg. Larkin's back hits the road in a hurtful sounding thud.

Using my forearms against his neck and ribs I prize myself free of his arm and kneeling over him savagely pump my right fist into his face. Three conscious separating knocks to the chin and his body goes limp and his eyes become still.

The victory is short-lived. A brain jarring boot to the underside of the jaw has my ears ringing and vision curtained by night and unbright stars. I roll, curl, and look through bars my forearms have instinctively made. A stomp comes and another and another, and my cage shakes and rattles in a street rodeo of shoe imprints and nihilism. Remembering past punishments my body soaks it up and the fuzz quickly clears.

Rolling into Bosenko I hook a heel and latch onto his leg with both hands. Bosenko tries to wriggle free, but I have the leg locked between head and shoulder. I rise and lift the leg. Bosenko hops, a plea for clemency forming on his lips. I chop him at the ankle, and he slams face first onto the unforgiving road.

Slack-mouthed and dazed, Bosenko is propped on his elbows gawping at a blood print on the grey concrete, that his nose and mouth are dribbling more blood onto. Damaged parts of his body compete for attention: a broken nose, a gashed elbow and swollen ankle are my guess.

I wiggle my jaw and the pain spurs me to boot him in the side a couple of times. Grunting he curls into a ball, adding breathlessness and sore ribs to the line-up of complaints. The dopey guy isn't so dopey after all and is ambling around the corner into Elfed Avenue.

Distraught and hateful, a stream of obscenities, curses and cries flow out of Jemma as she peels the jean leg away from her wound. Still spread out, Larkin appears as though he is sunning himself on the road. I pick up the weight and move closer to Jemma so I can look down on her. I say, 'You're an unfit mother and a vile human being, and it is just as well your daughter can hardly remember you now.'
The words pierce deep enough to momentarily take her mind off the dent in her shin. I'd sunk to the gutter, it wasn't hard, there wasn't far to go.

CHAPTER 12

The taxi takes me to London Row in Cwmavon and stops outside The Brit Pub. It is a detached house, painted white with a beer garden at the back overlooking the river Afan. It has a porch entrance and six grey-lined windows divided equally between upstairs and down. The typography has 'The Brit' written on the wall before the first top window, 'Fine Real Ales' before the second and 'Est 1845' before the third.

Inside there is an eclectic mix of exposed stone walls, Persian carpets, French chairs, and a log burning stove for the winter ramblers to warm their feet next to. Glamorous portraits from another century are printed onto the cushions of the wall seats and strikingly there is a lamp stand made out of a naked female mannequin, fastened to a pedestal and spray painted gold - her head replaced by four drooping Victorian era lamps. In all the decor manages to be quirky and cosy at the same time.

The bar is reclaimed wood and has a line of five ales on draught and a selection of specialised gins along the back counter. I choose a pint of draught Guinness and take it over to a window seat. My phone vibrates with a notification, and it is Stanner letting me know he's running ten minutes late. The pint is smooth and given my day simply glides down my throat.

As my phone is already out on the table, I decide to look over my case notes until Stanner arrives. It occurs to me that Jemma's assault doesn't fit with the others. I don't yet know the specifics of the attacks on Jodie Green and Eleri Parker-Evans. I do know from Olivia's notes that Jodie owned her own hair & beauty salon and Eleri was working at the time as an intensive care nurse in Singleton hospital. As far as I am aware Eleri, Jodie, Kelly, and Olivia were all successful, clean-cut professional women - Jemma possessed none of those attributes, except she was in the same age bracket - mid to late twenties.

Does the departure from victim type matter or is it irrelevant? The West Yorkshire Police made the costly assumption that The Yorkshire Ripper was deliberately killing prostitutes, when he was instead murdering those who were readily available to him. It was the killing and not who he was killing that was important as the police and subsequent victims were to find out. The difference is The Ripper prowled the streets scoping for any lone female, whereas our boy invades a home to rape a specific lone female - the difference in execution is substantial.

My train of thought is interrupted by the phone ringing. It is an unknown mobile number. I take a long swig and answer, 'Yes.'

'I want to make a deal,' says Sean King in a calm, measured voice.

'I'm listening, Sean.'

'I'll pay you three grand to cover the cost of the damage and we'll call it quits. No more hostility from me and none from you.'

'Lost your appetite for murder, eh Sean? What has made you change your tune?'

'Ibiza,' is the flat reply. 'I looked you up.'

'It is going to cost you more than a measly three grand, Sean ... now who is being cheap? I gave you four and a half two days ago. I want fifteen grand. Five for Gerald Jenkins, five for the damage your crew caused and five to help me feel less mean and vengeful.'

'Fifteen, that's steep, it's far too much.'

I feel calm and coldly detached when I say to him, 'The only reason at least one of your hapless crew isn't in a coma is because I didn't want them to be. So, ask yourself what is brain damage worth? Because I'll be introducing a .47 calibre ball bearing to that shiny dome of yours if I'm not compensated. Then your young girlfriend Kaylee can drive you around and wipe the dribble from your chops, or perhaps that'll have to be your son Jayden, because Kaylee will have fucked off for someone who can speak properly.'

He fumbles the words of a reply, 'I need time ... time to get it sorted, to get it together.'

'Time you don't have, borrow it if you have to. Fifteen thousand in my PayPal account by Saturday … oh, and Sean, send it as a friend,' and I terminate the call.

I finish my pint and go to the bar for another. The barman is pulling the pint when Anthony Stanner walks in. Almost reaching six feet tall, Stanner has long legs, a short, slim trunk, sloping shoulders and a swan-like neck. He has neatly trimmed swept-back white hair, and a pink hue to a clean-shaven complexion belonging to a face which defaulted to waggishness.

He looks well, as you do when you are relieved of stress and shift work and play golf all the time. He now wears an elegant pair of half-rim rectangle glasses, which previously were only worn for reading. He is smartly dressed in a navy brushed cotton chambray shirt, dapper sky-blue chinos, and a pair of tan stitched shoes.

'Will, you old dog.'

'Tony, how are you keeping?'

'Better than you by the look of your face, what happened?'

'Some old acquaintances ran into me outside Queens Court,' I answer, with as much significance as if I'd nicked myself shaving.

'Members of the Will Cutter fan club, hey?'

'Yes, you could say that.'

'What were you doing in that shithole?'

'Working a case.'

'Yeah, I heard you'd become a private dick,' he says with a snigger and a flex of his eyebrows.

'Well, as I was a public one before it was an easy transition,' I reply, joining in on the joke.

'What are you having?' I ask.

'I'll join you on the Guinness, thanks.'

We take our pints over to a window table near a stag's head and antlers mounted on the wall. 'You know Will, I shouldn't really be consorting with a notorious criminal, but my curiosity for a good yarn got the better of me,' he ribs. 'I read the story, but there is always an untold story, the one underneath … like how you got away with murder,' and the word is wickedly accentuated.

Tony is the same as I remember him - he likes to poke, stir, and provoke - a proper wind-up merchant.

'I've got an honest face,' I say drily.

'Yeah, right, as honest as a nine-pound note,' he scoffs.

'Says someone who looks like he fleeces grannies for a living.'

'I woo them, and they give me gifts,' he says with faux sincerity.

'From B&M Bargains,' and we both laugh at the invention of Tony Stanner, the cut-price gigolo from Bryn. 'I'll explain all later,' I say.

'Is that before or after you reveal your ulterior motive for our night out?' and his narrow, discerning eyes conduct a reconnaissance over the rough terrain of my face.

I smile and say, 'Never bullshit a bullshitter isn't that what they say?'

'They do,' Stanner chimes self-assuredly.

 'I want to ask you what you know about the slashings?'

'Oh, The Chair Rapist, why?' he says, and then it clicks, 'You're working the case ... for who?'

'One of the victims?'

He wrinkles his lips and I detect an inward roll of the eyes. He says, 'Believes in miracles, does she? No disrespect meant, but I've got more chance of hitting three holes in one on the bounce than you do of cracking the case.'

'I know ... I didn't want to take it on, but I couldn't say no. I suppose a forlorn hope is better than no hope at all,' I confess to him, fully aware of the dig - that my long shot is longer. 'To think, if only I'd carried one of those blue books under my arm and worn a snazzy mauve shirt and tie combo, I'd have a chance.' Tony throws his head back in a laugh, 'Quite true and don't forget a Parker pen to write in it with. The deductive magic can't happen without a decent pen.'

The smile given is sardonic and broken by the pint glass tipping the black stuff down my throat. Another smug detective looking down his beak at me. I have more street craft than all of them and gut-instinct too - the temptor and the guardian as I like to call it - the yes and the no.

Stanner poses a forefinger and says, 'Let me guess who it is who has hired you. It's not Kelly because she's dead, not Jodie because she is lost down a deep, deep rabbit hole that she is not coming out of anytime soon. It's definitely not Jemma, there is more chance of it being Kelly's ghost than her. That leaves Eleri and Olivia and I'd say it isn't Eleri because she changed her name and moved away. So, I'd bet a double whisky you are being employed by Olivia Holland.'

'You were on the case then, which means you wormed your way back onto CID … and you're right it is Olivia who has hired me to investigate the case … and if you'd like a whisky, I'll be happy to pick up the tab because I'm paying tonight.'

'Ask away, I don't mind singing for my supper.'

I raise my nearly empty glass to him and he copies the gesture. 'Okay, what can you tell me about the attack on Eleri?'

'Eleri was the first. The assault on her occurred in the early hours of Monday 4th March 2019. She lived here in Cwmavon with her husband at thirty-two Pine Valley. She was a highly-trained nurse and maybe has gone back to it, probably not though. The husband Alex Evans was a local plumber but because of his injuries isn't able to work anymore. A neighbour's CCTV picked up a hooded figure in dark baggy clothes marching quickly along the pavement with his head down at four minutes past three. Our arsehole walks up the driveway to the front door which is situated on the side of the house. He bends the door handle guard back with a pliers to expose the mechanism and then extracts the lock out of the door and he's in. If he knew what he was doing it would have taken him twenty seconds and made next to no noise. He then climbs the stairs and on the landing encounters an investigating Alex who must have heard the entry. He bludgeons him about the head with a hammer, not with the intention of killing him is the thinking of the investigation team, but with a sufficient severity that he isn't capable of being a problem. We know the attacker used a hammer because of the indentions it made in Alex's skull.'

Stan pauses for a drink, wipes the froth from his top lip and then carries on, 'Eleri wakes and manages a single scream before being subdued by the attacker. He straddles her on the bed, covers her mouth with his hand and puts a sharp blade to her neck. He tells her in what Eleri describes as a put-on satanic whisper, that if she makes so much as a whimper, he will cut her throat from ear to ear. He stuffs a sock into her mouth and then drags her downstairs to the living room. There he ties her hands behind her back with a cable tie and flips over a dining room chair. He pushes her through the upturned legs of the chair, places a video camera on a cradle in front of Eleri and sets it to record … he tells her this, that he is going to watch what he is going to do to her over and over. Then he cuts off her pyjamas and using a condom he rapes her. When he is done, he says to her that he is going to turn … a beautiful butterfly into an ugly caterpillar. Well, you know the next part … it defies belief what one human can do to another. It is one thing to momentarily lose your head and spontaneously commit an act of violence. It is another beast entirely, to coldly and with premeditation cut chunks out of a defenceless woman's face with a craft knife. He opened the curtains and left her in front of the window on display. A leaflet dropper saw her at ten o'clock and phoned it in; any later and Alex would have died.'

'Did he leave you anything?' I ask.

'Not much. We know he is about five feet eight, white, or at least has a light complexion. The black nylon stocking he wears obscures his features, but the victims could see that he is white. He is thickset and strong; all the victims describe his strength and the ease with which he controlled them. The Chair Rapist is careful and forensically aware. He's left no bodily traces whatsoever, except a size ten footprint belonging to a Converse All Star trainer. Wisely he doesn't carry a phone, no repeating number off masts or routers. The SIO believes he has considerable burgling experience, and a great deal of effort was directed to tracing, implicating, and eliminating known burglars, as well as the usual sex offenders. There were a couple that we initially fancied, though nothing came of it. Because of the distance between the victims, he must be using a vehicle. We did massive trawls for CCTV: houses, petrol garages and shops. We checked the ANPR cameras and what came up checked out, and what didn't we haven't seen again.'

'What do you mean?' I ask.

'In the Jodie Green case, a silver Peugeot 207 was picked up in Briton Ferry around four am and again at half-past five. It was on stolen plates and the driver had the sun visor down so the camera didn't capture his face.'

'Smart. Smart too, leaving it late to drive back when there would be cars on the road and tired police back in the nick,' I add.

'We haven't picked it up since and we tried. Our ANPR nerd Trevor Fordham enhanced the image and identified the 207 as an XR spec hatchback, five-door 2006-2009 model with a roof rack and dent in the front passenger door. Registration was put through national, local and partner agency databases, petrol stations, car parks you name it and added to the hotlist. Traffic pulled every grey Peugeot 207 they could find ... and nothing ... a bunch of ordinary Joes and Joannes that didn't fit the bill. I suspect it was used once and burned, car and plate. He shows discipline.'

'Discouraging.'

'Oh, yeah! As it went on morale sank all right, few leads and those we had hit dead ends, SIO Stuart Jones got the axe and was replaced by Detective Superintendent Ian Isaac who carried out a review. No real change, the leads dried up and the investigation floundered.'

'Jodie Green, how did that go down?'

'Same, except there was no bloke to hammer so he knocked her out instead, albeit after the disfiguring which included partly scalping her. Did a better job on the door handle this time and didn't wake his victim. The M.O. of the assault itself is identical including that creepy speech about turning a pretty butterfly into an ugly caterpillar. You know, she was a fragile soul before the attack and shattered into a thousand pieces after it,' he says dwelling on the final few words.

'Where in Neath?' I ask.

'Ten Gardners Lane at the top of the Melyn.'

'Is Jodie still in a catatonic state?

'I believe so, I bumped into Barry Kileen at Neath Market about three weeks ago. He's still working the case and he'd recently contacted her consultant for an update … and the poor woman is firmly locked inside her head.'

'Does she have any family I could speak to?' I ask.

'Yeah, if you don't mind taking a trip to Belfast,' answers Stan with a laugh.

'What, if any connections have been made between the attacks?' I ask.

'All white females … no, that's incorrect, Olivia is biracial, isn't she?' and I nod. 'All between twenty-five and thirty years old and all prettyish … including Jemma if you get beyond the chaviness, though no exact physical type, they were all slim or shapely women from sizes eight to fourteen. Four out of five in Port Talbot, four out of five home alone, four out of five building businesses or careers. Other than that, no real connections, or links between them,' and Tony displays his palms in a there-you-have-it gesture.

'Four out of five also feature that freaky bit about butterfly to caterpillar conversion; what's that all about?' I ask.

'The obvious answer is he hates attractive women; they all have that in common. It has probably because they've given him the cold shoulder or something and hurt his little feelings. I mean he hasn't attacked a munter, or even a plain Jane, so the attractiveness is important. Butterflies are beautiful and caterpillars are not … but why get hung up on insects? Fuck knows. Do you remember Bryn Edwards from Swansea Central CID?'

'Yeah, vaguely,' I reply, thinking of a gruff, fat detective with a reputation for perseverance.

'Well, he began calling him The Caterpillar Man, but it never took off. Around the office it was The Slasher or Chair Rapist, but mostly The Slasher because that is what the public and media refer to him as … and the chair thing sounds like a fetish, which of course it is.'

He finishes his pint and picks up a menu. I get another round of drinks and two double Johnnie Walkers, his with ice, mine as it comes. I swirl the blend, an amber enticement to accelerate the night - I take it and it takes me, and we're off and running.

We order food. Tony opts for lemon-infused hake, and I go for the cheese and leek pork Glamorgan sausages with creamy mash and onion gravy.

'Have you fully retired … got your hand in anything?' I ask.

He shows disinterest which morphs to a prurient gleam when he says, 'Never mind about that, quid pro quo, spill the beans. I want to know the dirty, bloody details of your misadventure in Ibiza.'

'Well, like any good story there was intrigue, sleaze, violence, and retribution …'

CHAPTER 13

I wake up with a foggy head and a strong sense of dislocation from how I've wound up in my bed. I make a strong spoon-standing coffee and sift through an alcohol doused memory for what Tony had told me last night - it doesn't add to a lot. I defer breakfast, chuck on a pair of blue jeans, a roll-neck Submariner's wool jumper, and the dependable Altbergs and leave the house.

Not having a better idea, I drive to Knights Road in Margam. I park the car between two drab Council-owned buildings housing six flats apiece that are found in the same design throughout the town. In front is a locked gate to the Groeswen playing fields and the football club I played in goals for as an eleven-year-old. 'Too short to cut grass' as one parent once commented when I got chipped and let a goal in over my head - it's funny the things you remember.

Adjacent to the changing rooms is the youth club where I did Judo for a bit, ate loads of chewy sweets, and learnt to play pool. I flashback to a Christmas disco in 1984, 'Like a Virgin' playing, me in my Pierre Cardin sweater that I wore far too often, lining the walls with all the other awkward pubescents in the first, nervous flushes of fancying one another.

Beyond the field and the railway line behind steam billows upwards from the coke oven quench towers. A northerly wind carries the emissions from the steel cooling process high over the field and the houses to the mountain behind - as usual, the future of the steel plant and consequently Port Talbot is uncertain.

I climb over the low wall that is at the side of the gate and walk clockwise around the edge of the playing fields. About seventy yards ahead of me is a man walking a dog off a lead. It is an Alaskan Malamute, and the man is throwing a ball for it using a red chucker. The man is walking a loop of the field in the same direction as me, and must have just passed the changing rooms before I arrived.

Whether it is just a listless morning after a heavy night before, or a deeper blue feeling of hopelessness that I feared would come from being utterly lost, I don't know, but dejected sums up my present state of mind as I plod over the wet green grass to another pointless enquiry - feeling not much more than a tourist on a gruesome tour.

The Malamute nudges the man's hand with his nose. The man isn't looking at him, instead, he is staring into the back garden of a house in Knox Street. The dog barks and the man absently scoops the ball up and flings it into the field. The dog chases, a pink tongue lolling out of its wolf's head and its bushy tail curving towards its back like a scorpion's sting; the man returns to his intent observation.

He has ginger hair and pasty-white skin and the powerful build of a stunted prop forward. Counting the houses from the junction with Knights Road, Jemma's is the eleventh along. I am passing the eighth, which by my reckoning is number twenty. Twenty-two, twenty-four and twenty-six where the man is standing and where I am going to, to do exactly the same as what he is doing. I can see he is about thirty and that the ginger hair is tousled on top and razor-cut on the back and sides. He has on a shadow-grey Parka coat with a fur-edged hood, grey workman's trousers featuring multiple pockets and black padded knees, and a pair of brown work boots.

The Malamute brushes his leg and drops the ball in front of his left foot. Turning and bending the man presses the chucker over the ball and when rising is facing me.

Although not small, his face is a squashed square of cramped features: baby ears, a short forehead, a piggy nose, and a pursed mouth. In contrast, he has expansive amber eyes as if the sockets had been filed down to give them centre stage and these eyes appear alarmed, though I don't see them change to become so. They stay that way as we exchange looks, then he turns and continues walking around the perimeter of the field.

Suspicion pricks me hard and my heart and stomach plunge. The man is the same physique, the same height and is showing what is perhaps an interest in one of the crime scenes.

A high-speed train is coming into the station and will barely stop - a handful of seconds to jump on or let that train pass. If I catch the ride I know where I want the train to go but have only my guts to say it will go there - this is what suspicion is and I love it - it is a bet on yourself.

I bite on my instinct and follow him the same way I had done so many times before but with much less at stake. Adrenaline backs instinct and I tingle and tremble in trepidation. I'm onto something or conning myself and I'm unsure which. I had got it wrong in the past and it could be he lived there as a child and had stopped to reminisce. I dismiss the second guess because like a missed shot it mattered little, you just had to keep courageously pulling the trigger and enough would fall, indeed plenty had.

I pretend to use my phone and dawdle as if I am distracted by other things. I put him on a long lead because some people, including me, don't like having someone too close behind them and will stop to let them pass.

The man bears right from the houses skirting a chain-link fence separating a band of pygmy trees and bushes buffering the Swansea to Paddington mainline. The man answers his phone and talks for a while. He stops throwing the ball for the Malamute and picks up his pace. The field slants alongside a recently built mini-housing estate called Clos Y Wern, and the man sticks to the thin track of trodden grass running around its border.

The field's fourth side is open and has many access points from a long unnamed lane running behind several streets. The man takes the main one which leads onto a piece of rough concrete adjoining the lane. Parked there is a blue Ford Transit Connect minivan. The man reaches into his Parka pocket and the indicator lights on the van flash. The van has livery on the side - it reads 'Margam Carpets & Flooring,' and has a telephone number underneath.

I tilt the phone and blind-fire the camera drive-by style. The man opens the driver's door, and the Malamute jumps in and over to the front passenger seat. He gets in and gives me a cursory look as I continue around the field towards the changing rooms - old memories scattering from a crossfire of thoughts zinging around a carpet fitter with disconcerting eyes.

The van is parked outside the store on Tollgate Road; a simple Google search had found it. It is the last but one in a row of houses that have had the ground floors converted into shops. It has a drab facade and is gloomy inside, looking like a business just starting or about to close. I am stationed in the Mazda further along the road with my eyes glued to the rear-view mirror.

The chill of the pastrami and mustard sandwich which I've just bought from the Co-op detracts from its taste, but the gurgling of my stomach wouldn't allow it time to warm. While I watch and wait, I listen to a Jordan B. Peterson podcast and sup my way through two bottles of cherry coke. The second becomes an uncomfortable mistake, and not wanting to break three hours of surveillance I lean forward in the seat and surreptitiously relieve myself into an empty bottle.

Twenty minutes later at a quarter-to-one, the man loads a carpet and underlay into the back of the van, and I ready the Mazda. The man gets in the van and drives up Tollgate Road and as it passes, I look down and scratch my head.

I tail him onto the main road and into Taibach where we stop at the traffic lights. He turns right and I follow. I'm directly behind him so hang back to create some space. The van's indicator signals left, and the van slows to turn into Field Terrace. The van approaches a roundabout and goes straight on towards a larger roundabout that has slip roads onto and off the M4 motorway.

I allow a car coming off the motorway to get in between us and I follow it and the van onto the roundabout and off at the second turning. I see the van slow and turn left into Park View and knowing that there are only three streets it could logically be going to, I drive on and take the next left into the street in front of it. I drive to the end of the street and its junction with Theodore Road. This road runs alongside a building that used to be the Port Talbot Arts Centre. It is now a school for expelled kids, and next to it is an infant school and an ambulance station.

I cruise along Theodore Road with its pavement trees, gable roofs, bay windows and tall ceilings, and see the van parked outside a house close to the junction with Parkview. The man is at the front of a porch and is speaking to an attractive woman standing at the door. He is wearing the same work trousers and boots, and a plain blue sweater that probably has the company name on the breast. In his right hand, he carries a toolbox. The woman steps aside and the man and his toolbox enter.

I decide not to hang about. The Mazda with its stand-out scar has had enough exposure for the day - the man inside and his white woolly jumper too. I ring Olivia and she answers immediately.

'Miss Holland, it's Will Cutter.'

'I know, I've saved you … your number I mean.'

'I'm nearby, could I call around?'

'You have something?' her voice lifting to a hopeful note.

'I have questions … which is a start.'

'Yes, yes call round, I've made another cake.'

Olivia Holland can bake a cake. I sit in the same winged leather chair relishing each mouthful of a moist, tangy, and indulgently sweet lemon drizzle cake. The coffee served alongside the cake is premium and with its hints of dark chocolate and tobacco is not like anything I've tried before - I feel spoiled.

'Fantastic cake, you should go on *The Great British Bake Off*,' and the moment the words leave my lips I wish I could pull them back.

She is curled in a defensive ball on the plump leather seat. The oversized wool jumper she is wearing drips off her like it is melting. She smiles an elongated smile looking like *The Joker* without the makeup and says, 'Perhaps when I can pluck up enough courage to allow another man to slice open my face I might. I'm not very photogenic at the moment as you can see.'

I want the floor to open up and swallow me. 'I'm sorry, that was insensitive of me.'

Olivia lights a cigarette and then says, 'No, I owe you an apology, I've made you feel bad. I lash out … my poor father gets it all the time. My therapist says it is one of several negative behaviours that I've developed. Speaking of facial injuries, what happened to you?'

I examine the brackets of broken skin on my knuckle and while pinching the greenish scab for pus say, 'An old grudge wanted settling … and it got settled.'

'I'm sorry you've been hurt. What have you got?'

'Probably nothing … a hunch that I'm following to see where it leads. Tell me, when did Jack and you buy the house in Ash Grove?'

'November 2019,' she answers, needling the pad of her thumb with the nail of the forefinger. 'We wanted to be together forever. I guess forever didn't include this,' and she circles a forefinger in front of her face.

I'm stumped for something appropriate to say so I shake my head and frown before carrying on with, 'Was it good to go or did it need work?'

'Chintzy and run down, it was a hangover from the eighties, it needed to be stripped back and modernised.'

'The Berber carpets, when did you have them fitted?'

Olivia exhales a long lungful of smoke before she answers, 'January 2020 I think, yeah, it was the start of the year.'

'What company did you use?'

'Carpet Masters on Western Avenue, I should still have the invoice in my Gmail.'

I tug at my beard twisting the hairs until it hurts - it is not the answer that I wanted. Olivia scrolls through her phone while the knuckles of my free hand tap an irritated beat on the armrest.

'January 18th order number twenty slash four, says Olivia, flexing her hacked eyebrows in anticipation and wriggling the tail of the thick scar leaving her hairline.

Nibbling my bottom lip, I let out a long sigh through my nose, fish out my phone and show her a rear profile photograph of the carpet fitter. 'Do you know this man?'

'Do you think it is him? she asks, venturing to the edge of her seat.

'Less so now, have you seen him before?'

Olivia pours her eyes onto the photograph and the scars yearn for it to be so. A tear comes to her eye, tips off the lid, and rolls into the bowl in her cheek before she can catch it.

'No … and if I have … I don't remember. Who is he?'

'A carpet fitter, but he either owns or works for a Margam firm. I don't know anything else about him, except that he had an intense interest in Jemma Vinson's old back garden in Knox Street. It was the route the rapist took into the house,' and I spread my hands to show that is all, and a pang of embarrassment radiates from a paper-thin offering now shredded.

'There were two of them that came to lay the carpets. An older guy who had bad knees did the speaking. I was getting in the way, so I went out for a ride on my bike and left them to it.'

I nod, sweat dampening my brow from the heat of the room, the hangover, the dead end.

During the drive home I get a phone call from a Swansea mush named Paris who wants her kidnapped dog retrieved from her ex-partner Crystal. Picking the bones out of her account it soon becomes obvious that the Labradoodle was a partnership pet bought together and is jointly owned. I tell Paris that I don't steal dogs and advise her to file a civil complaint at the County Court.

I wrap up the call on the road before my close. I slow and check my rear-view mirror and look into the closes before mine. A double-cross - King could be lulling me into one. Simple as ABC - accept nothing, believe nobody, challenge everything and on top of that assume the worst of people.

I warily enter the close, then with speed park and exit the car. The door key ready for the lock and a glance over the shoulder as I enter. The MX 5 roadster I see turning into the close and stopping in front of my drive belongs to Annabel.

She swings her long legs out and brings her svelte handbag from the front seat as I've drummed into her. Save for the dark brown hair, dimple on her chin and an olive complexion she is the spitting image of her mother. I added those ingredients to the mix and thankfully little else. The time and the fitted pinstripe trouser suit say she is calling on the way home from work.

The warm wide smile that she greets me with turns sour after she reads the trouble on my face. 'What the hell has happened to you now?'

'It's nothing, I'm fine.'

'You don't bloody look fine to me,' Bel's long eyelashes rise like a porcupine's quills.

'Well, I am … a small scrape, nothing to worry yourself about. Part of the job I am working on went south, it's over, done now.'

'Oh! So, you would be happy if I said that? Had your attitude. No, you wouldn't. You'd shout at me and then try to fix it.'

She is right. She has that about her mother too. 'Shall we take this inside?'

I make us both coffee and we sit in the conservatory. 'How is work?' I ask.

'Going really well, I've been given junior counsel in a juicy employment tribunal, it could be close to a million-pound settlement.'

'That's great …'

'Dad, what are you doing? Why are you still on the streets working these stupid, grubby cases and getting hurt? And don't say the money, not after Hannah offered you a job with her firm.'

'It's not a real job, is it? I don't get on with heights and I don't know anything about scaffolding.'

'Yes, Hannah knows that and is more than happy … really wants to, wants to give you two thousand a month to shuffle papers and answer the phone for what you did and lost. Dad, Hannah knows you blew your lump sum by hiring that big-shot lawyer to defend you, and that your police pension was stopped because of the criminal conviction. Hannah has grown the company and business is booming. She can easily afford it. Park your pride and take the bloody job, Dad!'

I lay my head against the back of the chair and puffing my lips out exhale a deep breath. 'I can't, not right now. I've picked something up that I can't just drop … I can't.'

'You've done enough, whatever it is, leave it to someone else … get yourself out of the bloody trenches and do something easy for once. God, I wish mum was alive, she'd lick you into shape, cut all your nonsense out,' and she looks mournfully up at the mountain, but I don't think it is what she is seeing.

'Bel, I've just got to give this job a month, exhaust the limited things I can do, and I will be able to tell my client with an honest heart that I have done all that I can.'

'Promise me, promise me, dad, that a month from now you will jack it in and go work for Hannah.'

'All right, I'll try. I promise to try.'

'Never mind trying, just do it,' she insists.

I rub my shoulders against the back of the chair like I'm a bear with an itch and move my mouth to say something that stays unsaid. She holds an expectant gaze and I say something else, 'How is Henry? I mean, how are you and him going?'

Smiling Annabel replies, 'He's fine and we're good … now stop deflecting.'

'Listen to you going all lawyer on me.'

'Yes, probably because growing up you were all police on me,' and her eyebrows arch in exclamation.

I meet her big brown eyes with a sense of disquiet, which greatens when I transpose Olivia's brutalised face onto that of my daughter's. Flesh sliced, peeled, and picked, crisscrossing lines of scars like spools of barbed wire over no man's land. I rub the image from her face and think of her as a young girl riding a little pink bike, instead of what she is - a beautiful woman soon to be twenty-five.

CHAPTER 14

The walls of the corridor are a submarine grey. It is a never-ending corridor until it abruptly ends in a heavy steel door. A bunch of keys jangle in the hand of a faceless guard and the lock of the door clacks open.

I follow the silent guard who then assumes a face, a shifting face as non-descript as that of a shop-window mannequin. We walk through twisting corridors and more stern steel doors for what seems like an age.

Then sunlight. Bright, joyous sunlight. I float towards a fifteen-foot gate festooned in barbed wire; road noises and the tweet of small birds beyond. My tipless ear is bleeding. I smell cordite. The bulletproof vest constricts my breathing. Once again, the forest-green gilet I'm wearing has two round holes in the pec and just below.

A disembodied voice echoes through the yard, 'Four years.' The hum of a motor gradually retracts the gate and the barbed wire slithers over the metal. On the other side is Beth. She is standing on the pavement looking more lovely than ever in a long floral summer dress and diamante sandals. Thick luscious auburn hair cascaded over her shoulders and a broad smile on her full lips.

The sunlight envelops us and is heavenly. The sun's brightness magnifies and becomes blinding, the intense whiteness obliterating line and form amidst the sound of a jet engine on full burn. The whiteness fades, a cell door slams, and the four walls laugh.

I awake with a start. It is 5:26. That dream or a variant of it, that has Jay dying no matter what I do torments my unconscious hours. I get up and go downstairs to make a coffee. It is an hour before dawn and outside blackness is beginning to leave the night. I sit in the conservatory watching the day arrive; my head as busy as a city centre bus station.

Three coffees later I'm on a workout mat grinding through fifty Turkish Get Ups, battling against a twenty-eight-kilo kettlebell. Into the forties and I am bathed in sweat and deep in oxygen debt. Using a heavier weight or in this case, fatigue introduces a further element of risk to the exercise and the last four are shaky. Whilst bridging on the penultimate rep my movement is sloppy and I almost lose control of the bell overhead. I lock the shoulder and correct the position a fraction before the tipping point where it could not be saved. Then, what is effectively a cannonball with a handle comes down and breaks what is unlucky enough to be underneath it.

Steam rises from my body as I slowly walk laps of the garden paying off the air owed. A sycamore tree leans over the wall of my house and between it and the roof of the house behind, chattering magpies mob one another. When sufficiently recovered, I use the same bell and finish the workout with two-hundred kettlebell swings.

After showering I treat myself to a cooked breakfast and decide to follow one of the ideas that had arrived this morning and stuck around.

Carpet Masters Limited sits between a Lloyds Pharmacy and a beauty salon named Body Solve. It is a warehouse-style building painted a warm beige with a navy roll shutter door to the right of the entrance that takes up the entire height of the building.

A short, grey-haired man with a stiff gait is outside and I see him press a fob on a set of keys. The door winds open. A chubby, bald bloke ducks under and wheels out a long trolley from underneath an orange shelf. In total, I count six shelves housing rolls of carpet. Following the instructions of the older guy, the chubby fella hauls a roll of red carpet onto the trolley.

I approach the older guy giving the orders and say, 'Good morning, are you the manager or owner?'

'Owner. How can I help you?' he answers in a nasally voice.

'Name is Will Cutter, and I'm a private investigator. I'd like to ask

you a couple of questions about a carpet your company fitted.'
'Oh!' he says with a puzzled look on his face. 'Whatever for?'
'I'm working for lady named Olivia Holland who engaged your services in January of 2020 to supply and fit Berber carpets at sixteen Ash Grove in Baglan. Two fitters worked on the job. I think one of them was you and I want to know who the other fitter was?'
Curling his bottom lip over the top one and squinting his eyes he asks, 'Why? Why do you want to know something like that?'

Questions, everyone has questions. At times like these, I miss wearing the uniform. People just answered it. I force a smile and say, 'I'm following a lead,' and as a prompt I produce the clearest photograph of the man saw in the field. 'This man, did he work for you?'
His eyes give it away. 'Yeah, he did, until he left me in the lurch to set up on his own.'
I sense the bitterness of a betrayal and realise that from here on in I'll get answers. 'When did he start with you? and when did he leave?'

He takes a moment and then says, 'Let's see … Dominic was with me for six years. He left last year after we came out of the second lockdown. No, it was a bit later than that, it was the tail-end of the summer, perhaps even September. So, it was sometime during 2015 that he started with me. I took him on without any experience and taught him the trade … and my mistake the business side of it too. That's gratitude for you, huh!'

'Yeah, I can see why you'd be miffed at that. So, would Dominic have fitted the carpet with you? It is order number four slash twenty, fitted on the 18th of January 2020 at sixteen Ash Grove, Baglan.'
'Toss-up between Phil and Dom,' and he flicks his thumb at the bald man loading the red carpet into the back of a van. 'I can check for you.'

We go inside the shop, and it is sample city: stands, rolls, racks and drapes of carpet, vinyl and laminate flooring hanging off the walls. He sits behind a desk, and I plonk myself down on one of the two chairs in front. And it occurs to me that Olivia and Jack had sat here too. They had browsed and discussed and selected their carpets before taking these seats. Was it Dominic that sat across from them that day? Was he courteous when he processed their order and took their payment? Was it then he sized her up for the cut?

'Computer is slow today,' he says.

'Are they ever quick?'

'No, I suppose not,' he says grinning. He lifts his eyes from the screen and considers me thoughtfully. 'When we met, I thought I recognized you and since then I've been trying to place your name and your face. You're that former Police Sergeant that got jailed in Spain, aren't you?'

'Yes, I am. Some crimes are justified and are worth paying the price for.'

'Shouldn't have gone to jail at all if you ask me,' and he continues working the mouse. 'Okay, yes, Dom and I did the job.'

'What do you remember from the job?'

'Nothing. If it goes smoothly and they pay, there isn't much to remember.'

'What is Dominic's last name?'

'Jane.'

I screw my brow, 'Jane?'

'Yes, like the girl's name Jane, spelt without the y. I heard he used to get teased about it in school. They'd be stupid to tease him now, that's for sure.'

'Why is that?'

'He's a powerlifting champion. He's won a couple of British championships in the light-heavyweight class and finished well in European competitions too.'

'What is he like as a person?'

'Quiet. Keeps himself to himself. Not really suited to sales ... more of a backroom guy than front of house if you know what I mean. You could get him talking about sport and he liked betting on it too. Was a good grafter ... but in the end disloyal,' he says with a snide smile.

'Anything else?'

'Dominic was unlucky with women. I don't think he had a proper girlfriend until Eva came along. I think she had a lot to do with him leaving and setting up on his own. She quit her job in Morrisons to manage the shop.'

His eyes cloud over in deep thought and then he says, 'Perhaps I'm being harsh on him. Eva probably spurred him on ... you know what women can be like? Mine cracks the whip in our house. Look, what is this about? Is my firm in any trouble?'

'No.'

'Well, is Dominic then?'

'Could be.'

'How? What for?' he pushes.

'You're being really helpful Mr ...'

'Richley, my name is Jeff Richley.'

I unfold a piece of lined notepaper from my shirt pocket and put it down on the desk in front of him. I stay leaning over the desk, smiling while encroaching on his space. My tone is a gauntlet in a velvet glove, 'Mr. Richley, on that sheet of paper, are five names and five addresses. I want you to tell me if your company has laid carpets for them and who were the fitters?'

I hear his brain tick and whirr: five women's names, five local addresses, a private eye prying into his business. Jeff starts to join the dots. 'That's right. Those are the names of the Slasher's victims and the home addresses where they were raped and mutilated.'

Jeff swallows hard and nervously licks his lips. 'I don't know ... data protection and all that.'

'The information you provide will be strictly off the record and stay between you and me. I've seen what this maniac has done to the faces of other men's daughters. Do you have daughters or nieces, Jeff?'

'I do,' he answers heavily.

'There's a link. Do your bit and help me find it.'

Jeff inputs the data and runs the checks. 'Thirty-two Pine Valley ... we did a job there in 2013 but nothing since. Ten

Gardner's Lane. Yes, on June 19th, 2018, Dom fitted laminate flooring in a study. The customer was Jodie Green. Ten Lupin close … no, we haven't done work there. Twenty-six Knox Street … that is also a no. And the last one sixteen Ash Grove we know about.'

'One last thing, what is Jane's date of birth?'
Jeff makes the face of someone going against their better judgement, but after rummaging in a drawer for a P45 says, '27th December 1991.'
'Thank you, Jeff.'

I leave the shop feeling charged, giddy, and somewhat daunted. Two connections. He'd been inside two of the houses, albeit over seven years - as a carpet fitter, he must have visited a thousand.

CHAPTER 15

A sparse, broken line of spectators are watching Cwmavon play rugby at home against Taibach. Calls from the pitch and shouts from the sidelines mingle with slaps, thuds, and grunts of thirty men crashing into one another. Nearest the clubhouse the line is at its most solid and I pick my way along it looking for Geraint Thomas. He is standing next to the halfway line, the last and most imposing figure in a group of four men.

I hear sharp, urgent voices overlapping one another as a Taibach centre intercepts the ball and sprints for the line. The centre gets just ahead of an ankle tap and runs the ball under the posts for a try and an easy conversion.

Emitting a loud groan Geraint throws his hands in the air and turns away from a jubilant Taibach. 'A sloppy, careless pass,' he complains, shaking his bull-like head in disappointment. 'But fair play to Taibach for capitalising on it,' he acknowledges, looking back to the field and offering a short, muted clap.

'Bad time to ask you for something?' I say smiling.
'No, not while we're still winning, though another score from them will change that. What can I do for you, Will?'
'I need a car for the case. One that is not my own. I need it to carry out a few hours of surveillance today and maybe again in the week. I want it to mix up the vehicles I'm using.'
'You onto something?' he asks.
'I might be. I came across this man, his name is Dominic Jane, he is a carpet fitter and a champion powerlifter. At the moment he's putting some ticks in some boxes. Did Kelly ever mention him? Do you know him?'
'No, and that is the kind of name you would remember.'

I show Geraint a photograph of Dominic Jane receiving a first-place trophy at a powerlifting competition. 'Nah, I don't know him, but you think he attacked my Kelly?'

The blue eyes harden and graveness seeps into the lines of a lived-in face. Graveness or is it menace? I must be careful with my words. I only have an inkling, and here I am striking matches in a hay barn. 'Geraint, I'm probably barking up the wrong tree. There is a ninety-five per cent chance I'm wrong on this.'

Geraint separates a Mercedes car key from a ring of keys and hands it to me. 'It's the old Benz parked outside the bungalow, and Will, here is my number, if you want to borrow it again.'

The drive to Great Western Terrace brought ghosts and they came out of the Penllyn Estate. Fucked-up Robbie Taylor is one of them. Poor bugger is dead twelve years now - off his head walking in the fast lane of a dual carriageway at night is what did it for him.

In one of those depressing, characterless flats I pounded his arms to make him let go of the bed. Dragged him with his tracksuit slipping down his thighs out of the top flat, his girlfriend screaming behind us, Robbie laughing his head off while trying to spit in our faces. PC Jon Derek and I wobbling down the metal steps, a gnat's hair from a tumble. Gob on our jackets, carrying him like a slain pig along the footpaths between the flats. The stone scraping the skin from his arse - and all because he bilked a taxi driver over a thirteen-pound fare.

The amount of violence I have inflicted and suffered over beer money and idle threats is lamentable. Once, I fought an Irish Traveller over old car batteries stolen from a scrapyard. The law matters but seems to matter less when you are fighting over its crumbs.

Geraint Thomas' car is an eighteen-year-old silver Class C Mercedes Benz with one hundred twenty-one thousand miles on the clock. I bring the seat forward, adjust the mirror and in doing so make the pine tree air freshener swing like a hanged man. Before more morbid thoughts arrive, I get the old girl going, and she takes me to the carpet shop on Tollgate Road.

According to the shop's Facebook page, it closes at five. I park further along in a layby next to the park where I have a good view of the entrance. I kill the thirty-minute wait by digging deeper into the company's pages. I find Eva. Eva Gregory likes Facebook and Instagram - is enamoured with social media in general. Eva is a prolific poster, an open book singing to the world.

In contrast, Jane is absent except where others post of him. Strangely, he doesn't promote his powerlifting achievements on any of the social media platforms. Second thoughts, if he is who I think he is then I wouldn't want to draw attention to myself either. Eva makes up for it though, and I glean several titbits of information.

They had met when he had fitted a carpet for her in May of 2021. Eva took a fancy to him and asked him out. The romance blossomed and by August Eva had moved in with Dominic. Pictures of a back garden barbeque hint to me that he lives somewhere on the Sandfields Estate. The couple had holidayed in Tenerife in August of this year.

There is a photograph taken by someone else of them arm in arm on the beach. Looks-wise they are a match. Eva has thin blonde hair, protruding ears, and a rather horsey face. Fat thighs are only partially hidden by a sarong and her arms are flabby. He, bone-white and pot-bellied with trapezius muscles like ramps, forearms that can hold three hundred kilos and legs that could jack up a car. She, showing her big teeth in a smile and him wearing an expression as if he were constipated. At the back end of August, the relationship hit the rocks and Eva moved out. Interesting.

I call Tony Stanner and ask him if the name Dominic Jane had found its way into the inquiry. He is in the middle of a round of golf and isn't keen to speak for long. Stanner tells me that at the high point in the inquiry there were over sixty detectives working on the case with thousands of actions initiated and completed, and the tens of thousands of pieces of information generated from those actions stored on the HOLMES 2 computer system. The name didn't ring a bell with him, he might have been spoken to through house-to-house enquiries, associate or vehicle enquiries and the like, but had not featured as a person of interest, a name on the board, of that much he was pretty certain.

At ten past five Jane and a young lad exit the shop. The lad jogs across the road and cuts through the park - keen probably at his age to get a Saturday night started. Jane locks up, stiffly gets into the minivan, and drives past me up Tollgate Road.

I U-turn the Merc, accelerate, the automatic gearbox lagging and lurching from the pressure of my foot. I catch sight of the minivan heading along Margam Road, and I follow it onto the slip road for the motorway. A stink of steelworks sulphur passes through the car as we travel through Margam towards Taibach; steam, smoke and gas funnelling out from the works and dispersing overhead.

He takes the slip road to Sunnycroft roundabout and from there heads to Sandfields. Onto Western Avenue passing a sign that warns you are entering a densely populated area.

I take it easy over the speed bumps and trail the van into St Helier Drive with its flower and colour closes. A queasy twinge of realisation and the heart kicks into gear. I hang back as he swings right into Long Vue Road, now, only a handful of streets and closes he could be going to.

I see him pass Aster View and turn right into St Kitts Place. It is a Cul-de-sac without garages or a garage compound access, so he'll be parking in the street or a driveway. Jane angles the minivan into the drive of either the last or the first house depending on how they are numbered.

I take a last-second turn into the opposite close, drive around an island in the centre of a turning circle that has a battered Nissan Micra dumped on it, and park facing St Kitts Place. I unfold a copy of *The Evening Post* over the steering wheel, read a paragraph about a fundraising mum, and then lift my eyes to the house.

It is a dreary wet-sand colour favoured by the Council and is one of a block of four. The drive is discoloured concrete and has weeds growing through the cracks. It looks unloved. I think about sticking a GPS tracker on the van because it appears to be the only vehicle he has. This thought is disturbed by the front door opening and the Malamute suspended over the doorstep straining against its lead. Jane tugs the dog to heel, and they set off on a walk.

I reach for the glovebox and pretend I'm looking for something. Jane crosses the close slicing through one of those idle swathes of grass before re-entering Long Vue Road the way he had come. I give him a lead, put on a baseball cap I have brought and then get out of the Benz to follow him.

Dark brooding clouds occupy the sky adding a heavy grey hue to everything underneath. A strong wind kicks an empty crisp packet along the pavement, and somewhere behind an empty aluminium can tinks and tonks a tune with the road. Rain is imminent and I zip up my jacket collar. Jane has changed into a pair of thick black joggers and a matching hoodie. With the hood worn up, he looks almost square. A square, black mass.

Jane must have been squatting the day before because his legs are as stiff as pokers and I force myself to walk unnaturally slow, to tread as if I were stalking a rabbit. Jane crosses over to my side of the road, the Malamute trying to pull him like a stuck sled. Jane approaches the T-junction with St Helier Drive. He's crossed the road so there'd be no sense in him going left. His intention could be to cut through the back of Purple Close, through the garage compound and onto Western Avenue.

Jane lops the corner off the junction and heads along St Helier Drive. Ahead of him Lupin Close and opposite it on the other side of the road Purple Close. I watch for a sign that he intends to cross over, but he looks to his right and takes the diagonal footpath into Lupin Close.

Jane ambles towards the back of the close, slow, wading through treacle slow, eyes fixed straight ahead at number ten. Jane reaches the slalom gate and stops. I mirror him, then realising just standing there I'm naked for a spot I nip into the nearest front garden.

Jane lingers, strokes the Malamute, and stares into the front living room. I hover by a front door, hand poised to knock, but with eyes glued on Jane. I see him put his phone to his ear, shift a little on the spot, but not avert his gaze. The Malamute is impatient. Jane winds the lead and it remains bolted to his leg.

I'm startled by the sound of the front door opening. An elderly man having a nose like a puffin's bill and skin speckled with liver spots asks crossly, 'Can I help you?'
'Is Andrea Thompson at home?' I ask while glancing back at Jane, who is still loitering outside Kelly Thomas' old house, holding what is presumably a quiet phone to his ear.
'No, whatever gave you that idea? I'm Mr. Milton and I've lived here for fifty-two years.'
'My mistake. Sorry to have troubled you.'

I turn away and Jane has gone through the gate. Clouds - pregnant with violence - glower and the close darkens. I feel the first picks of rain and then it absolutely slashes down.

CHAPTER 16

In my head, Dominic Jane is shaping up nicely. In reality, I have two-fifths of fuck all. Whilst walking his dog Jane has stared at two houses and fitted carpets in two others - so what? He vaguely fits the description - the keyword being vague - so would a lot of other people.

An open-source criminal background check of public court records draws a blank. On the one hand the fact that he hasn't appeared in a criminal court for any offences is a drawback. A red-warning light for cruelty to animals, flashing, peeping, sexual assault, or knives would provide another tick in another box. However, a guy with a clean sheet can fly under the radar. One of the first priorities of the investigation team would be sifting through known pervs to implicate or eliminate. Taking a microscope to each sad one of them until something rang wrong, but nothing had, they were all in the right places at the right time.

I recline on a chair in the conservatory listening to the rain lash against the roof mulling over which led to which? Did the route of the dog walk lead to the rape or did the rape shape the route of the walk? It could be either. But what if Jane regularly saw Kelly watering her flowerpots out the front? Jane taking the wolf for a walk after work and Kelly refreshing her flowers after coming back from the same. No one bats an eye at a man walking a dog. Jane could take that Malamute past her house three times a day and all that would be said is those dogs need some exercise.

Using the measuring stick on Google Earth it is only one hundred and eighty-nine metres as the crow flies from Kelly's house to Jane's. I can't be sure there wasn't another connection that spurred Jane to rape and disfigure her. Proximity though, wanting what you see, could be it.

Was it the same for Jemma Vinson? No. Jane didn't have the

shop then, had no reason to exercise the dog on playing fields across town in Margam, when there are others and the beach closer by. Not carpets either. Some other reason then?

Eleri Parker-Evans is also unconnected and disturbingly different. He breaks into a house with a husband inside. Knows this and takes a hammer to deal with him. This attack carried far more risk than the others. Did he learn from his mistake and thereafter select softer targets? Or did it have to be Eleri despite the risk?

My phone rings and I answer it.

'I've got the money,' says King.

'Then why hasn't it shown up in my account?'

'It's a cash business and cash is what I have.'

It is a fair point. Better to stick money under the floorboards than pass it under the scrutiny of a bank, the police, and the Inland Revenue. But now the pinch - the drop-off. King, me, and the potential for third parties and a knife in the back. Or does he greet me solo with the blast from a sawn-off shotgun? I don't know his pride, the standing he must protect, the face he needs to save with his bouncing buddies, the ones that now have holes in their bodies.

'Cutter, I will meet you at the entrance to the old BP works.'

'Like hell I will. We'll meet somewhere busy where there are cameras … or you could just drop the money on my doorstep. After all, you know where I live, don't you, Sean?'

'Yeah, right, as if I am going to give you an easy target.'

'I won't kill you on my driveway, Sean. What would my neighbours think? And what with my Hilux in the garage I don't think I could fold your seventeen stone into my little hatchback.'

'Funny. I'll think about it.'

'No, you won't, my house it is. Put the money in a shopping bag, knock three times and leave it on the drive … oh, and bring the X5 so I know it is you. It is seven o'clock now. I want it there for eight on the dot. Any shenanigans and I play for keeps.'

I hear him sigh down the phone, 'All right,' he says.

'Sean.'

'Yeah.'

'Don't try fucking me over. It won't end well for either of us. I'll be in jail, and you'll be having your arse wiped by home care.'

I peer through a slit in the blind scanning the close and street beside it. I've parked the Mazda in another close leaving nothing to hide behind and nothing to damage. The Titan is on Nathan's old bed and the pouch I have looped on my belt is weighted with lead shot. The spade leans in a corner at the top of the stairs. I walk to the entrance to the bathroom to check the back garden wall - no ladders or grappling hooks, yet. I go back to the darkness of Nathan's room to count down the final minutes.

King could just pay, though I don't want to let myself believe that he will. My corkscrew brain connives for him. King has a bomb hidden in the bag, has the money coated in Fentanyl, has bricks and petrol bombs coming through the living room window.

Seven fifty-nine. Rain in the headlights of a passing car, strafing puddles and drenching a coatless teenager; streetlights creating a sheen on the pavement. Two minutes past eight and still no X5. It convinces me of a setup; the disrespect peeves me more. King thinking I'd fall for a waste ground rendezvous at night. The street says I must follow through. An empty threat chisels away a piece of the person making it, injuring them like a self-inflicted gunshot, making them less, making them appear weak. As much as I don't want to, if I allowed King to regain his confidence, I'd be the one paying.

Three minutes past eight and the BMW X5 stops in the street outside my neighbour's house. Headlights at full beam, wipers going like the clappers. A slight man dressed in black sports clothes gets out of the front passenger seat holding a Lidl bag for life. Skipping puddles, he dashes across the mouth of the close; underneath the brim of his anorak hood is a thin, white face as twitchy as a squirrel's.

I hear three loud knocks on the front door, and then see him step back and set the bag down in the middle of the drive. For a couple of seconds, the thin man's eyes jump around the house.

Seeing no lights, no movement, or any kind of reaction he turns and runs back to the car. King's gofer jumps in. King performs a U-turn and the X5 mounts a kerb before speeding away.

Crouching down, I look through the landing window and survey the street. Nothing. Then, a thought pops into my head which excites and concerns me at the same time. It excites me because I've screwed my mind to think of it. It concerns me because it could be true.

I open the landing window, step onto the sill and carefully lower myself onto the garage roof. An easterly wind slants the rain into my face as I creep towards the side gate. Pinching a twelve-millimetre lead ball between finger and thumb I draw the sling and lean over the edge to view the side path. I expect to see someone pressed against the garage wall alert for the front door opening. This time suspicion isn't rewarded and no one is lurking.

I climb back into the house, collect the spade, and make my way down the stairs. Still wary, still distrusting, I open the front door. The wind has tipped the bag over and driven it against the boundary wall with my neighbour. The top of the bag is filled with scrunched disposable shopping bags and a loose one is about to fly off.

I shoot out, snatch up the bag and nip back in. I re-lock the door and consider what is in the bag: more plastic bags, used tampons, a dog turd, a pipe bomb? Gingerly, I remove the wet plastic bags and beneath them are uneven stacks of five, ten, and twenty pound notes belted by red elastic bands. Misery money squeezed out of poor desperate people. I count each of the fifteen bundles and none are light of a thousand pounds. I examine them under the kitchen light and they are legit. Smiling to myself I say, 'Well, what do you know.'

CHAPTER 17

It had stopped raining, though the streets and slabs of pavement remain a damp dark. The sky now over Aberavon is the colour and thickness of used cotton wool. A scrum of unruly seagulls cry and bicker over a spilled carton of Kebab meat and chips. Then they scatter in a hectic flapping of wings as a foggy-eyed man in night-out clothes, pitching forward and hunkering against the cold morning air, tramps unsteadily over their banquet on the way to an overdue bed.

There is a row going on in Olive Street. Thick southern Irish voices are rehashing a quarrel from the night before. I knock on Gerald's door and while waiting for him to answer inspect a balding tyre on the flatbed lorry.

He looks worse than he did before. The twenty feet from the chair to the door having the same effect on him as an ascent on the summit of Everest. Wheezing, his chest works like a blacksmith's bellows, and it rises and falls several times before he is able to speak. 'I have got ... the money ... I owe you.'
'No, Gerald. It is me that is going to give you money.'

Gerald shuffles into the living room and hungrily takes in oxygen from the tank next to his chair. I give him a minute to recover before saying, 'Gerald, I've been speaking to Sean King ... you know, the loan shark that Lloyd got in trouble with and ... he has had an attack of conscience, a change of heart and he no longer wants your money. So here it is with an additional five hundred pounds on top to cover your stress and inconvenience.'

I place a stuffed manilla envelope on the arm of his chair. Confusion plays on Gerald's ill face causing him to grasp for words, 'I, I ... don't know ... er, don't understand ... why would ...?'
'Don't worry about it, it's all been sorted. Now, is there somewhere safe where I can put your money? A place where

your carers and son won't find it.'

I get a sausage & egg McMuffin with a coffee from the nearby McDonald's at Water Street and drive to the beach. I eat in the car watching a parade of young families, dog walkers, joggers, and Sunday morning cyclists moving at various speeds along the promenade.

On the night of Jemma Vinson's attack, her boyfriend Conrad Harris had stayed with a mate. I had neglected to ask who that mate was and I sure as hell couldn't ask now. I had briefly bribed open a rickety condemned bridge which now lies irredeemably burnt in a pile of ashes. I don't know Conrad Harris, what he looks like, his age, whether he is a Port Talbot boy with connections to the town or has dropped in from someplace else.

What I do have in Conrad is an unusual name and apart from the accomplished violinist, there are only thirty-one others on Facebook and a couple less on Instagram and TikTok.

I sift through the first few eliminating a middle-aged Pastor from Little Rock, Arkansas, an events organiser from Adelaide, a coffee shop barista from Virginia and a product development scientist working in Berlin. Then there is an English teacher teaching in Lisbon, a retired solicitor from Dumbarton, a property developer from Kent, a bin man from Londonderry and a Buddhist Deliveroo rider from Newcastle. Closer to home there is an obese fifty-five-year-old from Bristol who collects porcelain figurines, and another that has the smack of South Wales about him.

Conrad Vegas Harris looks and fits the part of a Jemma Vinson boyfriend. He is jobless, short, scroaty and scrawny, makes moronic posts on social media and has a Cannabis sativa leaf tattoo on his flat white chest. Likes hip-hop, weed and ink, wears his hair in braids dyed blonde and red. Calls himself 'MC Vegas', thinks he can rap - is sadly mistaken as his travesties on TikTok bear out.

I run Conrad through 192.com and find a Conrad V. Harris listed in Port Talbot. I use a credit in my account to obtain

Conrad's address from the electoral register and his mobile number from the 192 records. A little research of Vegas shows him to have served four years of a six-year sentence for causing death by careless driving whilst under the influence of drink or drugs.

Back in 2011 when aged twenty, high on coke and weed, he swerved across a road smashing his Ford Fiesta into the driver's side of a Renault Clio. The impact killed its driver, twenty-four-year-old Morgan Williams instantly. The rest of his criminality is fraud, drug possession, harassment, and a distraction burglary on an eighty-five-year-old man - fair game then.

I drive to the centre of town, past the train station and Grand Hotel and then turn left at the Art Deco-inspired Plaza. The building was preserved after its life as a cinema and reinvented as a community hub for the arts. Into Eagle Street and then just before the Royal Mail sorting office I take another left to my destination Eagle Mews. I perform a three-point turn and leave the car next to the Paladin fence facing Eagle Street.

Exiting the car, I drop my car keys. I bend down to pick them up and my thighs register a late complaint about the Turkish Get-ups from the day before, and my right knee clicks and grates. A testament to the toughness of the workout, and to a body losing its fight with age creak by creak and ache by ache.

Conrad's house is an end of terrace one-up one-down in camel-coloured brick and brown UPVC. The front has a scraggy lawn strewn with divots and cigarette butts. No curtilage, just drainpipes to demarcate one uncared for patch from another. I smell weed, even though the windows are closed, and the curtains are drawn - I can smell it all right.

I knock on the front door and step back to observe any curtain twitch or furtive movement made. There is neither a wall-mounted CCTV camera or a doorbell monitoring camera, though the bedroom drapes are bunched on the sill and already have a small gap between them for someone to look through. I glance at my Garmin, it is nine fifty-eight - no way is he up and out. Harder rousing knocks this time, knocks to shift the smoke from his head. Still, no answer. Perhaps Conrad partied last night and crashed elsewhere?

Two black refuse bags slouch against the wooden side gate; the wood is blanched and rotting. Through the slats, I can see cracks in the concrete paving slabs and grass sprouting out of the gaps. I see a silver sheet of something and move nearer the gate to get a better look. It is a leftover piece of reflective insulation roll - effectively foil-coated bubble wrap, often used to trap the heat in a cannabis grow room. My initial suspicions are confirmed by the green bottle of 'Miracle Gro' discarded next to it.

I try to push open the gate and it doesn't budge. A cursory examination reveals the reason to be a length of two-by-four timber wedged under the latch and propped against the rise of an uneven slab.

I go back to the car and get the ball-peen hammer. I slip the hammer through a slit nearest to the latch, knock the timber sideways and then up. The first isn't hard enough and the timber falls back to the gate. I hit it harder, catching my fingers against a slat and grazing them across the knuckles. The piece of timber teeters in an upright position before falling backwards onto a soggy cardboard box.

Having no further need for the hammer I secrete the handle in the sleeve of my jacket and cradle the head in the cup of my hand. After checking over both shoulders I push the gate open and walk through to the backyard.

Bijou and low maintenance is how an estate agent would sell it. There is room enough for a small rotary clothesline, some more wet cardboard boxes scattered around the perimeter - these for LED grow lamps, and a three-by-five windowless shed. I hear whining and the sound of claws scratching against the wood of the door. This miserable crying is unmistakably that of a dog, a dog kept inside a shed.

The door is secured by a cheap bog-standard padlock which I'd be able to pick in ten seconds or break in three. On this side too I see that the curtains and blinds are shut to light and enquiry. No CCTV camera on this or the houses on either side.

The incessant whimpering and scraping pluck at my nerves initiating unwanted questions. I wonder if the dog is permanently kept like this? Is it injured, ill or starved? Then again dogs are caged in crates - is a shed any worse? But this is ten o'clock in the morning and the dog must have slept here overnight. I consider the lock again, one well-placed strike could do it, nevertheless, I'd need to make allowance for four to five cuffing blows. Four or five clangs sounding off like church bells on a quiet Sunday morning.

'Hey! You! What the fuck are you doing in my garden?'
I turn to the angry male voice and see blinds half hoisted and Conrad leaning out of an open upstairs window. I thought he'd looked ratty in his photographs and in the flesh this opinion is confirmed. His hair is like straw bashed out of a scarecrow, if that scarecrow had also had his beetroot brains kicked in and they had bled all over the stuffing.

'Are you deaf? I said, what the fuck are you doing in my garden?'
'Getting your attention.'
'Now that you've got it, what the fuck do you want?'
'I want to talk to you about Jemma Vinson.'
'Well, I don't. So, if that's it? Fuck along now and leave me to get some sleep,' and he makes a shooing motion with his fingers.
'Not yet, Conrad. I'll go after you've answered a couple of questions,' I say looking down at the toe of my boot and then tapping the steel cap against the concrete.

'If you don't fuck off, I'll phone the police,' and he makes a show of his phone and thumb hovering above the screen.
'Go ahead, phone the police and after we have agreed that trespass is a civil matter, I'll provide evidence to them that you're cultivating cannabis.'
'Snitches get stitches,' he threatens like he's used to dropping bodies and I am next.
'You're a funny little man. How about grasses jail asses? or thugs beat those that deal drugs? What do you think of those lines, Conrad? Tell me what I want to know, and I won't make it my

business to shut down your shop,' is my dismissive sounding reply.

'You're not a cop, or you would have said so already. Who are you?'

My name is Mike Frazier and I'm a loss adjuster for an insurance company.'

'Like fuck you are,' he scoffs, his face tainted with an underserved cockiness that will take a good beating or two to get rid of - I'd happily lend a hand.

'It doesn't matter who I am, only what I'll do to get the information I want,' I explain bluntly.

Conrad's mouth contorts through the decision as if his tongue is busy dislodging a stuck sweet from a tooth. 'All right ... five questions and that's it,' he says petulantly.

'On the night Jemma was attacked you were at a mate's house. Who was the mate? And what was the address?'

'I stayed at ... Jack Jones' flat ... flat four, twelve to fourteen Station Road,' he says with what looks to me to be an insolent smile.

Twelve to fourteen Station Road is a complete hole, which could give Queen's Court a run for its money for Port Talbot's shit pit crown. Dossers, druggies, and societal debris shamble in and out of its doors and dismal bedsits. Some stay awhile and by that, I mean a year or two, but most don't. They're evicted, they move on, they go to prison, they die on the floor with arms like pin cushions, livers like walnuts and vomit clogging their throats.

'Jack Jones, still in Station Road, is he?'

'Nah, moved back to London.'

'Got a number for this ... Jack Jones?'

'Nah, not anymore,' he says flippantly with a stupid smile on his lips.

'Kept in touch on social media then?'

'Nah, we fell out ... cunt owed me money.' He fans out the fingers of a hand, smiles widely and says, 'And that's your five.'

The dog's clawing, its desperate crying and Conrad's bullshit are putting me in an evil mood. I test the answers and decide to give them a shake to see if they stay the same, 'All very convenient and ... unsatisfactory. I don't believe you.'

'And!' he says in challenge.

'Harassment. I am going to harass you until you tell me,' I say with conviction.

I begin walking away and hear him shout, 'I've friends, people that will seriously fuck you up.'

'Better call them then.'

CHAPTER 18

Mr Holland is blasting soap suds off the CRV with a jet washer. We exchange nods and I press the blue-ringed doorbell. I look directly into its camera and smile. Olivia opens the door with her face buried in the cowl neck of a woollen jumper two sizes too big for her. Olivia's eyes are glassy, tired, and red - dirtied windows of the soul and indicators of past hours spent medicated, sleepless, and tearful.

'Come in, my father has almost finished cleaning the car for you. Would you like a coffee?'

'I always say yes to good coffee, thanks.'

The rottweiler's claws clip on the wooden flooring as it trots along the hallway to Olivia's side. She grips a fold of flesh on its neck and kneads it. Encouraging further attention, the rottweiler turns his head into her hand, but does not lose watch of the stranger at the door.

'Hector, is very protective of me, aren't you boy. If only I'd had you then ... you'd have torn the monster's throat out.'

Hector is a brute. A solid one hundred and forty pounds of dissuasion. Rust muzzle and paws, black everywhere else, powerful jaws and neck that could separate one body part from another. I want him to like me.

'This is Will, and he's a good man,' she says cutely to Hector in the way you'd speak to a three-year-old child.

The desire for vengeance burns the cloud away from her cast-down eyes and they take on an obsidian shine. 'I've had him trained by a former police dog handler to attack on command, and when I relive the event, I try to put Hector there, insert him into the memory and a knife into my own hand ... come on in and I'll make us coffee.'

Olivia leads me into her living room, and I take a seat in the wingback chair. The miasma of the space persists. The reek of smoke, the crowded ashtray, the heavy blackout drapes, the track of worn carpet, and on the Hatcher table a glass tumbler with a slice of wilted lemon hanging off the rim - vodka or gin to double down on the pills would be my guess.

Behind the tumbler is a silver picture frame holding a portrait photograph of a regal-looking black woman with large almond-shaped eyes. The woman is wearing a white Doctor's coat and is unmistakably Olivia's mother. Having not seen or heard of Mrs Holland I decide not to enquire. There is probably a sad tale involved and this room has more than enough misery already.

Olivia brings in coffee and shortcake biscuits. She passes on the biscuits and folds herself into the plump leather chair. She holds the mug at her lips like a cold orphan would and says from behind it, 'Tell me more about the surveillance you're conducting?'

'It is the man I showed you the picture of. His name is Dominic Jane and before setting up on his own he worked for Carpet Masters. He was the second man that laid your Berbers. He also put flooring down for Jodie Green and walks his dog past Kelly Thomas's house.'

'So, you think he formed the intention to when …?'

Inhaling deeply, I commit to it, 'Yes, I believe as he was fitting the carpets he was thinking about how he was going to attack you. He saw where you kept your keys, noted which stairs creaked, what bedroom you slept in, knew what dining room chairs you had and what he needed …' and I stop myself from crossing over into unnecessary detail.

'That would be sixteen months. Are you telling me he waited all that time?'

'The police have said the perpetrator is careful and disciplined, why wouldn't he be patient too? Did you or Jack mention on social media about Jack's deployment?'

Olivia thinks for a moment, blinks out tears and nods.

'He bided his time, created distance between attendance and invasion, waited for the right moment, planned each move … meticulous.'

Gently tugging at my beard, I drift into the back of my head, the word meticulous jarring with the chance of an unlocked door. Out of the corner of my eye I see Mr Holland in the doorway, shirt sleeves rolled up and a light sheen of sweat on his brow. 'The car is ready when you are,' he says softly.

Mr Holland passes me the key, his hand is unblemished, his body bookish as if all that was required of it is turning pages and pressing buttons. 'Thank you, Mr Holland, I'll have it back tonight.'

Olivia gives her father a curt smile and he takes the hint and leaves. 'You've got your father twisted around your little finger, haven't you?' I say half humorously with the other half disapproving of her rudeness.

'Of course, I do, I'm daddy's ruined princess. He knows no one else will love me.'

Jane is out somewhere in the van. I wait nearby in Dolphin Close and occupy myself reading a Wikipedia article on The English Civil War. After an hour I park on Long Vue Road and continue to watch the house from there.

After another fruitless hour, I station the Honda further down the street. Conscious that if I stay too long in one spot someone might phone the police that there is a burglar, hitman, or paedophile loitering outside their house. There are enough paranoid people involved in feuds, persecuted by ex-partners, or running from debts to think of me as an agent in their enemy's machinations.

This position only offers a vantage of the entrance to St Kitts Place and not of Jane's house itself. I contemplate parking for a while at the back end of St Kitts, in the bowl of the close. Jane's house is at a tip of the U-shape, and he has no need to drive to the back - it seems a safe spot.

My finger moves away from the ignition as the minivan comes out of Wyvern Avenue. It heads towards me on Long Vue Road and turns into St Kitts. My fingertips play a tuneless tap on the steering wheel as I mull over what to do next. It is too risky placing the magnetic GPS tracker on the undercarriage of the van. Jane has two security cameras and these if triggered could send an alert to a phone or tablet. I'd have to fit the tracker when the van is parked in the street, preferably when Jane is occupied at a job.

The decision is made for me when Jane walks around the corner in a black street-style tracksuit highlighted in red and white graffiti. His right hand is tempering the eagerness of the Malamute, while the left holds onto a bulging plastic bag stretched to the point of breaking.

He walks on the pavement towards the Honda in a rolling motion, his shoulders dipping side to side. Chalk dust on his pockets and strands of hair stuck to his forehead provide clues that he's just come from the gym. I make a pretence of reading the article, my head aligned with the screen of the phone, but my eyes above on the contents of the bag. Bottles with black sealed tops, slender necks and amber liquid in their glass bodies protrude, push against, and weigh down on the thin bag.

Having past the Honda Jane crosses the road. I watch him through the rear windshield and then by adjusting the offside wing mirror, observe him turn into Border Road. I make a three-point-turn and keeping the hybrid engine running on electric glide to the junction of Border Road.

Jane crosses the road again and enters a front garden of tall grass with tussocks of even longer grass, and a knot of brambles spreading out from a corner. The house is in the same state of decline, the gate is riddled with rust, the windows are frosted with dirt and moss has taken a grip of the rendering. Inside I'd expect to find dead flies littering the windowsill and a toilet caked in shit.

Jane lets himself in and leaves the door open. Uncertain what to do next I hover at the junction. The door left open suggests a flying visit.

A car horn toots from behind. Prompted, I drive to the end of Long Vue Road, take a quick left into Southdown View and follow the curve of the street to where it meets the other side of

Border Road. To complete a lap, I make another left and cruise along the street. I see Jane, hand now free of the bag dragging the gate shut - somebody inside the better or worse for four bottles of whisky. Even the lowest-priced supermarket own brand and you're talking fifty quid.

Fixing my eyes ahead I speed past Jane. At the junction, I give way to a fat cyclist with a bag of takeaway hanging off the handlebars. The drop-off looked like a late Sunday lunch for an alcoholic; a relative maybe? And more than likely they paid forward or back.

I park the car on the wrong side of the road at the top of St Helier Drive. From here I have an uninterrupted view of the entrance to Lupin Close. A half-hour passes before I see a black, square shape at the bottom of the road, then the dog and the unmistakable rolling gait.

As I watch Jane approach, I make a bet with the world that he will turn into Jasmin Close. He does. I check the time and check it again when he emerges from Lupin Close - too long. Loitering in the garage compound tying his shoelaces or some other subterfuge; side view of the house this time with maybe a glance over the shoulder into the living room. I lean across the passenger seat and fiddle with the glovebox, and when I sit back up, I see the back of him heading home. The clock on the dashboard reads 15:41; just enough time to visit the fish counter at Morrisons for an eat-by-today fish.

Geraint had provided me with a list of Kelly's friends, and I spend the rest of Sunday afternoon and early evening calling them. Four of the five went out with Kelly to Bar Gallois and watched Wales thrash Italy 42 - 0 in the opening match of the Six Nations championship. The women spoke of a great day out, of having a good craic as an afternoon of drinking extended into the evening. There were no dramas, peculiarities, or faintest hint of what was to come. Four of the friends hadn't seen Jane before but one had.

Dana Francis grew up on Sandfields Estate and went to school with Jane. Dana described him then as quiet, scruffy and a bit of an oddball. When the other kids were being kind they called him Dommy and when they weren't, which was far more often, they called him Duminic, Dom the Dum, Gingernut, Janet and a host of other spiteful names. Or they'd just call him Jane using a horrible feminine voice. There was physical bullying too: wedgies, Chinese burns, dead arms and dead legs, trips, and shoves. Dana didn't recall seeing him that day or Kelly ever mentioning him.

Kelly hadn't confided to any of her friends that she was being stalked and I figured as much - the investigation team would have homed in on that like a heat-seeking missile. It is clear that if none of the enquiries had led to Jane then the investigation team would not know of him. I had chanced upon Jane, and I am working from him and not to him. There is a danger in finding evidence to fit a suspect instead of following evidence to a suspect - that was the old way the police conducted business, and led to miscarriages of justice. Am I resurrecting bad habits and leaning towards Jane more than I should?

CHAPTER 19

It is twelve minutes past three on a Monday morning when the credits for *Carlito's Way* roll up the screen. I've watched the film four or maybe five times, and despite knowing the ending I always pull for Carlito to make it. I finish my coffee and switch the television off. I rest my phone on the arm of the chair, put on a thin, black windbreaker to match the black jeans I am wearing and leave the house.

From its avenue of lights, the motorway is cast in an amber glow and a solitary car proceeds over the mostly sleeping town. At night the works is a sprawl of white lights and orange gas, like a dystopian city at the edge of the sea - it never sleeps.

I slip off at junction 40, drive to the end of Tanygroes Street and park the Mazda in a quiet unlit lane running off Eagle Street. I take the spray can out of the glovebox and feel for the lock pick wallet and jemmy under the driver's seat.

I press the door closed and pull up the hood of the jacket and raise the snood over my face. Using the cover of a line of cars I walk briskly to Eagle Mews. No lights or movement at number eleven. Head dropped low I move purposely to the front window and spray the word 'Grass' across it. Then over to the slatted gate, where using the jemmy I repeat the trick of dislodging the buttress onto the cardboard box. I tread noiselessly to the shed, glance back at lifeless windows, and take out the wallet from my pocket. The tension wrench selected is an L-shaped tool with a flat head. I stick the head into the bottom of the keyway and after turning it three hours clockwise hold it in position with my left thumb. Next, I use a city rake, so-called because it resembles a city skyline. I don't see it myself, to me, it looks like a mountain range.

The rake is inserted above the tension wrench. Wriggling the pick in small in-and-out motions the lock is massaged open in the time it takes to put on and button a coat. I pocket the padlock and wipe over the latch with the sleeve of the jacket, then keeping the sleeve over my hand I open the shed door and release a foetid smell of dog waste.

Cowering inside is a pathetic-looking lurcher pup. Rangy and bony it seems to be a whippet crossed with a wired-haired terrier of some kind; black with a white chest and about six months old. It is a bag of bones shivering on a soiled curtain, its uneven coat matted by the shit it is forced to lie in.

'It's all right boy,' I whisper as I fasten the lead clipped collar around his long neck. I coax him out and he follows me meekly as though the world is about to fall on his head. I haven't finished with Vegas, not by a long chalk.

We walk back to the car, and I encourage him onto the passenger seat. Under the interior light, he appears more pitiful still with ribs like a xylophone and atrophied thighs. I loop the lead around the headrest and after starting the car put the heaters on. I drive home using the motorway again because there is less chance of being stopped by the police.

Once home, I lift the dog into a lukewarm bath and using a shampoo scrub his fur clean. He doesn't like the water and eyes me suspiciously as someone else that means him harm, but fearful as he is he doesn't bark or bite. After drying him off with a towel I inspect him for obvious infection and injury, and thankfully he appears free from both.

I put down a bowl of fresh water and he vigorously laps it up, his thin tongue slapping and sloshing the water over the floor. I get a pack of shredded chicken from the fridge, tooty down and offer some of it to him off the palm of my hand. Hunger and the scent of chicken draws the dog to my hand. Having owned dogs before I only feed him two palms worth, too much too quickly and his hunger-tight stomach will likely throw it right back up.

A bed is made for him in the hallway using a doubled over quilt from Nathan's room. He quickly settles on the quilt, instinctively knowing that his bones and a ceramic tiled floor are poor bedfellows. I cover him with a thick fleece blanket and block the stairs with a wooden pallet that is destined to be chainsawed into chunks and fed to the log burner. After all, there are few worse experiences than just getting out of bed and squishing your bare toes through a poo.

Over a breakfast of bacon and eggs I name the lurcher Buddy. Buddy has some too and his taste buds lose the plot. I take Buddy out for a ten-minute walk around the estate; just enough to stretch his legs and about enough for a starved, boxed-up dog. It is evident that Buddy doesn't understand the limits of a lead and has had little experience outside of that poky backyard and shed. Inquisitive, nervous, and overwhelmed by the new neighbourhood he sniffs, pees and velcros himself to my leg whenever a dog, person or car comes into sight.

Back at the house, Buddy nuzzles into my lap working his pointy snout underneath the cushion I'm resting the iPad on. Feeling a warm pity I stroke his bone-ridged back and decide that I'm going to keep him.

Using a combination of Google Earth and Maps I soon identify the whisky swiller's hovel as twelve Border Road. Helpfully the street view has a picture of the neighbour's wheelie bin outside on the pavement and this has a large white ten daubed on it. Next, I run the house number through the electoral register and find that a Bernard Quinn is the only person listed as living at the address. The register also tells me that he is between sixty and sixty-four years old.

Switching over to another tool of the trade I enter Jane's name and date of birth into a record of births, deaths and marriages and tick the box for birth. On the certificate, the father is named as Darren Mark Jane, born on 18th July 1972, and the mother as Sarah Elizabeth Higgs, born on the 4th of April 1974. The family home was given as forty-two Chrome Avenue in Sandfields. I dig around, exploring my Ancestry account to expand the Jane/ Higgs family tree. I soon learn that the address in Chrome Avenue is the home of Higgs' parents Marilyn and David Higgs and that Sarah continued to live there. Darren Jane moves to

Swansea, gets married to a Joanne Brown in 2002, and then both show up living at Alaska Street in Hull.

On the 18th of June 1994, Sarah Higgs married Daniel Thomas Blackwell at St. Paul's church. At that time of tying the knot, her occupation was listed as a cleaner and Blackwell's as a railway worker; the marital home was recorded as twenty-nine Verdi Road, Sandfields.

The marriage was ended by death and not divorce. At only twenty-eight-years-old Blackwell died on the 9th of August 1998. He was in a crew of six Rail Track workers carrying out maintenance on the London to Paddington mainline near Cardiff when he was struck by a train and killed instantly. The inquest blamed a signalling breakdown amongst the team. The point man was slow to relay the message of an approaching train and the receiver, whose job it was to get the men off the track, was not looking because he was relieving himself in a bush.

Twenty-nine Verdi Road exchanges hands shortly after with new residents recorded in the 2001 National Census. The same census documents a sad split - nine-year-old Dominic Jane is back living in Chrome Avenue with his grandparents, sans mother, who is absent.

She surfaces briefly in Cardiff at a supported accommodation run by a homeless charity. She was registered to vote there in 2003, but not the following year, and from there she simply drops off the map.

The coordinates pointed to a downward course, and I envisage the chain of events leading to a life on the streets of the nation's capital. Grief aided by substance abuse, a mental breakdown or maybe both. A loss of employment, then abandonment or removal of a child, deepening mental health problems and substance misuse likely leading to eviction and a family break-up.

Homeless and with ties to the town cut, Sarah like many who find themselves in this position relocated to the city. I check for a death certificate and find one. Sarah Blackwell died in Bristol on the 14th of December 2012 of acute alcohol poisoning.

I examine the branches of the Quinn family tree looking for connections with the families of Blackwell, Jane, and Higgs, and as far as I can tell the Quinns are a separate entity. A friend of the family possibly? The permutations of how that could have come to be are mind-boggling and ultimately unknowable without asking.

I inspect the packet of fresh mackerel turning bad on a shelf in the conservatory. It had sat there since yesterday afternoon and now in between showers, the sun shone strongly through the glass. I sniff at the small hole I've made in the cling film and the fish is spoiling nicely. Another sixteen hours at room temperature and it'll stink to high heaven.

CHAPTER 20

I forget the tiredness left from the early-hour foray; the distraction from eye-picking light-headedness is my lovely Hilux, the gun-metal now restored and gleaming in the garage car park. Climbing in I admonish myself for putting it up for sale, in the same way that you can't understand what you did, how there can be two versions of yourself capable of making wholly different decisions.

I drive to town, park in Llewellyn Street, and walk briskly into Argos. There, I pay forty quid in cash for a prepaid Vodafone Alcatel 1 phone. It comes loaded with three gigabytes of data and two hundred and fifty minutes of talk time. I charge the phone off the Hilux and make a call.

'Baglan Taxis.'

'I'd like a taxi from eleven Eagle Mews to go to The Twelve Knights in Margam please.'

'For what time?'

'As soon as possible.'

'What is the name?'

'Conrad Harris.'

'Will fifteen minutes be all right?'

'Fifteen minutes will be dandy,' I say.

Under the name Mickey Wise, I create a fake Facebook account using a randomly generated email from Tenminutemail.com. I find Conrad's page and post this:

'the weed u solt me is rank ass ditch weed u ripped me off and i c u soon !!!! gimpy prick'

The Hilux powers up Baglan Hill and with no traffic coming the other way shoots across the carriageway onto the Bwlch mountain road. Before the bends, I work the horn warning and watching for those flippant to the danger of the thin twisting road.

I drop down into Cwmavon winding around streets of former Council houses to the entrance of Pine Valley. It is an eighty-house estate set midway on the mountain, and I suppose semi-affluent as far as Port Talbot goes. They are white houses, mostly detached and well set apart. More than half are bungalows fringed with shaped hedges, shrubs, and trees.

Number thirty-two is situated at the bottom of the estate and is amongst a dozen semi-detached houses of lower value. It has a red-brick terraced garden in the front filled with shingle, potted plants, and miniature conifers. A plain concrete driveway runs along the side of the house to a garage in the rear garden. I walk down the driveway to a side front entrance covered by a portico roof and rap the brass knocker on the white UPVC door.

A balding, overweight man wearing two-day-old salt and pepper stubble answers. He appears slightly out of breath, and I notice a considerable amount of sawdust caught up on the fibres of his navy woollen jumper.

'Good afternoon, my name is William Cutter, and I am a private investigator; no need to worry, what I am looking into doesn't really concern you, but you could be of help.' The man frowns sceptically like I'm about to pitch him something that he doesn't need, or worse, attempt to get into the house under false pretences.

I stand back from the doorway and giving him an easy-going smile say, 'Three and a half years ago Eleri Parker-Evans and her husband Alex Evans were living here. I need to find Eleri and I was wondering if you were given an address to forward any mail to?'

'No, I've lived here two years and haven't received a thing for those poor souls. Now, if that's all, I've got a birdhouse that I want to get back to.'

'Last question, who did you buy the house off?'

'Payton Jewell Caines in Station Road,' he answers, his mouth setting to a pissed-off smile.

'Thanks for your help,' I say while thinking it a stroke of luck that those estate agents were used.

I knock on some doors. I start with thirty-one and a no reply, move to thirty and another daytime worker. Try thirty-three and see the shimmer of a figure in the opaque glass. A man around sixty answers, short mostly black hair with a jazzy quiff curl and a moustache like a Victorian bartender. Guy has a barbell body and the late-life tattoos of a man who hasn't accepted decrepitude. A Fitted mustard polo shirt with the top button done up, drainpipe jeans and brown Chukka boots complete a dapper look. We eye each other in faint recognition.

'I know you from somewhere,' he says, wagging his forefinger as if it will help him remember.

I surprise myself when I get there before him, 'You were Justin Hurley's best mate … Richie. I went out with his younger sister Beth. If I remember right, you were working on the North Sea oil rigs as a commercial diver.'

'That's right … and I'm sorry, I can't quite remember your name, though I recall seeing you at Just's house, and one time him and I watching you box for a Welsh title at the Afan Lido.'

'Will Cutter.'

'Richie Grange. What is Just doing these days?' and he offers his hand.

We shake with equal firmness, and I answer his question, 'He and Karen emigrated to Australia about twenty years ago.'

'Before the internet people just lost touch. The North Sea, the Philippines, Nigeria, Mexico, I've worked the lot. I've been a rolling stone for nearly thirty years,' he says in a rather muddled accent that has picked up bits of others along the way.

'Retired now?'

'Partly, these days I consult and teach. I moved back four years ago after my mum became ill; this was my parent's house. What about you? Did you try your hand in the professional game?' he asks.

'No, I became a different kind of punch bag, I became a police officer and now for my sins, I'm a private investigator,' I say, flicking my head in a woe-is-me-nod, like it is some heavy cross

I've had nailed to my back and been told to carry around.

The conversation lulls for a second, I could fill it with more chat, but I choose to fill it with the obvious. 'Right, you are probably wondering the reason I've knocked on your door, well, it is to do with the horror show that went on in number thirty-two. I am looking for Eleri Parker-Evans or her husband Alex Evans. Do you know the families? Or did you ever speak to the parents … like in the aftermath when they were sorting out the sale of the house?'

'No,' he answers, 'I can't help you with that I'm afraid.'

'No worries, it was a bit of a punt.'

'Look, I'd like to invite you in for a coffee and have a catch-up, but I have a work appointment at Swansea Marina I have got to get to,' and he smiles one-sidedly in a what-can-you-do way.

'Of course. Just one last thing, do you know this guy?' and I show him a powerlifting photo of Jane.

'Yeah, I do, that is Dom, and he trains in the same gym I go to, he's a fucking animal.'

'Yes, he most definitely is. Which gym is that?'

'Warehouse Fitness in Taibach.'

'How well do you know him?' I ask.

'To say hello to at the gym and occasionally we've spotted for one another. When I moved in, I put my stamp on the place and totally re-decorated it. He was one of the guys I had in to lay the carpets and the woodblock flooring. He was here for about three days, and we got talking about weights and gyms. I was looking for a place to train and he recommended his.'

'Was that soon after you moved in?'

'I think so … wait, it was March, maybe April or May 2018 when I … no, mum died in March, and so it was April, then a month or two after that I suppose. Breathing Trimix for thirty years makes your brain all squiffy. Definitely spring or summer of 2018 though, I would say.'

Richie makes a show of looking at his chunky diver's watch and says, 'Sorry, I've got to fly.'

'Of course, thanks for your time … small world, isn't it?'

I walk back to the Hilux. If he was there while they were there he might have seen, wanted, and put a mark on her. Was it as straightforward as that? A few sightings of an attractive woman - leering leading to an attempted murder, rape, and mutilation - is that it? No tipping point reached, or great lever pulled, just a psycho ripe for his revealing.

Their logo are the letters PJC squashed together into an orange square, and your eyes have to perform the trick of pulling them apart from each other to make sense of it. Across the rest of the blue facade is Payton Jewell Caines. Above, there is the first floor of a terraced house, a bay window, and a single window each covered by sets of natty net curtains. Probably a flat and accessed from the rear by a fire escape staircase.

I push on the left double door and go in. My luck holds and Natalie Ferguson is behind the desk. She is a solidly built woman with uncommonly wide shoulders, dusky skin and black hair presented today in a box-braid bun. Her father Ledell Ferguson runs the boxing club where I've trained and informally coached for years.

'Oi, oi, look what the cat dragged in, here to buy a house or here to kick my arse back to the gym,' she cracks, beaming an ivory-toothed smile.

'I can't say anything, I've skipped a week myself, and in any case, I am not sure I could kick your arse,' I reply smiling and with a hint of flirtation.

'I don't know, you're a rough old boy,' she says, and her eyes twinkle mischievously.

'Less of the old if you don't mind.'

I take the punter's seat thinking that if I was five years younger I might ask her out, though I was never any good at asking women out - I needed a pub and my inhibitions drowned and theirs left in the bottom of a glass too. She is my type though - playful, sassy, and well-put-together.

'So, you're looking to move, and you thought you'd give me the commission?'

'Afraid not, I'm after a favour.'

'Sounds ominous,' she says in faux dread as she takes a seat on the business side of the desk.

'No, what I'm going to ask you to do is all above board. Thirty-two Pine Valley, your firm sold it sometime in 2020. I need to know the particulars of the person who was selling it. I want you to contact that person, explain to them who I am, emphasising my credentials and trustworthiness,' I say, conveying it with a straight face and heavy sarcasm.

She rips into me with, 'I am a bloody good saleswoman, but I am not a magician.'

'Right, you get the gist, sell me as someone who is on the level. Tell them I am working for one of the victims of The Port Talbot Slasher, that I have a lead in the case that I want to discuss with them and pass my number. Could you do that for me, Natalie?'

'Sure, have you really found something?

'I hope so.'

I hear snippets of Natalie's conversation as she paces the back of the office. She returns to me shaking her head and with her lips pressed up against her nose in an expression of disappointment. 'I tried and I ... succeeded,' she says with a smile escaping across her naturally generous lips.

Pinching a corner of a yellow post-it note between her fingers she leans over me, and I allow her the pleasure of sticking it to my forehead. I peel it off and read:

Sandra Parker
55 Chrome Avenue
07664239188

The address jumps off the paper. It is the street where Jane spent the second part of his childhood - the traumatised part.

'It's the mum, she wants to speak to you in person, asked that you call around this afternoon, just give her a ring to let her know what time.'

Getting up I say, 'Natalie, you're a star.'

Giving a cheeky wink she replies, 'I know.'

I stop by the house, fuss over Buddy, feed him and take him for another short walk. While Buddy is busy sniffing the hell out of a tree, I message Sandra that I am on my way.

One street behind the seafront Chrome Avenue bends from Golden Avenue to Marine Drive. The properties are all semi-detached houses featuring slit-like bathroom windows more suited to defending a castle than a home.

The Parkers have paved their driveway in terracotta and iron-grey stone. Then used the same coloured bricks for the porch and curtilage wall. A Payton Jewell Caines sign announces the house is up for sale. The metal gates are open, and I walk around the side of a 21 plate Vauxhall Mocca to the half-glass porch door. The doorbell plays the classic eight-note Westminster chime, and as it ends, I see the distorted figure of a man through a stained-glass depiction of two soaring doves in courtship.

A man I know as Alan opens the door. Alan is or was one of the security team at the Aberafan shopping centre and also a volunteer boatman at the local RNLI station. Both occupations worked closely with the police, and I knew him from numerous shoplifters and reports of distressed people walking into the sea. Mid-fifties and looking it, he has a florid face marked by a repaired harelip and a no-nonsense short back and sides haircut.

'Sergeant Cutter ... I mean William?' and he cants his head in question.

'Hello Alan, you never knew my first name and I never knew your last. I'm sorry that it has taken this awful business to learn them,' the tone of my voice lowered and subdued, as it always does when broaching grief.

I am invited to take a seat in the front living room. I sit in a brown and cream plaid chair next to a lace curtained window. Across from me Alan and Sandra perch on the edge of a two-seater sofa of the same suite; both their backs are rigid in anticipation. There is the smell of pine air freshener, the loud tick-tock of an old mantel clock and a stripped-back tidiness. I notice a black dog-eared bible on the coffee table and a plaque above the gas fire stating, *'Bless This House'*. Thirty-two Pine Valley had not been blessed and I wonder how they reconciled their faith with the grotesque indifference of the universe - I never could understand.

Tentatively I speak. After all these years I am still not fluent and never will be in the language of sorrow and condolence. 'As Natalie has told you, one of the other victims has hired me to look into the attacks and by luck, I think I've stumbled upon a suspect. It is all very circumstantial at the moment, even speculative, but I could be on to something … well I believe I am.'

I become aware that I'm mimicking their sitting position, only I'm leaning forward and playing with my hands more than a sincere man should. 'I'd like to ask Eleri and yourselves about Dominic Jane?'

It hangs there like a foul smell. Alan's eyes screw incredulously, and Sandra's mouth is catching flies.

'Dominic Jane! The ginger lad from across the street who works in the carpet shop on Western Avenue?' questions Alan disbelievingly. 'He's your suspect?'

I nod my head to confirm and say, 'Yes, that Dominic Jane, he is my suspect.'

'But Dominic and Eleri went through school together; his grandparents David and Marilyn are Methodists, as are we,' protests Sandra.

I don't say what I am thinking that religious parenting didn't save their daughter Sarah from fornication and the demon drink.

'Why do you think it is Dominic?' Alan asks.

'Connections, coincidences, observations,' I answer as if that is a good enough explanation. 'Eleri and Dominic, what was their relationship?'

Modest and proper like a vicar's wife Sandra adjusts her position to sit side-saddle with her hands interlocked on her lap. She is on the doughy side, has short side-parted hair that has mostly lost its colour, and wears oversized glasses that dominate her small round face. The frumpy look continues in a long muted skirt and cardigan, plain white blouse, and laced grey genderless shoes.

In a meek voice, she says, 'They were childhood friends. When Dominic's stepfather died his mother Sarah moved back with her parents. Dominic's real father abandoned him, and Sarah had her struggles … it wasn't easy for Dominic, he was quiet and didn't make friends easily. Eleri and our son Rhodri are non-identical twins and we encouraged them to befriend Dominic. Back then Eleri was a bit of a tomboy, so she didn't mind typical boy activities.'

'Were they close?' I ask.

'Not really no, but as Methodists, we believe in doing good, and giving companionship to a lonely child is an unquestionable good,' Sandra replies.

'Of course, it is,' I concur, smiling. 'So, this … encouraged relationship, what happened to it?'

Sandra is the one to answer, 'When Eleri left junior school and went to the local comprehensive, she came out of herself, and found a group of girls to be friendly with. It petered out after that. Rhodri stayed friendly with Dominic, and they played youth rugby together at Baglan RFC.'

'Are Rhodri and Dominic still friends?'

Alan shakes his head and says, 'No, Dominic dropped out of the team … didn't like team sports is what Rhodri said. Dominic got into weightlifting, and they … went their separate ways.'

'Did Dominic ever show any sexual interest in Eleri or Eleri in Dominic?'

'No, no, I don't think so,' she dismisses with a priggish twitch of her nose, and I am left with the impression that Sandra isn't a mother that Eleri could confide in - too moral, too uncomfortable and inflexible around sin and temptation.

'I would like to speak to Eleri, there may be more to this than you are able to tell me,' I say.

'I doubt she'd want to speak to you. Eleri has moved on, moved to new pastures, and with the Lord's eternal grace has forgiven her defiler and rebuilt her life, praise be to the Lord our saviour,' the meek voice suddenly gaining a preacher's strength and conviction.

'Amen,' affirms Alan crossing himself.

'I'm in the eye for an eye and tooth for a tooth camp myself. And where forgiveness is indeed a powerful thing, it won't prevent the wolf from slaughtering the flock.'

I eye the both of them, allowing the sharpness of the words to penetrate the baser parts of their nature that we all possess, however tall or grand the edifices laid on top. Alan closes the matter by saying, 'We do want justice, for him to atone for what he has done in this world before the next. We will speak to Eleri and pass on your number.'

'When did Eleri and Alex move to Pine Valley?'

'After they were married, which was August 19th, 2017,' states Sandra with an unmissable air of propriety.

'One last thing … is Bernard Quinn, an alcoholic from Border Road, anything to do with Jane's family?'

'I have no idea,' replies Alan and Sandra nods in unison.

I rise and begin moving to the door. Alan stands up, cross confusion rippling over his face, 'You've not oncementioned evidence; have you any against the man you say is a suspect?'

'Alan, there is a certain kind of policing that works like faith. You trust in subtle signs and follow a feeling that you can't always define, that won't stand scrutiny and the evidence comes from your belief … it is a beautiful and capricious thing. At the moment I have scraps of evidence, but they're adding up … and in time I hope to be able to sew enough of them together to make a case for his arrest.'

I exit into a low autumn sun hepped up on a whiff of future glory - Eleri Parker-Evans, a would-be Eleri Parker-Jane - I'd bet big on it. A childhood crush of a damaged boy - unrequited yet kept, contained without an outlet to turn rancid.

CHAPTER 21

After sending another taxi and a pizza to Conrad's house I bombard his Facebook friends with malicious rumours - Operation Cat Amongst the Pigeons. I make another bogus account that mirrors an existing user named Wallace Dobbs. Dobbs is a violent drug dealer from Neath and his profile name is Wally Dobbs. Mine is Wally Dobbes and I use it to post:

'I herd u been talkin to the police bout me ... better not be tru.'

Using the same method, I also masquerade as Conrad and troll his friends and the friends of his friends and succeed in stirring some trouble.

At eight o'clock I log in to Chess.com and video call Xavier. 'Buenas noches, Xavier.'

'Nos da, Guillermo.'

'Even I know that's goodnight in Welsh for when you are going to bed,' I say laughing.

'What should I have said then?' Xavier replies, stifling his own mirth.

'I don't know, you're bilingual and I'm not.'

'Anyway, how are you this evening?' he asks.

'Pretty good, how about you?' hoping he isn't going to lead the conversation to where he will probably lead it.

'I've been for a long run and I feel relaxed. But what I mean and what I meant to ask before ... is given how you were in Algeciras ... how are you feeling psychologically now?'

I look away and comb my hand through my hair, words jammed in my head and not wanting to unjam them, 'Fine ... fine now I'm not marked for death.'

Xavier nods and speaks soothingly, 'Yes, the strain was immense. I was worried for you with how paranoid you got.'

In prison, Xavier consumed books and was particularly

interested in those on psychiatry and psychology. The downside is he fancies himself as Sigmund Freud and it is the one aspect of his personality that annoys me.

Guaranteed every third game he'll probe and prod my mental health and apply some cod psychobabble to it. I am a friend and a practice patient rolled into one.

'You say paranoid, I prefer to say acutely suspicious. Not everyone had to watch out for the Romanian Mafia … and I know what you're going to bring up, Aleksi Spasov. Yes, I got it wrong, he was a fucking Bulgarian … but they could have contracted him … and the sly bastard had been watching me … and he was walking towards me with his hand in his pants for fuck sake! How was I to know, he was just scratching his balls … was I supposed to wait until he shivved me to find out?' I sound off my temper fraying.

'I wasn't going to bring that unfortunate incident up, Guillermo, I am just concerned about you,' placates Xavier. 'It is not easy for other people to understand what you went through.'

'I know you mean well, but I have a handle on it. I have it in a box labelled leave alone. So, let us just play, shall we?'

We do and I get massacred. During the game, stray thoughts intrude and ricochet around my head, concentration leaks into other areas and my position becomes untenable but fifteen moves into the game.

I am finishing off a light supper of crackers and cheese in front of the living room fire when my mobile phone rings. It is a couple of minutes after nine and from an unknown number. I pause the Joe Frazier tribute video on YouTube and answer, half expecting a torrent of intoxicated abuse and threats, instead, I hear a clear, sweet-sounding female voice.

'Good evening, I hope it is not too late to phone you, it's Eleri. Is it William Cutter I'm speaking to?'

'Yes, I'm Will and no, it is not too late to phone me, I don't keep regular hours. I am glad you called.'

'I was going to phone earlier, but I got cold feet, then when I made up my mind I would speak to you, I couldn't leave it until tomorrow,' she explains politely.

'No problem,' I say soothingly, while at the same time reaching for a bottle of half-drunk Birra Moretti. 'I take it your parents have informed you that I am a private investigator working for another victim, and briefed you on what I told them about Dominic Jane?'

'Yes, it is quite a shock. I don't know what to say, except it changes what happened to me. If it was Dominic, then the assault was personal ... and it makes me feel worse about it if that is possible,' and hurt can be heard in her words causing them to falter.

'Sandra, told me that you and Dominic were friends up until you went to the comprehensive and got in with a crowd of girls, is that right?' I ask.

'It is.'

I take a long gulp of the still cold beer and ask, 'So, you stopped bothering with each other around ... twelve to thirteen years of age?'

'Yes, I became more interested in hanging around with girls ... playing netball and hockey and shopping for clothes and accessories, you know?'

'Sure ... did Dominic ever show any interest in you as a girlfriend or were you ever made aware that he liked you in that way?'

I finish the beer and while waiting for an answer watch the dregs rolling down the sides of the bottle to the bottom. Flames riot behind the glass from the fire rolling over like waves and the heat becomes too much for Buddy to bear. He gets up from his bed and joins me on the two-seater Lay-Z-Boy.

Finally, Eleri says, 'In our final year of comp, this would have been 2007, he left an envelope in my school bag. I found it and opened it while in class. It was a letter declaring his feelings for me ... he said that he loved me and wanted us to go out together. I wasn't interested in him, and if the truth be told, I didn't really like him as a person either.'

Eleri takes a deep quivering breath and I hear the air vibrate, as it and a chestful of emotion come out of her lungs. 'I'm not happy … no … I'm ashamed of what happened next. I read it to a friend, and she blurted it to the class, and it spread like wildfire through the year … and Dom got taunted because of it. Dear God … is that why? No! not twelve years after, twelve years without speaking, ten years without seeing, surely sweet Jesus no … just because, because I shared a personal letter.'

I'd introduced a complete head fuck to a damaged psyche. I try consoling her, 'Eleri, your assailant is a sick puppy and was predisposed to commit abhorrent crimes. His genetic makeup, his upbringing, a cracked moral compass, and an unfettered will to inflict harm led him to do what he did. He was a gun with a hair-trigger ready to go off, the only question was at who. I think he saw you not long after you and Alex moved into Pine Valley. Dominic lays carpets for a living and was fitting out a house across the road from you sometime in May or June of 2018. You with Alex, his unrequited feelings for you, and a head of steam already building.'

I swish the bottle and suck the suds out of the bottom - it is the last and that is not a word I like where booze is concerned.

'Did my parents tell you that I have forgiven my attacker and rebuilt my life?'

'Yes, they were keen to make that clear to me. They seem proud of you.'

'I put on a brave face for them. They don't know that I'm on four different mood and sleep medications, that I have PTSD and suffer night terrors. I had a crisis of faith which I couldn't share with them, can't share with Alex because he now has the mental capacity of a child. I couldn't deal with the stigma or the fear of living in Port Talbot, so I changed my name and moved to another part of the country. I struggle Mr Cutter, I want you to know that. My parents think faith in God solves everything and it doesn't. I can't really speak to them, I can't be honest about how I feel. I contemplate suicide nearly every day and I have graphic revenge fantasies where I torture and kill the bastard … and now I have a name and a face to scorn and stab.'

This isn't the picture her parents painted and the best I can do is say, 'It's understandable. If it was my daughter, I'd roast his nuts over an open fire.'

'I'm somebody's daughter,' she says plaintively.

'Yes, you are,' I say, and for a moment in the silence between sentences it is Annabel on the other side of the line, and my mind too disconnects from investigation to a simpler form of justice.

'How do you know it is him?' she frets, the sweet voice now jagged.

'I don't, Eleri, but I believe it. I just got to put enough stink on Jane, so the police take a sniff in his direction.'

CHAPTER 22

A reveille bugle alarm wakes me at four o'clock. I silence the alarm and lie in bed for a minute thinking that sleep may be more important than what I plan to do. I brush those thoughts away, roll out of bed and put on the black clothing I'd readied the night before. I run my hand over the right pocket of the light Storm windbreaker, and feeling a tube-like shape know that I hadn't forgotten to place it there.

I drink a mug of strong Colombian coffee as I liquidise the rotting fish with a pint of milk that is also on the turn. I switch the outside garden light on and unscrew the top off the empty squeezy washing up bottle that I'd left in preparation next to the back door. I detach the liquidiser jug and carry both out to the drain in the back garden. Over the drain I fill the bottle, then wash the jug out thoroughly with a hosepipe. I replace the top and put the bottle in a disposable plastic bag.

On the way in the car, I listen to *Research Chemicals by Viagra Boys* and the dirty, driving cacophony gets me in gear for the mischief ahead. I park in Manor Street on a corner of the Aberavon rugby ground. I get out to crisp morning air and an industrial orange sky dispersing over Taibach.

Hooded and gloved, I stride along the double yellow-lined lane into Eagle Street and pass the Telephone Exchange building. I disturb a black and white moggy on the prowl and it scurries under a parked car. Ahead I hear coughing, then see a short woman huddled in a long coat walk out of one of the terraced houses, and sucking on a cigarette she moves towards Talbot Road. A car pulls into the car park of the Post Office Depot; there are lights on in the yard and mail vans in a line ready to go.

My watch glows four twenty-five - a time for the industrious and the wicked or in this case both. The early bird gets to fuck around with the worm is my take on it. I'm waiting for a qualm that isn't coming, a moral quandary that doesn't exist - all the lights are green. Four years ago, I patrolled these very streets looking for people up to no good; I silently chuckle to myself about how tables turn.

The internal mirth continues when I envisage Conrad calling the police in the morning, being put into the 101 queue, and having his crime allocated to a telephone investigation team - which to be blunt is a landfill site for crimes. The officer phoning him back would get Conrad to do his own house to house and CCTV enquiries. If there is no named suspect, or positive and fairly easy lines of enquiry the crime would be finalised pending any results from Crime Scene Investigation, who themselves after assessing the probable forensic opportunities may not attend. No, unless I run into a patrol car the chances of getting caught are as remote as Easter Island.

Into the Mews and a bank of dormant grey windows. I unscrew the top of the bottle, carefully lift the letterbox guard, and squirt the stinking sludge through. I leave half and squeeze out the remainder over the front door. Using my gloves, I wipe off any fingerprints on the bottle and toss it on the lawn.

Next, I take out the small tube of Loctite from the windbreaker pocket and insert the glue into and over the keyhole. Satisfied with inflicting another two small cuts in a campaign of a hundred if need be, I march back to the car and home to see Conrad's former dog.

It is daybreak when I take Buddy around the block, and the smell of freshly baked pasties wafting from behind the Baglan Bakery makes me salivate for one. I walk three laps of the estate and use the time to review the case. Jane is a suspect on supposition alone, and however seductive that supposition is, it is no more tangible than vapour. I need a piece of hard evidence like the size ten Converse trainer he wore entering Jemma Vinson's house.

The thought doesn't make it far before getting gunned down by acumen and experience. What would build a case would be the same thing to demolish one. You can't enjoy fruit from a poisoned tree, there is legislation and procedures for the police to follow and use, which I as a freelancer aren't authorised to access. They can obtain search warrants and use what they find, whereas I would have to resort to a burglary, and couldn't use what I discovered without copping to a fairly serious crime.

An additional impediment is not being able to find out the means, motive, opportunity, whereabouts, and alibi. With a Magistrates extension the police could hold Jane for a total of ninety-six hours. In that time they'd dissect his life, tie him to times, places and people and dismantle any lies he put forward in defence.

No, the best I can do is connect Jane to the victims. Each link on its own is insignificant - probably fifty per cent of the town has an association with at least one of the victims, but five links are suspicious, five links are a chain that he can be locked onto. Add Jane's stature, physique and strength, use of a Stanley knife in his work and you have a person of interest. All I needed to do is to find an association with Jemma. Once established, I will compile all the information into a report giving one copy to Olivia and the other to the investigation team - job done.

Comp kids dawdle from the shops to school, some of them eating breakfast bars, some knocking back energy drinks and a handful of them having the first fag of the day. The girls wear short skirts, some practically pelmets worn with black tights now that the weather is turning cold. A few the boys wear hiked up trousers to the calf and white socks pulled up to meet the cuffs, which seems to be this year's delinquent's fashion with the uniform.

A delivery truck prevents Jane from parking the carpet van outside the shop, so he slots it in one of the diagonal bays across the road and next to the park. Jane climbs out attired in a blue crew-neck sweater and holstered workman's trousers with black padded knee bands. Although the crew neck isn't a muscle poser Jane's physique imposes itself through it. It is as if melons had been cut in two and their halves stuck on his shoulders and chest, either side of his back, and hunks of it packed onto his arms.

Sixty yards away in the Hilux I watch him lumber across the road, open the shop, and go inside. I drop the glove box lid and take out a magnetic GPS tracker. Out of the cab and a spring in my step eats the yards to the van. I slide through the gap with another car and jog across the road to beat an oncoming Transit van.

I nip into the Co-op and buy an *Evening Post,* a chicken salad sandwich, a bottle of cherry coke, a bar of Toblerone chocolate, a jar of fair-trade Guatemalan coffee, a bottle of Jameson whisky and a packet of spearmint chewing gum. I add a bag for life to the amount and put what I'd bought inside.

At the shop door, I slip the tracker on top of the folded newspaper and plot a line to the nearside of the van. It is slanted at a forty-five-degree angle, and an approach to the nearside obscured what could be observed through the carpet shop window. I drop the bag, kneel like a knight, and clamp the magnet to the van's underside. Then up and onto the pavement that shoulders the chain-link fence to the park.

Back in the Hilux, I use the burner phone to send Harris a message, adding drug references that he wouldn't want the police to view:

'Drug dealer drug dealer how does your garden grow
With a lamp's heat reflected by a foil sheet and cannabis plants lined in a row.

Are you ready to tell me what I want to know? Because there are plenty of tricks left in the box if you are not - dirtier and nastier tricks. What is worse than a drug dealer? What is worse than a cheat? What is worse than a grass? What label is the lowest of the low? That's the label I'm going to stick on you if you don't tell me the truth.'

From the spot on Tollgate Road where I have positioned the

Hilux, it is a slingshot to Knox Road. I take a left through a nothing road called Maxim that doesn't reach ten houses and I am there. After getting out of the Hilux I stretch and yawn. A late night followed by an early start, and I owed myself sleep - round-the-clock harassment is tiring.

I knock on the doors around number twenty-six and after getting a couple of no replies, I kick myself that I didn't conduct the house to house before fixing the tracker. I do a dozen and in just over half someone comes to the door. I ask about Jemma and Jane, show a photo of his powerlifting prowess and get a mixture of blank and bemused faces - the rest I'll have to mop up outside of office hours.

I take a stroll around to the playing field and make my way to the back of Jemma's old home. Only a waist-height concrete block wall stood in Jane's way. A scraggy tree leans on the wall like a battered boxer held up by the ropes. A kid's swing showing the signs of rust at the joints, and its colour washed out by rain takes up most of the lawn. Past the lawn there is an old coal shed and a grey-slabbed patio leading to a backdoor.

On the left side of the door is a kitchen window and further along on the right side a bigger reception room window. The window is split into two sections of glass with a bar of UPVC separating them. Two-thirds of it is a fixed panel of glass and the remaining third is an opening window, and presumably a full side opening window, as opposed to a tilting design otherwise Jane could not have gained entry.

I stand there absorbed in twisted thought. Did Jane deviate on this one? Did he wing it? Go out on the hunt to see what would come his way? One of many night-time forages with one ending in Jemma's open window. Mixing up the meticulous with the rush of a rash action. There were no dining room chairs after all, and he had dealt with a man before too if one had been there - so a lucky dip perhaps? Insert a blind hand and see what you come out with.

But what of kids and if she was fat, fifty and not much to look at? Despite all the self-destruction I had to admit Jemma was curiously pretty, not now, not in herself as a person, but back then a tricky-kind-of attractive that threw up questions. The random victim scenario is unhelpful - is a big bloody Bluebottle in the ointment of a consistent M.O.

Pacing back and forth I reject the idea, partly because it doesn't fit the narrative and thankfully more so, if it were left to luck, Jane could intrude on a sweaty sixty-year-old man with a bad case of piles. So, back to him knowing the target beforehand and a planned attack.

Jane couldn't count on the window being open because Jemma generally kept it closed. Probably, he planned a different entry, one that was perhaps more difficult, and then seeing the window open took advantage of the easier access. I think hard, slowly spinning through the crimes like the chambers of a revolver. Commonalities - night-time break-ins, recorded rape and mutilation, victims all twenty-five to thirty years old and pretty.

Differences - Jemma was knocked out from the start and not spoken to, why? - the others were all verbally degraded. I imagine for him the degradation is like the sauce in a dish, creating a frisson to savour before the slashing begins. The malicious whispering of the words, and the tormenting of the blade are both a sequence in a perverted ritual. Jane skipped this part, didn't speak, knocked her out because, because - he was concerned that she might recognize him. Yes, he controlled the others with a threat yet chose to knock her out, didn't say a word to her and sliced her face from behind.

Eleri knew him as well, but as a teenage schoolboy separated by a dozen years of fading memory and sixty pounds of muscle. The shutting down of her senses and the restriction of information to identify him meant that there was a risk of Jemma recognizing Jane.

Walking back to the Hilux I roll the idea around that Jemma's involvement with Jane must be recent or have depth. I need to speak to her again, extend an olive branch of money and put forward my best patter, whilst not forgetting to watch my back, and for that matter my front and side too - the last hurdle is going to be the tallest.

A basic beep and squeak ringtone emanates from the glovebox. I dig out the prepaid phone and answer it with silence.

'You fucking prick, cunt … any more shit and I'll set your house on fire with you and your fucking kids in it… and that is not a threat it is a fucking promise. I know who you are and where you live … and your whole street is going to fucking smell of cooked pork … do you feel me?' rants Harris in a fake London accent of a Roadman.

'Have you finished?' I dismiss, putting gravel in my voice and dropping it a pitch lower in case he chooses to selectively record sections of the conversation.

'No, I don't stop, I don't ever stop, I'm like Duracell … I'll stab you dead every-fucking-day of the week you cum stain. What have you done with my dog? I want him back now!' and he screams the last word like a histrionic teenager.

I am calm and removed from his filthy squawking. I am sitting on top of my head pulling levers and pushing buttons like a crane driver moving a stack of stupid to the place I want it to be. 'Have you finished? There are levels to this. I know what you did. You've caused a loss that you haven't properly paid for, and I have no qualms about making you settle that bill. I want the name and address of who you stayed with the night Jemma Vinson got attacked, or we go up a level of intensity and harm. I don't see MC Pedo getting many gigs, do you?'

'You can't do that, I'm not a pedo … I'm not.'

'It doesn't matter, it's what people believe that counts. I'll make people think that you like little boys … and after that I'll get really serious about destroying your life.'

There are seconds of what I hope is a reflective silence.

'Who are you? Are you one of Morgan's uncles or is his father paying you to fuck with me?'

'I told you before I'm a loss adjuster and the only thing this has to do with Morgan's death is it gives me the go-ahead to be mean to you because you deserve it. My purpose is Jemma and what you tell me will have come from someplace else.'

'I slept at a mate's flat, Austin Ashworth, lives at fifteen Vivian Court, do you know it?'

'Yes,' and I'd heard of Austin Ashworth too, not much of him, but enough to know that he isn't made up.

'Is that the truth?'

'Yeah.'

'Do you know a powerlifter named Dominic Jane?'

'No,' is his brusque reply and I can't read into it either way.

'Are you sure?'

'Yeah, I'm sure. Can you see me hanging around with a roidhead?'

Jane and Harris do make an incongruous pairing, but an expansive answer and one that sought to convince has me suspicious of a lie. Then again, you would want to be believed. You'd want to persuade a man who threatened to make you as popular as Jimmy Saville.

'I'll root about and check, mind you.'

'Do what you like … now, what about getting my dog back?'

'I heard he didn't like the box he was living in and found himself a better place to live. At least that is what he told me anyway. He also told me to tell you … to take a long fucking walk off a short pier.'

CHAPTER 23

White City is a rundown island in old Aberavon. Glyn Street, Enfield Street, Henshaw Street, Glenavon Street, Borough Street, Isaacs Place, part of Ysguthan Road, Burrows Yard and Vivian Court. A circular road cut the area off from the rest of the district and made it distinct.

Corrugated iron, rubble, weeds, and refuse stand in Burrows Yard. Formerly a Council depot and now a walled-off wasteland that at one time was going to be transformed into a small retail park. For over ten years the skeletal girders of two outlets that never were stood as a stark reminder of abandonment and neglect.

The backs of long grey warehouses are the looming end to Borough Street. A five-unit industrial estate is squashed into a single compound at the tail of Henshaw Street: an auto repair shop, a heating engineering firm, and an upholstery company. Rough, filthy, and broken back lanes running behind cramped terraced housing make up the rest of the city. Sold signs, boarded-up windows, bare floors, the smell of damp and depression - a slum landlord's bread and butter.

Vivian Court is social housing stock built in the early 2000s. Built with small pine-coloured bricks, a band of red bricks through the middle like a ribbon and white Georgian windows underlined by the same. The rear of the houses face onto Henshaw Street and Enfield Street, while the front of them is accessed via a footpath off Ysguthan Road or a back lane behind Enfield Street.

I reluctantly leave the Hilux at the top of Henshaw Street and walk a few yards around to the alley off Ysguthan Road. A heavyset woman in black leggings and a blue Hilfiger sweater pushes a stroller over the zebra crossing. The strapped in toddler is sucking on a sippy cup filled with a black fizzy drink. I glance again and unfortunately I am right that it is Coca-Cola, and that the kid probably won't have a tooth in its head by the time she is four. The woman arches eyebrows as wide as strips of electrical tape and throws me a baleful stare. Before anything is said, I turn away from her harshly bronzed and contoured face, and slip into the narrow alleyway.

I walk through looking at door numbers to the back lane where a bracket of houses forms a court of sorts. A cheap black plastic or low-grade leather sofa is upturned against a wall. Its cushions and back have puncture wounds, actual knife cuts by the looks of it. The houses are bordered by black hooped-top metal fencing that have white canvas recycling bags hung off the hoops - presumably because there are no sheds or garages to store them in. One resident must have started it and the others followed suit.

The houses are split into upstairs and downstairs flats and have separate doors. The upstairs flats are accessed via a side porch door which leads directly onto a set of stairs. The downstairs door is situated in the front of the house. Number fifteen is a downstairs flat and I give the door a knock, then another and finally a third. Having no joy, I go back to the Hilux to wait for Austin to return.

To be able to know him when I see him, I search for Austin on social media. On Instagram, I find a shrine to the self, a topless, tattooed gun show portraying a faux high life far removed from the White City. It is a page of carefully constructed and filtered photographs, like a portfolio for *Love Island,* or some other phoney reality show.

I switch to the front passenger seat, so I have a viewing angle into the back lane. I eat my sandwich and between glances read the local newspaper. The front-page story is that plans to build the Swansea Bay Tidal Lagoon power plant have, after much opposition, finally been given the go-ahead.

A section of page four contains a report on the inquest of Callum Tolton, a divorced father of two and former Vizor glass factory employee. Tolton was found hanging from the crossbar of goalposts in the Ynys Park football ground on March 16th of this year - he was twenty-nine years old. The inquest revealed that he was a chronic gambler dealing with an insurmountable debt, and associated loss of home and family. Prone throughout his life to bouts of depression he pinned a suicide note to his chest and hung himself with a length of garden hosepipe. I recount my own brush with being suspended by the neck until dead, albeit in mine it was others who tied the knot and sent the suicide note.

I break a triangle of Toblerone off and remember Jay and I sharing a bar accompanied by two fingers of Monkey Shoulder - 'Vigilante rations' I had called it and Jay had agreed he could easily march on whisky and chocolate. The smile is a hurtful one in remembrance of a good friend had and a good friend lost.

My eyes are out of focus when I see a purple and black figure emerge out of the alley, cross the lane and hover outside Ashworth's flat. I push out maudlin thoughts and sharpen my eyes to see the figure is a schoolgirl from the nearby St. Joseph's Catholic Comprehensive. The shiny purple puffer jacket is worn open, and the loose fat knot of the green and yellow striped tie is the tell. She has her hair in a bushy ponytail and is wearing a short black skirt and tights.

At ten past eleven it is too early for a school lunch break, so she must be bunking off from class. She knocks on the door, then looks around, is pulling a phone out of her pocket, when from the other side of the lane a man on a mountain bike rides up behind her and stops. The man surprises the girl and they both laugh. She puts her hand on the back of his arm and he dismounts from the bike. She grabs his hand, he squeezes hers, and there is a moment leading to a kiss - her on tiptoes, him bending his head to meet her, mouths just an inch apart. Then, like having an icy glass of water poured down his back he pulls away from public gaze, but not before I have filmed their illicit liaison.

I eject myself from the car as if it is on fire and march toward Austin and the girl. He wheels the bike to the front door, retrieves a key from his pocket and while making furtive glances sees my hurried approach. His eyes go to the teenage girl who I can now better see is only fourteen or fifteen years old, to their proximity and the stranger closing. 'Can I help you pal?' he challenges in a nervously belligerent tone.

I stop within private speaking distance, 'Yes, you, can, Austin,' I say spacing the words out for emphasis. 'The name is Mike Frazier, and I'm a private investigator, and I have a couple of questions that you'll know the answer to, and which you've already told the police.'

'Now is not a good time,' he says blinking, then he blinks again more violently, and I realise it is a squint - a single detraction from an otherwise bedroom-poster face. We are eye-to-eye, mine heavy and still, his blues flashing like hazard lights.

'It is a good time because this looks about as right as a duck driving a car,' I say, conveying a cold knowing smile. 'You! you better get back to school young lady.'

The girl looks at Austin and he nods his consent.

Although I have the recording I imprint her face to memory, the button nose, the cute freckles on either side, the black beauty spot on the left side of her chin, and the bitten-down fingernails - a sure sign of a troubled girl. I assess her age again - an advanced thirteen, probably fourteen, barely fifteen if she is that, but fourteen if I had to commit to it.

'Silly girl has got a crush on me. I mean what can you do? I keep telling her no and she keeps turning up at my flat,' he dissembles, tucking his fingers into the elastic waistband of the joggers, and showcasing on the back of his hand a black tattoo of a rose head in full bloom. My deteriorating eyes pair with a guess to make out the word '*Love*' written across the knuckles.

'Yeah, girls these days ... what are you going to do,' I parrot empathetically while forcing down the lid on my disgust.

He is in his late twenties, has a head of thick black styled hair, a fake Mediterranean tan, and teeth as white as piano keys. A solid five feet nine inches is figured into a classic V-shape - I reckon three inches and a squint had kept him in Port Toilet. He is wearing a quality fleece-lined navy jogging pants and sweater combo, and grey red-toed Reebok gym trainers. A slim cord-tied gym bag is worn like a bandolier over the right shoulder.

I hear a door opening and flick my head in the direction of the noise. An elderly man is outside number six picking up his green food recycling bin. He slaps his lips together as if he is eating, though he will need to put his teeth in first. He has wild white hair like Albert Einstein and crazy far-away eyes. I leave him chewing on nothing and fire off a question, 'Conrad Harris has said that the night Jemma Vinson was raped he stayed over your place, is that right?'

A small shrug, a crinkle of the top lip, an expression implying that it is easier to answer than not.

'Yeah, he did, crashed here for one night and it had to be the night the skank got raped ... I had police bugging me for days after.'

Independent of conscious thought I start to size him up. A match for height and build, is no doubt strong, dry on compassion, dislikes Jemma and with a penchant for underage girls is a nonce. Already a dirty line crossed, how far over does the deviancy go? I look at the shoes and they are about a size nine.

'One night you say. Who was Conrad staying with before you put him up?'

'He did say I think, but after two years I can't remember.'

'Jemma told me that the two of you were drinking, what time did you call it a night?'

'It wasn't just two of us ... it was a bit of a party, a few of the boys and some girls. I got my end away and Conrad got the couch,' and he grins smugly like a guy who carves notches on his bedpost.

'How do you know Jemma?' I ask.

Austin points through the alley to the streets across the encircling road and says, 'I grew up with her. As a kid, I lived on Pendarvis Terrace and the Vinsons were around the corner on Stair Street. Jem and me went through school together, then I used to see her around the pubs and clubs ... and I banged her a few times too, that was before she had the kid and became a junkie and a slag. Didn't see much of her after … I'd bump into her in town every now and then, when she was pinching or on the mooch for money. It was only when Conrad started going there that I got to know her a bit again, but I wouldn't have the light-fingered bitch at my flat and we fell out.'

'What about Conrad?'

'He's a fucking leech as well, sponging little prick owes me money,' spits Austin, setting his bike against the side of his door. 'But how do you know him?' I press.

'Conrad is a Neath boy who moved over here … I don't know, say five years ago. He used to live in Harvey Crescent, and we used to play pool for the Fanny Stars in the Port Talbot league.'

I snigger and comment, 'That can't be the official name of the side?'

'The name of the Green Stars RFC pool team is Fanny Stars, it's on the league's website. He now plays for the Railway Club side Kev's Ten Bears, thank fuck.'

'Do you know Dominic Jane?' and the question is loaded with anticipation.

'Yeah, he used to train at the Vitality Health and Fitness gym where I am an instructor, he's an absolute beast,' he answers, exaggerating the lip movements of the words to emphasise the compliment.

'Does Conrad or Gemma know him?'

'He's mates with Conrad, at least he was, I don't know about Jemma,' and he shrugs what I notice are thinly manicured eyebrows.

I smile as a category four firework goes off in my head and explodes in an incandescent yes. Intrigued, I want to know more, 'What have they got in common? Why are they friends?'

'Weed. You wouldn't think it would you? Dominic enjoys a smoke and Conrad supplies him his weed, grows the stuff, proper little farmer he is. They're mates as well, but that's what connects them.'

'Were they mates around the time Jemma was raped?'

'Definitely, because come to think of it he may have been dossing at Dom's before he stayed at mine.'

'Was Dominic at your party?'

'Nah, he's not the partying type, and from what I've seen he's not much fun,' he says grinning, which tells me as much about him as it does about Jane.

'I've spoken to some people who would agree with you.'

I get a puzzled look from him, but he has something else on his mind and curiosity isn't it. He leans forward like a confidant and says, 'What you saw … I helped you. Whatever it is you're working on, I helped you with it … and that has got to count for something right?' and his head slants to one side soliciting agreement.

My face is as still as a millpond before I set about disabusing him of this notion, 'You are dreaming if you think helping me buys you my silence to molest an underage girl. You are a nonce, and they don't get a pass, not ever!'

Austin scrunches his face, squints like an electrode has been jammed into his eye socket and expands his chest. Stepping forward he limbers his fingers and protests angrily and fearfully, his eyes projecting a feverish gleam like a trapped fox about to be shot, 'She is sixteen … and I haven't done nothing, you said you understood.'

'Not everything said is meant,' I goad. 'And you! you're fair game for lies, you stink of guilt, you double negative, didn't do nothing, kiddie … fiddling … clown.'

I see him clench his teeth and advertise a right hook that I'm not buying. I duck under the square-stanced punch and drive a short right hand into his solar plexus like I've drilled innumerable times. I feel the satisfying sensation of my fist sinking into the space between the lowest ribs. My fist tells the truth, the guttural noise he makes is the truth - it is a wholly honest transaction.

Hips reloaded I spring off the left foot, rotate violently upwards, and wallop him as he is teetering on his heels with a clubbing left hook. The punch makes a sweet connection with his jaw and slumps him against his neighbour's front door - it is over in little over a second.

Glassy eyed and semi-conscious Austin makes a mouth like a landed fish, his spasming diaphragm is forgetting how to breathe and his senses, all scrambled up like a dog's dinner, are unable to help him remember.

I walk back to the Hilux feeling good about the morning's work, and thinking there aren't going to be any one-punch shootouts in the roofing trade.

CHAPTER 24

Jemma deserved to know and might be able to add to the picture. Jemma's life is a series of collisions and abrasions. Drama is the default setting, turbulence the norm and a great many people had drifted in, and crashed out of her life. What would she have to say about Dominic Jane? Would she even remember him?

I am sitting in the Hilux at the top end of Victoria Road with eyes on Queens Court pondering this and what part of the daily graft she is engaged in, because being a junkie is a full-time gig. For a thief like Jemma, it is an endless cycle of stealing, selling, buying, and using. Graft done, Jemma could be holed up in room fifteen sucking on a crack pipe and rowing with Nicky Larkin. But crack is a hungry beast that needs constant feeding - sooner or later they'd have to come back or leave, and begin the hustle again.

While I wait, I transfer the Austin footage from my regular phone to the burner phone. Next, I visit the South Wales Police website and file an anonymous online report of child sexual exploitation throwing in keywords such as vulnerability, grooming and sexual predator. I name Austin and where he works, name the school, give a description of the girl, and highlight her age. I upload the footage and submit the report understanding that I'd just flushed Casanova's gym job down the toilet. His nature being what it is, it is better that he is digging roads than correcting the lifting form of young women.

I go into the GPS tracker app and see that Jane has been to Rice Street in Aberavon and Windsor Village on the Baglan Moors. It then occurs to me that the tracker is of limited use. It will tell me his day-to-day business: work, shopping, gym, associates, but not inform me of his crimes.

A cheating spouse takes a tracked car to the house of the person they are cheating with. A bad-back absentee from work drives a tracked car to the golf club. Jane is not going to use his van to commit a crime - he's much smarter than that, he uses an old banger wearing false plates that he can dump and burn up the mountain after. This segues into another thought of when he will attack next. It has been sixteen months since the last rape and mutilation - a long time not to scratch an itch, to vent that hatred.

Coinciding with the hiatus in activity is Dominic Jane's relationship with Eva Gregory. I suspect it had quelled the urge, restrained it, or provided an outlet to satiate his violent lust. I would like to speak to Eva to explore their bedroom habits. I would bet a pound to a pinch of shit that it involved sadomasochistic activity. It could be why she dumped him - it got too real. That said, it is not a conversation I'd expect she would be prepared to have with a stranger. I'll leave a female detective to broach the subject sensitively at a later date. The break-up was in August, and now as October approaches has Jane a new victim in the pipeline? It is prudent to presume so.

At six minutes past three, I notice Jemma limping along the pavement towards Queens Court. She is on her own and putting the least weight she can on the shin I left a dent in. I get out of the Hilux and cross the road to intercept her. I see her wince in pain before she sees me, then jut her chin out in a grimacing underbite when she does. The hard eyes flood with contempt and she drags a lungful of air through her nose like an angry dragon. If she could breathe fire, I would be incinerated.

'Don't hit women huh? You're worse than I ever thought you were ... lying two-faced cunt. Going to smack me around some more are you?'

'Dominic Jane,' I state emphatically as if I am the foreman of a jury delivering a verdict.

The name is as sobering as a slap and shuts her foul mouth. 'Blocky-looking fucker, immensely strong, didn't speak to you as he did the others because you'd recognize his voice. Knocked you out and didn't let you look at him, knew you were on your own, because he knew Conrad was staying at Austin's.'

A brisk wind coming off the sea buffets my back and ruffles my hair. It pulls at the skirt of Jemma's knee-length shoplifting coat, and compresses and lifts the hood to uncover the signature of a madman on her brow. Conflict recedes, tension ebbs, the face reposed for once as her clever, messed-up brain unpacks what I just said.

'I saw him stare into the back of your old house, reliving what he did to you, and he has a connection to all the other victims. I just need you to put aside your hatred for me for five minutes, and give me some answers.'

I look over my shoulder to the entrance to Queens Court; all I need now is for Larkin to show up. I turn back to her, and the fidgeting ticing mouth has returned, the squirrely eyes, and the irrhythmic movements of her body.

'Nicky is on remand, he and Ricky got charged with four burglaries and dangerous driving on Sunday.' Her voice is hard, yet brittle, and although it sounds most of the time like tin being slashed, a softer emotion creeps into it when she appeals to me, 'You're not fucking with me are you, Cutter, not over this? I know you think I'm trash, lower than shit on a shoe, but I'm … I'm a person, a human fucking being, and however much I hate your fucking guts, I wouldn't want you to go through what he did to me.'

If nothing else, we have distrust in common. I gaze at her and with all the solemn gravity I can muster say, 'No, I am telling you the truth, I believe Dominic Jane raped and disfigured you, Jemma, and after speaking to you I'm reporting what I've found out to the police.'

'What do you want to know?' she asks in a semi-pleasant way suggesting a genuine desire to cooperate.

'When you kicked Conrad out, did he stay with Dominic?'

She nods her head definitively, 'Yeah, stayed with him first … he phoned from there begging to come back, then after three or four days Conrad slept at Austin's. Conrad was at Austin's getting fucked up the night I got ripped to shreds.'

'How well do you know Dominic?'

'Not well, he doesn't say a lot. He's given us a lift in his car a few times and called at my house to buy some grass off Conrad.'

'Did the two of you have words or a falling out, anything like that? Or was he perhaps interested in you?'

'No, no, never got that vibe,' and then thinking about it harder, she says, 'He called to buy grass one time and Conrad asked him to stay for a smoke. Conrad likes that Dom is big … makes him feel safe having a big mate that could stick up for him. Craig and Leeza were there too, there were flagons on the table and some whizz going around. I don't remember how it started … I think it was banter that went too far, but Conrad said something nasty, and I topped him … I said he had a soft baby dick that was no use to any woman. Dom told me that I shouldn't have said that, and I told him to keep his fucking pug-dog nose out of it, and he did.'

'Jane didn't say anything to that, just took it?' I say shaking my head lightly.

'Yeah, pretty much. He gave me the eye and I thought lovely boy I can stare too, so I gave it back and he turned away … and a little bit later he left. That is all it was.'

'Did you mention this to the police?'

'No, why would I? It was weeks before, it was nothing.'

In the whole scheme of Jemma's war-torn life, it was nothing. It was, however, a significant event for Jane and consequently became a significant event for Jemma. I say to her, 'Listen, Jemma, it's important that you don't say anything, don't fly off the handle, okay? Let me inform the police and let them deal with it, all right?'

'What could I do?' she asks if she were Jodie, Eleri or Olivia and it comes across as disingenuous, especially as I know her to be a walking hand grenade with its pin pulled.

'Jemma, a shorter answer is what you're not capable of.'

She smiles at that and then her eyes angle off me to Queens Court. She bites her cracked lip and says, 'I got to go and … '

'I know,' and we go on to what each of us is compelled to do.

Whilst listening to a Spotify playlist featuring *The Kills*, *St.*

Vincent, The Doves and others I set about writing the report. Midway through I take a break to throw some kettlebells around. I select a pair of twenty-four-kilo bells, and after a shadow boxing warm-up perform a hundred and twenty double snatches in laddered sets of four to eight reps. I finish the workout using the same kettlebells to bear walk around the garden, and after exhausting myself completing ten one-minute sets I knock it on the head.

After showering and eating I go back to the report and complete it. I re-read it and make some corrections, then read it again. The sum of my effort is no more than a paltry page. There is no space for instinct and intuition - that is a meat that has to be left off these bones. I remind myself that what I have put down on the page is not there to convict, but to point a finger at.

CHAPTER 25

I drop down from the Hilux and close the door. A gust of wind whips up a swirl of crispy brown leaves from the trees lining the Dyfed Road tennis courts, and blows them about me as if I am a figure in a snow globe.

I am dressed for my attendance at the police station in a blue checked flannel shirt, navy fleece gilet, matching chinos and Skechers deck shoes. I walk down the road clutching the brown A4 envelope and rehearsing a spiel. My heart thumps a peculiar effect around my body, a queasy yet exhilarated feeling made up of trepidation and anticipated praise. I round the corner into Gnoll Park Road, pass the Kwik Fit tyre garage and walk into Neath Police Station.

It was built as a bland, space-saving exercise in the mid-nineties, I had worked there, and it wasn't to my taste - too pokey, rooms like cubicles and toilet cubicles as tight as coffins. On top of that, the constant air conditioning dried out your skin and caused it to dehydrate.

I go through the glass push doors and walk across a blue plastic Lego brick floor to the front desk hatch. I press the bell and the desk enquiry officer appears from behind the alcove where the computer, monitor and phone are. She is an unfamiliar face framed in a tinsel-red pageboy haircut.

I clear my throat and say, 'My name is William Cutter, and I have important information concerning the Port Talbot Slasher. I'd like to speak to someone from Major Crime please?'

'If you would like to take a seat, I will phone upstairs and find out if there is a detective available to come down and speak with you.'

I nod, breathe deeply, and walk aimless circuits of the empty foyer.

I meander uneasily for five or so minutes until I hear the lock of the foyer door click. I turn sharply and half of DC Katrina Szerbo is leaning through an open door. At five foot and a spit, she was always too short and petite for the street, but is smart, thorough, and inquisitive enough for the blue-book brigade.

Her chestnut-brown hair hadn't lightened or darkened in the intervening years since I saw her last and is worn in a ponytail. I calculate her service and it must be around twelve years - and her, about thirty-five - a good thirty-five. She still has cheekbones you could hang a hat on, blazing blue eyes that often seemed judgemental, and fat bunched lips poised as if to kiss - and many of the boys had tried until it became known that she is lesbian.

Nevertheless, some still tried hoping that she went both ways, but she only liked women and older motherly ones at that. Her bust creates a shelf in a tight beige cashmere sweater that I notice a tad too long, and the tailored black trousers are criminally flattering to a pair of shapely legs.

I lift my eyes up and say, 'Hi Kat, I see you've moved up in the world.'

'DS now too,' she adds with humour, although she wants me to know it.

'Come through, Will,' and she leads me to what was once the Bronze Inspector's office for the Neath & Port Talbot Division. It was absorbed by Swansea and became the Western Basic Command Unit, and the Inspector's office went over there. In this room I had explained myself a great deal, had my arse kicked and my back patted, and even though the praise outweighed the bollickings, it is the bad I remember, always the bad. It is now a witness interview room where statements are taken.

The walls are an off-white, the floor a drab blue anti-slip plastic composite. The room is windowless, and a fierce fluorescent strip light's white illumination is as harsh on the eyes as an operating theatre's stark glare. There is a poster informing complainants and reminding officers of the Victim's Code, and another of the Force's mantra - to be Proud, Professional, and Positive.

A metal legged desk with a laminate wood top supports two wide-screen monitors, a mouse, a keyboard, and an electronic signature pad. One violet-blue cushioned office chair is behind the desk while two black fixed-legged chairs are to the right of the desk, one for the witness and one for an appropriate adult or interpreter.

I park myself on one of the standard chairs, with my back tilting forward and forearms resting on my knees. The envelope is pinched by the fingertips of both hands as though it just received a coat of wet paint. Kat takes the interview chair and brings out from underneath her arm a blue hardback A4 size notebook. She crosses her legs and props the book on her thigh. She then removes a fancy ballpoint pen clipped onto the page she opened the book to.

When we make eye contact again, I hand her the thin envelope. She pulls out the single A4 sheet and reads it, flips it over and seeing the absence of any more writing flips it back. I should have used a larger font and used more paragraphs.

She flicks her eyes up at me, re-reads it, and then puts the sheet on the desk. She inhales deeply like people do when they are about to say something difficult. The glossy puckered lips are flattened into a straight line, an unimpressed, underwhelmed shape of disappointment that many a human mouth makes.

'It's a bit of a leap, Will, even for you,' and this time humour doesn't clothe the words.

I feel a warm flush of embarrassment, which turns cold, then mean. Two can play this game and I prepare to fire a snide bullet of my own, then thinking better of it, put the pistol back in its holster. 'Kat, it's a pointer, not a case,' and I go about implicating Dominic Jane, touting the ticks and colouring his hands an incriminating red.

'What size shoes does he wear?' and her question severs my argument, more so as the way she asks implies that she already knows the answer.

A reply stumbles out of my mouth, 'I don't know exactly ... about a size nine or so I reckon, I couldn't measure.'

'Jane is a size eight. His name cropped up in the Vinson rape and we measured his shoes along with her partner, ex-boyfriends, and associates. We've been thorough,' and the last words are lingered on long enough to hurt. A two-piece combo, one to the liver and one to the jaw has me floored and my head spinning in its stupidity.

Without a knock the door swings wide open, and standing there arms akimbo, imperious like an Emperor of Rome is Alexander Pritchard-Hayes. The blow-dried and swept up coiffure of his dyed-black hair reminds me of the late mafia boss John Gotti. It tops his head like a crown, and he does everything to encourage the illusion. The slate-grey reptilian eyes are the same - detached and desolate, and when a person is in their gaze, they could be forgiven for thinking that they are in the presence of a different species of human - one whose natural instinct is to throw people under buses. If I was stranded on a lifeboat with Pritchard-Hayes, the first order of business to ensure survival would be to club him over the head with an oar, then throw him over the side.

In his early fifties and of medium height, he has a smooth impassive white face unmarred by lines of concern and the burdens of conscience. The Chief Inspector is a diamond shape, broad across the beam with meatless sloping shoulders and legs tapering into a narrow ankle-touching stance. From the way he holds himself he has the appearance of a ten-pin skittle.

He is dressed in a funeral-black business suit, salmon-pink shirt, and matching tie. Behind him in the corridor is the six-foot-seven mass of DC Mike Porter; not here to provide his insight I suspect, more as an insurance policy to cover the Chief's mouth.

'William Jon Cutter, vainglorious thug, liar, convict, and former disgrace to the uniform,' the senior officer announces as if it is my official title.

The chair suddenly feels very uncomfortable, and I shift position, inflate my chest, and cock my head at him impudently to say, 'What are you trying to look good on now butterfly? still flitting around the Force stealing credit for things you haven't done, and chopping people's legs off at the knees while doing it?'

'You are addressing Detective Superintendent Prichard-Hayes senior investigating officer in the Slasher Case, is that substantial enough for you?' he declares pompously. In another era, in another part of the world, he'd be a tyrant having people put on trains.

'Every time I see you, Alexander, you've gone up a rank and hiked further up your own arse,' I retort.

Kat stifles a grin, and the Super bares his teeth how crocodiles do in neither a smile nor a grimace. 'After three years in a Spanish jail I'd say that you'd definitely know more about anal invasion than I, Cutter.'

Porter gives a short, cough-type laugh and Kat's chest convulses, before letting out what mirth she can't contain in a single snort. A predictable and easy comeback, though effective nonetheless. Prisons and sodomy go together like biscuits and tea - an aspersion doesn't need to be anywhere near true.

Pritchard-Hayes moves in fussy little steps across the room to the desk and picks up the report - the single sheet bending away from him and seemingly drooping in shame. I hang on the ropes waiting for a barrage, a clinical finish with the sheet as the knuckledusters.

There is a gripe from the plastic flooring as he turns on his heels, and knowing he is the most important person in the room he takes his god-damn time.

'This slim offering is a departure from the last work of fiction I read from you in the Larkin complaint, a better reflection of your capabilities I'd say, Cutter.'

A smirk breaks the bust of stoicism that is his face, 'Poor, flimsy, desperate, amateurish and so ... wrong. You're like a sad glory hound barking up the first tree it finds ... pissing against a tree is all you're good for, Cutter' and though you could hardly tell the extension of the metaphor amuses him.

'You see, Cutter, last night we arrested a man on suspicion of the slashings. We have the Chair Rapist in custody, and he wants to confess his crimes. Oh, this is too sweet a gift. Not only do I solve the case, but you serve yourself to me with this!' and pivoting again he struts over to the confidential waste bin. 'The shame and embarrassment you must be feeling now,' he gloats, and in a theatrical flourish, he consigns the report to the shredder, the mechanical teeth gnashing the paper in a cacophony of grinding gears.

Kate mouths the word sorry, but I don't know that she is, I'm not sure of anything. As silent and obedient as a golem Porter blots the doorway. Pritchard-Hayes radiates a gloating heat of triumph, pride, conceit and vanity - the temperature created is unbearable. My blood boils and cooks the wits out of my brain. Hubris would not visit him today, because it had already pushed me off a tall building instead.

The best I can manage is an insult. I rise to my feet and hiss, 'You're a snake, a charlatan, an insufferable prick, and as well thought of as herpes. My one hope is that you're found out.'
'Stick to finding cats Cutter, the right one mind,' and I hear their cruel mocking laughter trail me to the foyer.

Back on the street I feel stripped, deconstructed, and exposed. The sound of traffic is muted, and cars appear out of focus being reduced to barely recognizable shapes of colour. The pavement is a lengthy grey slab devoid of shade, contour, and detail. In a self-induced daze of introspection, I walk back to the Hilux on autopilot. I climb into the cab and drop my forehead against the steering wheel, while an identity constructed over thirty years comes tumbling down around my ears.

CHAPTER 26

The taste of whisky is on my lips as I scoot into the front seat of the taxi. Buddy, me, and a hip flask had gone for a walk around my estate, and while Buddy stopped and sniffed, I partook of a sly snifter. The cabby tries some small talk which I kill off with one-word replies and a sour look that could make a flower wilt. I pay the man and trudge up the long drive to the Edwardian house where this all started and would now end.

Over the mountain black pregnant clouds make a promise of rain and have turned a dimmer switch on the early afternoon. I huff at the doorbell, ring it, and hear Hector growling from behind the door. I hear Olivia coax him into a back room and a door being closed. The slap of shoes can be heard in the hall. Then Olivia covered like a desert traveller by a scarf wound around her nose and mouth answers.

My drunken despondency must have reached out to greet her because her first words are, 'What's wrong?'
'I delivered my report to Major Crime and if you'll pardon my language, they took a piss on it.'
'Look, Will, come on in and we'll talk.'

Her backless mule slippers flap against her socked heel, and a grey woollen jumper hangs like a surgical gown around the back of black leggings. We go to our meeting room and surprisingly the day's miserable light has been allowed access. I plop in the wing-backed chair, muzzy, recriminating thoughts scattering like startled crows, and my mind drawing to a place of failure, and how to explain it. I caress my bearded chin and pluck at a clump of hairs to acquire the sensation of physical pain - a pain preferred over the psychological kind.

Olivia discards the scarf and ties herself in a ball on the enveloping chair. From behind her knees, she says exuberantly, 'The police have got him; you were right they didn't give up and they've got him. His name is Martin Sloper, he's a thirty-eight-year-old unemployed man from the Neath area. He was arrested for indecent exposure along the Neath Canal path and came clean on the attacks … it is amazing news.'

There is a litre bottle of Absolut vodka underneath the overhang of the fat drooping chair, two thirds full and I want a glass. I lick dry lips and pointing my nose in the direction of the vodka comment, 'Cause for celebration?'

'Oh, the voddy … that comes after many causes, is a cause for itself,' and in smiling the extended line of her mouth disjoints into three sections. 'Can I make you a coffee or would you prefer something stronger?'

'Stronger is good. I'll have a screwdriver made with plenty of screw and no rocks please, Olivia.' I order it like it is an old favourite, and although I have a penchant for refined whisky, the truth is I am not particular, I am promiscuous around alcohol - an unfaithful tart that will go with almost anything.

With light now permitted into the sanctum, I can see there is a drinks trolley near the bay window. Olivia fixes me a screwdriver in a heavy cut-glass tumbler and brings it over. I sip the simple cocktail and pleasingly it has plenty of Russian influence.

'What an interesting morning we've both had. I've clashed with Major Crime, and they dismantled me, murdered my dignity, and dumped it in a ditch. You receive a flimsy little report from me connecting Jane to all the victims, when really in a small town there are probably only a few degrees of separation with anyone. I liked him for it, and I fell into a classic trap … I made it fit, although ironically it is the foot that doesn't fit which rules Jane out. Then, you get a major breakthrough with an arrest, and not only that the suspect is singing like a canary. I was right in the first instance, I shouldn't have taken the case, it was beyond me.'

Feeling flatter than a flounder I take a gulp from the screwdriver and tug some more on my chin. She looks at me like I am a dripping-wet puppy missing a ear and tries consoling me, 'Don't be so tough on yourself, Will, you tried and that's all I asked that you do. I know you worked hard and did the best that you could. It did add up and make sense, so don't beat yourself up, all right.'

I gaze at her admiringly; a person who wears a crown of thorns and thinks of someone else's discomfort. Touched I say, 'I've refunded you half the fee and the sixty that is left out of the expenses. I've attached a note on what they went on, getting people to speak to me mostly.'

'There was no need for that,' she says, fanning the palms of her hands outward.

'Yes, there was, I have some kind of integrity left. Did they tell you anything else about the case?'

'Only that they are searching properties and seizing vehicles then going to interview him later on today.'

I nod and drain the glass. 'Olivia, I wish you well. I hope that you gain a great deal of closure after the bastard is put over the wall, so you can begin the process of healing yourself.'

She smiles awkwardly and her sad cow eyes gleam from a film of tears. 'It's nice of you to say.'

Getting up from the chair I chuckle sadly and say, 'I don't often get associated with that word.'

I walk to the door a little more squiffy than when I came in and stepping outside part with the words, 'If Hector ever goes missing and you need someone to find him ... give me a call.'

I opt for the shortcut through the motorway underpass and accompanied by my old friend self-pity plod through the back streets of Aberavon towards town. On Station Road, a whim takes me into The Pig Iron Tavern - a chain pub acknowledging Port Talbot's historic iron and steel industry. The place is dated but not in a quaint or retro-stylish way. Dark wood tables and panelling, deep-brown leather-backed chairs and a hideous floral-patterned carpet of a long-dead great grandmother make up the decor.

I buy a pint of San Miguel and sit next to the bank of tall windows looking out onto the street. The Wednesday afternoon crowd is a gathering of old pubbers. A grumpy, dissipated gaggle of white-haired men suffering with hacking coughs, in near-to-grubby clothes, stooping over cheap, nearly out-of-date beer.

After a grab-and-go breakfast and no lunch, the lager drops down my throat to an idle stomach. I glug sections off the pint to dull the pain of character assassination. Criminals had abused me for years and their crude words would bounce away like rain off a boulder. The key to inflicting harm is truth and Pritchard-Hayes had thrust it through me like a stiletto. It is a trait I'm vulnerable to. I recognize it and allow it to strike home. Bull-headed people, egomaniacs, and narcissists, they're incapable of seeing themselves as they actually are so can't be hurt by the truth. I doubt I disturbed the Detective Superintendent's unshakeable belief in himself one iota. I could make him nervous as I had before, just the two of us in an office with the door shut and me giving him both barrels in resignation - the vitriol teetering at the edge of violence and Pritchard-Hayes squirming. I smile to myself that I'm reinforcing his point.

I get out my regular phone and go onto *Walesonline* and the arrest of the Port Talbot Slasher is front-page news. The article is light on detail as they always are and contains a cringe-inducing quote from Emperor Caligula himself. Olivia had said the suspect was arrested for exposing himself to a woman on the Neath Canal path. It seemed odd, a climb down, a significant de-escalation to go from slashing to flashing. The tendency is for the scale to increase - greater depravity, greater violence, greater suffering - greater satisfaction.

The Caterpillar Man is an apex predator in the sexual offender food chain, and viewed through a certain optic is worse than a murderer. The godlike sensation of selecting a victim, the delayed gratification, the long meticulous preparation, the charge of invasion, and the absolute power there and thereafter of the violation made him a monster, a feared creature, a bogeyman figure in the shared imagination of a town and beyond. Wiggling a dick at a dog walker and getting caught is pathetic in comparison and doesn't stack up - the dynamics are different. It's like a high-end jewel thief stealing a bag of crisps from the local convenience store. But, what the hell do I know, I suppose even a Cordon Bleu Chef sometimes ate a Maccy D. I'd got it wrong, and in the shoe size overlooked a basic level of corroboration. I'm not fit to be part of the conversation.

I get another pint in and sit amongst the deadbeats, the retired and the lonely, those who haven't anywhere better to be, or with, on a dreary Wednesday afternoon.

CHAPTER 27

The fire is now a blackened husk underlaid by ash. It was roaring beautifully before my eyelids were weighed closed by the day's excess. Buddy is curled next to me on the La-Z-Boy, and I am reclined right back like I'm about to have my teeth examined. The tv is on and Film Four has gone off air. I lower myself, switch off the box and let Buddy out the back garden.

It is dark outside, and I blink sleep-stuck eyes to make out the time on the wall clock, it is a few minutes after four. There is an unfinished whisky on the table and I don't let it go to waste. The thought of changing for bed defeats me and I crash face first on the L-shaped sofa in the conservatory. Buddy cuddles up to the back of my legs and sleep comes again.

At daybreak a fat magpie is skittering noisily across the roof, its skewering beak rooting for insects in the sills and troughs. It sees me peel myself off the sofa and flits to the rooftop of the house behind. I shower and change into a clean set of loungewear, make myself a strong coffee and feed the dog. I microwave a small bowl of honey-doused porridge and put the news on.

On mornings such as these after the night before regret hangs just above my head like a tied-on party balloon. And when I'm not regretting the copious amounts of booze I drank, I am feeling anxious and displaced.

Outside the day is cold, bright and windy with the earth sodden from the previous night's heavy rain. I could lie about feeling listless all day, or I could sweat out the poison with a bracing walk up the mountain.

Dressed in cargo trousers, a thermal long-sleeved top, gilet, and woollen beanie hat I look for my walking boots. They are found in the cupboard underneath the stairs but considering how wet it is I leave them there and go into the garage for my wellies.

They are hunter-green calf-length ones and I take them into the hall and to the foot of the stairs. They are my shooting wellies, and I haven't worn them for three and a half years. I slip them on, and they are loose, spurring the memory that I deliberately bought them a size up from the nine and a half I usually take in footwear. I run up the stairs and from my sock drawer get the extra thick fleece-lined thermal socks I bought for winter outings. I go back down and pull the wellies on for a snugger fit.

I am wiggling my feet into them when it hits me like a bullet right between the eyes. It doesn't matter that Jane takes a size eight shoe and the Converse is a size ten. Two, or three pairs of socks would fill out his feet and make them fit. Jeez, could he be that clever? And assuming such intelligence was applied - was the footprint left purposely? Jane, aware of his orbit around Jemma took a precaution to divert blame away. Like Cinderella's slipper, the footprint informed Major Crime's thinking and eliminated Jane. I think back to OJ Simpson at his televised murder trial struggling to put on the blood-shrunk gloves, and how persuasive that image was of his innocence.

If that was contrived, was the open window contrived too? Jemma said she didn't leave it open. The invasion into Olivia Holland's home is also deceptive, the unlocked door just doesn't ring true. My excitement crashes like a wave when cold reality intrudes - it has a man called Sloper sitting in a police interview room admitting the crimes.

The hike up is hard, but worth it for the fresh air and clear panoramic view of the town and Swansea Bay. I let Buddy off the lead, and he scampers happily back and forth on the trail in front of me. We walk the crown of the mountain stopping every now and then for me to loose off a few shots with the Titan at a knot in a tree, or a flat rock I'd set on its edge like a tombstone.

On the way back down, I receive a phone call. My brow tenses in the reflection of the screen as I see it is Olivia Holland. 'Hello, Oliv ...' and I am cut off by a runaway train.

'No further action. Released without any further action. It's not Sloper, he's a liar, an attention-seeking fantasist, a fucking nut job that gets his jollies pretending to be people he's not, and wasting everyone's time in the process. Tom Whelan, from Major Crime, just told me. Told me also that seven years ago Sloper admitted to a gangland murder in Manchester that he had nothing to do with, he didn't even expose himself to the woman in Neath, it was just a warm-up for the big show. He was in Portugal at the time of one of the attacks and a patient in a secure mental health ward during another … aarrrhh!'

I pull my head away from the phone and hear the scream transform into sobbing. I hear the clink of ice against a glass and the careless slosh of liquid being poured. 'Olivia, I know you must be feeling awful at the moment, but are you all right? is your father there with you?'

'Will, the carpet man, how sure are you of him? Is it him?' she asks plaintively ignoring my concern.

'Olivia, I don't know anymore, I don't.'

My confidence has taken a shoeing and although one of those dents to it had been popped back into place by the NFA of Sloper, I still feel tender from the kicking and unsure of myself.

'I trust you and you thought it was him. Deep down you think it is Dominic Jane, don't you, don't you Will?' and from the rapidity of the words, I'm not sure whether she is asking or insisting.

My answer is deflated and said in the past tense as if it no longer mattered. 'My gut said it was him, if he were a horse in a race and that race was who was guilty, at the time I would have bet my house on him. It is not enough though and the SIO won't touch it because it is me that brought it to him. We need hard evidence … facts not feelings.'

'Find it, do what it takes, stick on him and find it … stop him, get what you need and stop him!'

I had never heard something said so desperately, so urgently as if life depended on it and her words move me. It is as if at this moment I held the thin piece of rope that she is clinging onto. It is mine to hold and or mine to release. Neither choice is without consequences, some I can see, others like snakes in tall grass lie hidden and waiting, invisible to you, yet you know that they're there.

'I have some reservations, Olivia, about what it is you expect me to do?'

Shedding weaker sentiment her voice becomes as hard as a diamond-tipped drill, 'You're a capable man, expedient and resourceful … I'll leave that to you. I've taken the liberty of sending two weeks' wages plus expenses to your account.'

'Presumptuous of you,' I say, feeling ambivalent about the double-edged flattery, and not at all annoyed by her insistence.

'As I told you before Will, I'm a ruined princess, and princesses are used to getting what they want,' and she cackles in a slightly demented way completing the gamut of human emotion.

CHAPTER 28

A residual hangover leads to a sluggish session on the heavy bag. After a shower, I fix a breakfast of scrambled eggs on toast, and for the rest of the morning, I drink coffee and apply my menial street copper's acumen to the subject of the slashings. Because I have nothing else and because of what I suspect, I continue to build a case centred on Jane.

The Caterpillar Man is clever, cautious, patient and disciplined and I credit Jane with those qualities too. The rapist has equipment: a vehicle, false registration plates, burglar tools, camcorder, clothing, rucksack, cable ties, socks, lube, condoms, latex gloves, stocking, size ten trainers and a Stanley knife.

Jane has to store his rape kit somewhere and given he is cautious the likelihood is it is someplace other than his house. If I was him, I would buy the stuff I needed well in advance, from far afield and with cash, and then keep it at arm's length at a deniable location. Murderers had been caught on the day of the deed on local shop CCTV buying black bags and butchers' knives. The most serious thing they'll ever do and bugger all prep.

The tracker is still on Jane's van, and I examine its movements over the last few days. Typically, the van leaves St Kitts just after half-past eight and arrives at Tollgate Road shops just before a quarter to nine. From there it travels to a total of three addresses in Port Talbot, and one out of town on the Marlas Estate in Pyle. The duration of time at these locations would suggest he is fitting carpets. He drives from Tollgate Road at quarter past five and stops twice on the way home at Morrisons Supermarket on Baglan Moors. Tuesday and Thursday evenings, he is at his gym for seven o'clock. Jane is home for nine and the van doesn't move after that. There is also another stop at Groeswen playing fields and a detour to Ash Grove where he parks in the curl of the close near number sixteen. Five minutes there, too long just to drop a carpet sample off and too short to measure a job up, but Goldilocks for a little leering trip down memory lane.

The sun is a frozen camera flash shining through dishwater-grey clouds, and a cold breeze riffles through the grey worn streets of Sandfields Estate. The greenery in the gardens of Border Road is interspersed with the beautiful death colours of Autumn. Buddy walks ahead on the retractable lead and we enter Long Vue Road. Behind Jane's house is a compound of garages. The road in is on Long Vue Road, then six houses further is the turn into St Kitts.

I walk along the short diagonal road into a loosely rectangular compound running parallel with the back of Southville Road. Corrugated garages resembling shanty town shacks are aligned to the rear gardens. I count sixteen on the Southville side, seven on the St Kitts side and two set at accommodating angles where the compound pinched to a point at the end.

I know from my time working the beat here that the ownership of garages does not correlate with the houses they are aligned with. With sixteen garages spread over the span of eight houses residents from Southville, Long Vue, St Kitts, Dolphin Place or anyplace else could own them. The same is also true of the seven other garages on the St Kitts side.

Most of the garage compounds in Port Talbot are maintained by the council and rented, and this won't be information contained on the databases I subscribe to. So, with deduction and research out of the window, I'd have to resort to door-to-door enquiries. I could use the pretence of having just moved to the area and having a need for a garage. I'd tell the resident that the council had said that there were no vacancies, and if they are renting a garage would they for a fee give me notice if they choose to give it up.

I bounce the idea around and a few cracks appear. To seem genuine, I'd have to leave a card with a name and mobile number, which I have but with William Cutter Private Investigator as a title. A more significant problem are the other garage compounds to account for in nearby Jasmin Close, Lupin Close, Iris Close, Southdown View and so on. The corners of my mouth turn down as the size of the task looms high and dwarfs me. I bin the idea and walk back to where I'd left the Mazda in Southdown View.

On the way home I stop off at Pets at Home to buy a box of Wainwright's meat trays and a pack of peanut butter and chicken chews. Subway is in the same retail park and for lunch, I pick up a foot-long steak and cheese.

In the afternoon I visit a Turkish barbershop in Station Road for a haircut and shave. The barber takes it down to a number three on the sides. He shortens the wavy top giving more of a tufty point to my hair, which has the effect of making my big old head seem more oval. Then using a cutthroat razor, he reduces my beard to a chevron moustache. In the barber's mirror, I look quite different, like an older version of how Jay used to look when he served in the Parachute Regiment. I pop home and change into more casual, knockabout clothes - a pair of grey Skechers Go Walks, black jeans and a black-peppered grey Superdry hoodie. Then with Buddy in the Mazda, I return to Sandfields Estate.

The sudoku puzzle was easy at first and gave up all the sevens. I worked out quite a few of the fives and filled a line - then it dried up. My eyes scrutinise the numbers, lines, and boxes running over them like a Spaniel chasing seagulls. A sigh is made, and I switch over to my Google feed - I'd go back to it later with a fresh outlook. The clock reads twenty past five; I'd give it another ten minutes.

For the second time today, I use Buddy for cover and walk him along Border Road. Taking scant notice of my immediate surroundings my eyes scout ahead to Long Vue Road, and when I approach its junction, they rove to the corner of St Kitts. Not seeing what I'm looking for I turn and walk to Southdown View.

I hear the throaty, staccato revs of a scrambler engine coming from the subway running underneath the dual carriageway. A red and white dirt bike bursts out from the tunnel, narrowly avoids the bollard that prevents small cars from being driven through there and zips over the pavement onto the road. The rider is a white, raw-faced youth with bright devil-may-care eyes, and fine blonde hair fluttering wildly on his head. Fearful, Buddy entangles the lead around my legs and the youth tears along Southdown View.

I twist us free and walk past a T-shaped flat complex and into Iris Close where there is another standing opposite. Excluding the flats, there are only eight houses in the close and the road soon veers to the right and into the garage compound behind. This one is smaller, having only five garages on one side of the close. They are irregularly spaced apart and in the gaps between them are splintered slabs of concrete and sprouting grass where garages once stood.

One door is rolled back and a lean man about forty is spray painting the tyreless frame of a mountain bike a garish orange. The door of the garage next to it has a bottom corner bent back like a partially opened can of baked beans. The two after are side by side and are nearly identical. They have grey metal strip doors and T-handles with keyholes in the centre.

The last garage is tucked into a corner of the compound and nestled by overhanging trees from the rear gardens of the adjoining street and close. I walk over to its onyx-black metal door; it is a Henderson up-and-over type with a reflective L-shaped handle the same as black gravestone marble. At the foot of the door and at its centre is a T-bar called a Garage Defender. It is bolted to the ground and is obstructing the door from being lifted further than a couple of inches. The garage probably houses a high-performance motorbike or expensive workshop that the owner doesn't want thieved.

I backtrack and take Buddy through the short rat-run leading to Border Road, and pass Bernard Quinn's house on the way to Long Vue Road again. Checking my watch I loiter at the junction, then cross the road to Gloucester House, one of the ubiquitous two-floor flat complexes dotted around the estate.

I stand on the communal path listening to a woman trying

to settle a crying baby in the flat above. The tracker app shows the van has returned home. I give it a minute, pull up the hood, put on my reading glasses and edge out along the path to the street. Jane appears striding out of St Kitts. He has the lead of the Malamute in one hand and a laden carrier bag in the other.

I go down on one knee and retie the laces of my right trainer and when Jane still hasn't passed, I retie the laces of the left. The Malamute barks at Buddy and the lurcher pup runs behind me. The lead snaps tight and I am pulled over onto my backside. Jane grins, brings the Malamute to heel, and carries on.

I roll to my feet, reel the dog in and stroll out into the street. Jane turns into Border Road and crosses over the other side. There is booze in the bag, dumpy turquoise and blue bottles of Frosty Jack peek out of the top - mini scuba tank size shells of white cider incoming to Bernard Quinn is my guess.

Sure enough, Jane lumbers into the overgrown garden, places the bag down by the door, reaches into a work trouser pocket, produces a key, and lets himself into the manky house. I pass and walk back through the rat-run into the garage compound behind. There is no access to the compound from the back of Quinn's house; it is hedged in by the back gardens of Iris Close - Jane would have to use either of the ways I had.

The lean man is inspecting the coverage of the bright orange paint and applying more where necessary. He has an angular face covered by a short scraggy beard, and curly shoulder-length brown hair tied messily into a man bun. I approach him and say, 'I'm a fan of the standout colours myself.'

For a second, he looks at me like I could be taking the piss, but when I nod with unguarded eyes and a smile he returns the gesture, and whilst smiling says humorously, 'It'll help mountain rescue find me when I come off. Do you ride?'

'I used to have a mate who was really into it, he loved all the adrenaline sports and he'd take me on the Afan Argoed trails. Is that where you go?'

'Yeah, mostly, but I travel too. I really like the routes in North Wales.'

Inside the garage, there is a white-framed road bike hanging from pegs on the wall, and suspended alongside it in the same way is an expensive-looking mountain bike. Below them leaning against the wall are bits of bikes and some almost formed but with parts missing. There are two rows of spare wheels in the corner, a workbench in the centre and a rack of cycle clothing on the opposite wall to the bikes.

'Hey, I've just moved into Gloucester House and I'm looking for a garage to rent, somewhere to store a punch bag and a few weights, do you know who owns these?' and I wave my hand across the four garages.

He turns a curved thumb in the direction of the broken door garage and says, 'Old Ron living next door to me owns this one, and the local cats use it more than he does. Jim from Iris Close rents this one for his fishing gear and Paul who is a neighbour of Jim's rents this one for his scrambler,' and the thumb is jerked twice in more or less the same direction. 'The one in the corner I'm not sure of. I think it belongs to somebody living on Border Road. I don't see it getting used.'

'Looks to be in good nick, perhaps if I can find out who he or she is, and if they have no use for it, they will sub-let it to me. Any more information on who the somebody is?' and I look over in speculation at the backend of Border Road.

'Jim would probably know, he is a local councillor, has his nose in everyone's business and runs the neighbourhood watch.'

With my hands in my pockets, I turn towards Iris Close lifting my right foot off the ground as if in readiness to move in whatever direction he sends me. Widening my eyes and smiling like a chancer I ask, 'Which house is Jim's?'

'Number seven and you can say you spoke to Steve.'

For a moment I forget to thank him, because at that moment I'm dumbfounded by how readily Steve passed information to a stranger - gave it away like a week-old newspaper. Then I remember my manners and show my gratitude.

Seven and eight Iris Close are semi-detached houses attached to one another. Number eight is on the end and has a triangle for a front garden to allow for the lane into the compound. Number seven is perpendicular to number six and because they share the same front space, and both have gardens divided into triangles. Absurdly number six has a motor home crammed into theirs, which enhances the perception of number seven being wedged in like an afterthought.

I enter a bland concrete yard and knock on a half-glass porch door. I stand back and notice I'm being watched by a wall-mounted CCTV system. I smile unpleasantly and lightly shake my head at being nailed to a time and place.

A man steps into the porch, he is pot-bellied and of medium height and in his mid-sixties. He has long blood-flushed ears, bushy eyebrows, and a prominent brown mole on the tip of his nose. A thick black moustache sits on top of heart-shaped lips and what is left of his hair is combed over the top. He has on a checked grey shirt, a pair of shapeless blue jeans and wrinkled brown leather slippers.

The man who I presume is Jim puts the chain on the latch before opening the door. His baggy brown eyes regard me warily through the slit that the chain will allow. There is a vague recognition of him that may be real or imagined, that could be swayed by a suggestion to a time and place. An active member of the community, public-spirited, a busybody with years on the clock, and me a former tempest of the town with my own high mileage - I play it safe that our paths have crossed.

Showing my card I say, 'Hello, my name is Will Cutter and I'm a private investigator, although for a long time before that I was a copper around here.'

'Ah, I remember you now, about fifteen years ago you were the local Neighbourhood Policing Sergeant. You look different,' and he fully opens the door.

'Feel it too,' I say smiling, 'Community meetings?'

'Yes, Sandfields West at the community centre in Mozart Drive. I still go and at least half a dozen Sergeants have come after you. There is no commitment, no investment in relationships.'

My mind conjures a faint memory of an awkward bugger with

his heart in the right place. 'Yes, that's the police for you, a right merry-go-round,' and I twirl a finger carelessly.

'Well, Will, what can I do for you?'

'The garage in the top corner of the compound, the one with the black door, who does it belong to?'

'Bernard Quinn, lives behind me on Border Road,' and the left side of his mouth curls upwards dimpling the cheek above in a self-satisfied expression - our conversation has turned to his specialised subject.

'What can you tell me about him?'

'Sad, story, very sad. Back in the day, Bernard was quite the sportsman. He played football and cricket and also enjoyed the social side,' and along with a reproving smile, Jim holds an invisible glass and tips it back and forth. 'Later, when he could no longer dash about the pitch, he replaced the football with darts and played in the pub league for The Dunes. The cricket club, The Dunes, and especially as The Dunes is just around the corner and he was doing a lot of drinking. His wife Catherine met a man more sober and divorced him. Thankfully there were no children involved and she moved away ... to a village in Devon is what I heard. Bernard's drinking got worse, and he took a redundancy package from the Council. They were cutting back after the awful recession of 2008, and sensibly he opted to jump before he was pushed. Now, he hardly goes out and the bottle bin is overflowing. Sad how he's killing himself and how he's left the house to deteriorate like that. I've complained to the Council, but they've said as he owns the house there's nothing they can do.'

'Are you sure Bernard still rents that garage?'

Jim rolls his eyes and answers, 'Yes, Bernard has had that garage for forty years,' then double-tapping a forefinger on his temple continues, 'I know this is still the case because the big ginger lad that puts his bins out for him was over there last week.'

'Actually inside?

'Yes, I went over to mine last Tuesday night, well, a week last Tuesday at ten o'clock and he was coming out. You see, my wife doesn't like me bringing my fishing gear into the house and cluttering up the hallway any earlier. Some kit goes in the car and the rest is laid out ready to go for a six am start,' and the self-satisfied look gets a second showing. 'Anyway, we each gave the other a little fright and he locks the garage door, and then locks it again at the bottom with the T-bar. I asked if the T-bar was easy to fit and he grunted a yes and left.'

'Do you know what the relationship is?'

'No, I don't. Bernard comes from a large catholic family … he's one of seven, so he could be a nephew,' he speculates turning tightened lips in the opposite direction to the knowing grin.

I nod appreciatively and unknowingly my hands are clasped together in front of my chest, gripping, and rubbing each other as if I'd just come into money.

'Why the interest in Bernard's garage? What's this about?' he asks, and the crescent-bagged eyes brighten with curiosity.

'I can't say anything yet, Jim, so keep it under your hat that I asked, okay? But when it is done you will know.'

CHAPTER 29

According to the Screwfix website, they have the PBJ Garage Defender in stock for £59:99, and the branch on the Baglan Industrial Estate is open until eight o'clock tonight. On the way home I pay in cash and pick one up.

I make myself a Guatemalan coffee, get my lockpicking wallet out from the sideboard drawer and sit down at the dining table with the Garage Defender. I open the box and take out the brass-coloured floor plate, two raw bolts, red T-bar and rectangular padlock. The solid steel floor plate is secured via two of three available bolt holes into the ground and under the garage door. At the front of the plate there is a raised fixture to accept the T-bar and to fix the padlock onto. Cleverly, the T-bar has a triangular bracket in which the padlock is housed and protected after it is fixed. I construct the lock and it forces the opening of the padlock to be made an inch off the ground and to the side - it's going to be a bastard of a position to pick from.

Along the top of the T is a sticker with the name of the product, and on its neck is a sticker which brings me confidence. The sticker says, 'Sold Secure' has a picture of a keyhole with rings around it and beneath that the words 'Domestic Security Bronze.' Out of the five printed words the most important one is bronze. Bronze is the minimum security standard of the Sold Secure Scheme. It lowers the price of insurance but not as much as silver, gold and diamond ratings which will withstand increasing levels of prolonged and robust attack.

The bar seems sturdy, the bolts fixing it to the ground are long and thick, and the bracket affords the padlock protection from bolt cutters and hammer blows. A smile creeps across my lips as I speculate the hidden difficulty of the lock mechanism itself. Typically, a thief will use brute force to prize, smash, dig around, pierce or cut open security features and that is what is protected against. A thief picking a lock is rare, which is why there can be less effort put into the defence; it is all about cost.

The smile persists as I stick a tension wrench into the bottom part of the keyway and with my thumb apply varying torque. I take out a city rake and after pushing it in above the wrench and noting the time, begin a filing motion, gentle as first, then more vigorously as if I am scrubbing a stubborn stain off the cooker. At two minutes and twelve seconds the lock gives. On the second try it releases after one minute and fifty-seven seconds of coercion. A third attempt takes longer at two minutes and fifty-one seconds, and a fourth longer still at three minutes and four seconds. A fifth go brings the time taken back down and I get it open in one minute and forty-nine seconds.

I try to beat that time and it requires two minutes and twenty-five seconds of raking and nudging the wrench to get those pins doing what I want them to without a key. I convert minutes to seconds and add the six times up and then divide by six. Two minutes and twenty-three seconds is the average time, the likely time that I will be lying on my side on the cold concrete floor at the back of Iris Close.

I cook myself a twelve-ounce medium-rare fillet steak, some fat chips, peas, and fried garlic tomatoes. At the dining table I eat it accompanied with a generous amount of Coleman's English mustard, and a tall glass of orange juice. I put the fat, gristle, and couple of chunks of steak in Buddy's bowl and he hoovers them up. The taste of the steak acts like cocaine and for five minutes after he's sniffing around for more. Standing up on his back legs he puts his front paws onto the kitchen worktop, straining his snout to the bloody plate where I settled the steak.

There is some crossover between burgling equipment and shooting kit. For instance, the elastic strap head torch that I used for night-time hunts which has degrees of white and red light will do nicely for the search inside the garage. Likewise, the latex gloves that I would wear to clean rabbits and wood pigeons will keep my fingers nimble and printless. A canvas shooting bag with a shoulder strap and a wide flap can hold the second GPS tracker I have and my Nikon DS5300 camera. I decide to include a crosshead and flathead screwdriver and put them in a separate compartment of the bag.

I opt to wear loose-fitting black jeans, a black jumper, a dull black windbreaker and the dark-grey Skecher Go Walks. I finish the outfit with a petrol-green baseball cap and flectarn snood to be worn around the neck.

Feeling too charged for sleep I lay the clothing on the dining room table, and have another crack at the sudoku puzzle that I got stuck on earlier. Straight away I find a three, then another which then helps me place a two in the bottom left box. Then I stall, and for five minutes the blank boxes remain that. I stick with it and work out a nine which triggers a chain of deductions and the back of the puzzle being broken. From there the numbers come in frequent intervals until completed.

I kill time until the burgling hour by watching boxing biographies and classic fights on Youtube. I try to distract myself and not overthink about what I'm going to do; plan yes, question the whys and what fors no. I have surrendered to the need to know - I must know. I am in the tall grass wading to the other side - so far in - perhaps not too far to go - certainly too far to turn back. The jeering of the witness room, the piercing disrespect, the construction of worth, and the need for vindication drown any voice to pull back. I will know, and the inside of that garage, or another garage or even Jane's house is where I'm going to find out.

The super-noon shift knocks off at three o'clock. It is an extended afternoon shift providing a five-hour crossover with the night shift to help cope with peak demand over the weekend. After that, it is a Sergeant and six, which with leave and sickness is more likely a Sergeant and four. Put two at Morriston Hospital or at custody with a prisoner and that left one double-crewed car to cover the town, and they'd be at a call or back at the nick taking a breather.

Jacked up on coffee and minus my phone I exit the house at twenty to four. After storing the shooting bag under the front passenger seat, I bite off a line of black electrical tape, squat down to the number plates and convert a D into a B and then a 5 into an 8.

I ease the car off the drive then stop, get out and remove the tape from the number plates. If I am successful there won't be a crime to investigate. If I botch the job and damage the lock, I'll be undone by Jimbo when the house to house is conducted. If I get stopped by the police, I could say I'm an insomniac driving to the seafront for a stroll along the promenade. I could sell that story but not the altered plates. A simple vehicle registration check against the Police National Computer and the handcuffs would be going on.

At this time of Friday night in a small steel town the roads are quiet. No large nightclubs, casinos, all-night diners, or an Accident & Emergency Department to keep traffic circulating. An occasional car, a four-up taxi, and an ambulance on a blue light run is all I encounter as I reach my destination.

It is a layby on the arterial road to all the housing estates on Baglan Moors. Next to it are the bungalows of Pentre Afan, and across the road a path to a blue metal footbridge going over Afan Way and dropping into Southdown View. Having checked that the coast is clear I retrieve the bag, get out and jog across the road.

The footpath is tarmacked and framed by two tubular metal barriers that look like contorted ladders turned on their side. I climb the zig-zag ramp onto the bridge, my breath funnelling in front like a kettle on the boil. The stars are out tonight, tiny holes of scintillating cold light set in perfect blackness. No smearing grey clouds or radiating orange gas from the works to pollute the magnificence.

While going over there is a loud fast sigh of a car passing underneath and soon the fading hush sound diminishes to silence - the dead of night arriving full of illicit possibility. Striding to the other side I descend the ramp into a corridor of panelled fencing and emerge in Southdown View. The street is shaped like the letter J, a long-bottomed J that can't sit up straight. I come out in its slouched back.

Left I go, snood up, using parked cars as cover, keen eyes ahead and behind and all around. After Daffodil Close, I cross the road and jump over the low wall of the flat complex on the corner of Iris Close. I cut across the dewy grass passing its limited number of houses. I circumvent the building and hurdle the low wall, passing the side of number eight and into the compound.

On go the latex gloves as I march past the ordinary garages to the special one in the corner. I look around the darkened windows of the surrounding houses and it occurs to me that this is what Jane sees, this is what Jane does and a chill runs down my spine, as I contemplate that my nefarious night could also be his. I look anxiously at the rat run, hell knows when or whether he'd appear, as I am now dressed in black.

I get out the two picking tools I'd separated from the wallet - the wrench and the rake that I'd used in the house and drop down onto my side. I wriggle the wrench and the rake into the lock, then as practised vary the tension with my thumb, while prodding and pulling at the pins as if I'm sawing steak with a butter knife. The ground is wet from earlier rain, and my crackling arthritic neck aches from suspending itself above the fall of my wide shoulders.

In the theatre of the moment, the lock does not relent. I keep raking and the fingers ache in sympathy with the neck. Then when I'm considering a different tack it yields. I remove the T-bar and move onto the L-handle lock. Not expecting much from it I roughhouse the plug with the wrench and rake, until in no time at all the handle goes from horizontal to vertical.

My heart detonates in my chest like a series of depth charges as I lift the door and discover a car. I bend under and pull it down behind me, and what is a low rumbling murmur sounds as loud to me as a lorry carrying scrap metal over a potholed road. I wince, and wait a few seconds for something to happen that doesn't.

I stretch the head torch over my head and press the squidgy button for a dim red light. Inside the walls are plain brickwork and are sprayed in cobwebs wherever there are corners and edges. The place is dusty with a smell reminiscent of mouldy potatoes.

The emblem on the bonnet of the car is Kia and in the red light I'm unable to tell what colour it is. I switch over to a weak-white light and the body work is a pea-green. In the thin corridor between the car and the wall I crab walk to the back of the vehicle. I see Picanto in small case embossed on the hatchback door. The registration plate is LB11TNK which makes it an eleven-and-a-half-year-old car. I crouch down to inspect it closer and notice that the caps covering the two screws fixing the plate to the car are missing, but that the screw heads are pristine and not rusted.

The interior is tidy with no food wrappers or bottles in the cubby holes, or muck on the floor mats. There is just a woman's arse air freshener hanging off the interior mirror - disembodied, rounded, in a red thong. The car looks like it was throughly cleaned before being sold and kept immaculate through non-use.

I try a door handle expecting it to be locked and it opens, and a sweet strawberry aroma pleases my nostrils. I check the glove box, underneath the front seats and the back and discover nothing. I pull down the driver's sun visor and a single car key falls out - odd, but not so if you don't want any link to the car. I put it back how I found it and press the car door shut. The boot is clean and empty except for a full green plastic petrol can, which I surmise is an accelerant to torch the car after use.

I lift the flap of the shooting bag and remove the Micro Magnetic 4 Covert GPS car tracker. After switching it on I clamp the two magnetic disks of the palm-size unit to a section of metal undercarriage at the back of the Picanto.

At the back of the garage, there is a scarred wooden workbench and a dusty and battered chest of drawers that had at one time, though not recently, been a feature of someone's bedroom. On top of the workbench there are crusted tins of paint marked along their length by permanent teardrop tracks. I count five cans, two are five-litre cans of Dulux white matt emulsion paint, two are two and a half litre tins of Ronseal floor varnish, and the last is a newer two and a half litre can of Dulux Sapphire Salute paint. Further along the bench is a foot pump, a bottle of engine oil, a bottle of engine coolant and an oily rag.

Being mindful not to disturb the layer of dust settled on top of the chest of drawers I ease out the highest drawer. On the left side folded neatly with collar facing upwards is a fresh smelling and unblemished black boiler suit, next to it is an open cardboard box of disposable blue vinyl gloves, a set of red-handled screwdrivers, a pair of sturdy pliers, a wooden-handled ball pein hammer with a silver head, and underneath them all front and back number plates displaying the index FG61MMG.

I draw the Nikon out of the bag and photograph the contents, turn, and making sure that the registration plate is in focus photograph the back of the car.

I try the next drawer down. Inside there is a small aerodynamic black rucksack with a chest clasp to fix the shoulder straps in place. Next to it are a carefully folded hooded black tracksuit top and bottoms. They are plain charcoal-black, thin, and inexpensive and appear to be new or as far as I can tell practically unused. I photograph them in situ.

I unzip the main compartment of the rucksack and find a GoPro 10 camcorder attached to a mini tripod. My heart flutters with indecision as to whether to interrogate the camera for recordings or leave it as it is. Curiosity as usual outweighs caution and I switch the device on. I touch the nine-dot navigation icon and the recording gallery is empty, or as is more probable has been wiped of the ghastly scenes it once held. He must have transferred them to a USB stick and hidden it well in the house to watch and relive.

I switch the camera off and zip it back in the rucksack. In the outer secondary compartment, there is a hand bottle of water-based lubricant and a packet of Durex extra-thick condoms - keep remembering he is careful and takes precautions, don't ever think he is a dummy, let that be your guiding light.

In the third drawer, my beam highlights a packet of antiseptic wipes, a roll of bin bags, two pairs of thick grey sports socks, and a pair of black hard-shelled tennis trainers positioned on their soles side by side and facing; I see a leaping Puma logo on the tongue.

I pick the right shoe up and bend the tongue back to look for the size and slam dunk it is a ten. He had ditched the Converse like he will the tracksuit and the car. Nothing is brought back to the house or from the house to here, and that goes for the van too. This is Jane's locker room, his depot and toolbox - his separate place of work. I click away and the flashes illuminate the garage like an avant-garde nightclub.

The bottom drawer catches and requires a light jiggling motion to open. Here is the sharp end of the operation, a bunch of triangular-toothed cable ties, a roll of shiny grey seventy-two mm wide duct tape, a pair of black stockings compressed into fat irregular rings, two soft nylon socks joined and rolled into a ball, and the instruments of mutilation themselves.

The first is a folding Hawkbill carpet knife and opening it out it looks like its name. It is a ripping tool for cutting carpet, leather, or other tough fabric. It has a three-inch downward curving blade which is an inch wide, narrows to a sharp piercing point, and is held by a palm-moulded wooden handle.

The second is holstered in a protective leather sheath. Drawn from the sheath it is a silver-metal Stanley knife housing a short triangular blade and with a diamond-pattern grip. I pull down the slide to retract the blade and it is stuck. I examine the blade more closely and in fact there are two. There is some kind of thin spacer between them jammed into the housing. My mouth contorts into a grinning grimace of astonishment and understanding. I put it back and in closing the stubborn drawer a light perspiration becomes clammy, and the dark, cramped confines of the garage becomes as claustrophobic as a priest hole.

I take a deep breath and then another to compose myself. I can't go just yet, there are places to search and perhaps more to discover. Hanging from two pegs on the opposite wall to the one I had crab walked along is a Voodoo Bizango mountain bike equipped with road tyres. Staring at it I start to think of what its purpose is in the mission. A mid-range alternative to the car maybe? Or with back seats flattened and crammed into the car, it could be a method of transport home after a secluded burning of the vehicle.

After seeing that there is nothing else stored below the bike, I look behind and under the bench and drawers, and only finding a cracked aerosol top return my attention to the tins of paint and varnish. To my suspicious mind their presence is incongruous. This garage is a deviant's workshop where everything has a place, has a point, has use in the plan. Jane doesn't store extraneous things that he would need to keep popping in and out for - exposure and attachment to the garage is kept to a minimum.

I'd been on a drugs warrant where a can of paint had been used to conceal a zip-locked bag of amphetamine. I inspect the lids for prize marks and although the cans of Ronseal each have one, they are crusty wounds congealed by rust and varnish. The cans of Dulux white paint bear similarly aged marks of neglect and feel empty in weight. I shake them, and they are noiseless.

A section of the rim of the Sapphire Salute paint lid is chewed up. A flathead screwdriver or other such tool has prized the lid open several times and kinked it. I pick up the can and it has fill weight. I shake the can and its contents slosh inside and something rattles slowly and dully against the sides.

I pull out the flathead screwdriver from the bag and placing it into the damaged lip jack the lid up. I remove it and the can is filled to an inch of the brim with water, and bobbing on the surface is a hard plastic case.

Forming a pincer with thumb and middle finger I lift it out and place it on top of a paint tin. It is black and has the same dimensions and design of a spectacle case. If it is a spectacle case it is intended for divers, military personal or survival enthusiasts. It opens with the stiffness of a clam. Inside, pressed still on a sandwich of dry charcoal foam are four round-backed mechanically cut door keys. They are silver and Yale made, and each has a different coloured dot sticker placed in the centre of the round back. From left to right are green, purple, grey and red.

Like a breath blowing dust from a page of a book, what was obscured is shown, and the light that had once glinted and winked through the foliage of the trees becomes full and brilliant and overwhelming. Suddenly washed by a flood of understanding I have to steady my brain and slot the keys into the crimes, but not here, not while burgling the monster's lair. I turn away from a rabble of competing thoughts, and carefully photograph the mementos of a serial rapist.

The case snaps shut with the force of a bear trap, and I'm convinced jug-eared Jim will hear it across the compound. I put it back in its hiding place and secure the lid. I check that I've left everything as it was, and not noticing any evidence of my presence, I lift the garage door and crawl out. While intermittently looking over my shoulder I relock the L-handle and fix the padlock back on the Garage Defender.

I slink back to the car struggling to keep alert, the crimes intent on barging to the front of my mind. I drive home, pour a hefty Jameson, and sit down to click it all into place.

First as first, Eleri. Eleri, married and making a happy home with Alex was the trigger. It could be that he was close anyway, was nurturing sinister fantasies, while he was on his knees cutting-up carpets in the homes of hopeful newlyweds and expectant couples. The swell of jealousy, resentment, and malice must have been totally overwhelming and pushed him over the edge and some way beyond. So, it was going to be Eleri, despite any difficulty, but eventually it would have been someone else that felt his cold rage.

It did not go according to plan, Alex and Eleri heard the entry, Alex came to investigate, and Eleri screamed. Jane had to adapt and recover the mission, but with moving parts it could have easily slipped out of his control and ended in a bungled attempt.

Jane used a burgling technique that he probably picked up

from the internet. He is not a burglar, hasn't served a thieving apprenticeship, so wasn't shown the tricks of the trade, or schooled in prison by other burglars. He got in, but he wasn't quiet, wasn't refined and he didn't fancy just committing common burglaries to get good - so back to the drawing board.

Jane has access to houses and sometimes has the run of them. He would see keys left in locks or on hallway tables, or hung up on hooks in the kitchen. He took a liking to Jodie Green, and while fitting laminate flooring in her study the opportunity presented itself to pocket a front door key. All he had to do then was make an excuse for why he needed to pop out for twenty minutes. Perhaps he told Jodie he was getting lunch, and maybe he did, and at Neath Market got a Thai tray curry to go and a key copied from the shoe repairman. Then eleven months later armed with this key he smoothly and quietly let himself in.

However, an entry that did not disturb or cause damage signposted to an unlocked door, or a key opened door and Jane wouldn't want those questions asked. This posed a problem, albeit one that came with a simple solution - create a detectable point of entry. So, post burglary Jane bends the door handle guard back and removes the lock barrel, but he doesn't want Jodie to hear him doing this, and that is why he must punch her unconscious before leaving.

On the camera display I look at the photographs I took of the keys. The first one has a green dot sticker and assuming they are in the order in which they were used, and correspond meaningfully with the colour code chosen, then the first is the key for Jodie's front door.

The next attack on Kelly Thomas occurred at Ten Lupin Close. Jane had not carried out work at the house and there was no connection to Kelly that would have granted him access. This didn't matter because Jane had scoped and cased the house during regular dog walks past the address. He worked out that the cat flap provided a viable point of entry, and an ability to remove the key.

Onto Jemma Vinson and a definite use of a key. A purple

sticker: Jemma, Vinson, Knox Street, no violet flowers in the garden, Vinson, vine, vineyard, grapes - purple? Conrad had the back door key and he stayed with Jane for a few days. I check my notes and Jemma had phoned Conrad to get the key back, and Conrad had said that he would give it back when they made up. Jane must have overheard the conversation because he sneaked that key out and got it copied. It made sense now, why Jane dragged Jemma into the hallway. He intentionally put her out of sight and earshot from the rigging of the back window. It wasn't left open, and Jane didn't need it to be, he knew how he was going to get in because he no longer left anything to chance.

The third key is a light grey or could be described as an ash-grey, and is an easy deduction for Ash Grove. For some unknown reason, there was no diversionary point of entry for Olivia Holland's rape - it was left to the carelessness of an unlocked door. Jane might have got spooked, forgotten his pliers, or just the massive ego-boosting confidence of getting away with it went to his head, and made him complacent, as complacent as a god.

The red dot key is a pass to a future violation. One night, tomorrow, next week, the week after that, Jane is going to drive to a house with dying red roses, a lush burgundy carpet fitted by his hand, that has a lone woman sleeping inside called Rosie or Scarlet, or has a family name like Redmond or Redmayne, and he will cut agony into her life.

CHAPTER 30

The mirror above the sink shows a man with a sallow complexion. The yellow tinge to the skin and hazy eyes brought about by three hours sleep, and short-changing the unconscious hours of several nights before that. I slap cold water on my face, rub and wipe it partly dry with my hands, and leave the remaining wetness to wake me up. I shave the moustache off and dislike my bare face. I will grow another beard – I look better with one.

I feed Buddy a bowl of kibble and then drink two jar-tipping coffees back-to-back. Although I feel like binge-watching a series, lazing around on the settee, and eating sugary junk all day Buddy is boisterous and in need of exercise. Five days of good food and care are already showing on his frame, and he is now lean instead of skinny sick.

I head out the door in my brown Altberg boots, a pair of tan chinos, a thin black insulate top, and black ribbed gilet. The day is as sombre as a funeral, and I stay around the estate in case the heavy bruised clouds decide to open up.

I've walked a lap and a half when I see a dog walker that I say hello to come out of a close. He is a tall fella named Richard, is a dead ringer for Captain Birdseye and is slim as a polecat from all the dog walking he does. We are twenty yards from one another when I acknowledge him with a nod and a, 'All right.'

'Yeah, you?'

'Suppose so,' I answer with a sigh.

'New dog, Will?'

'Yeah, he's a rescue.'

Richard looks him over and asks, 'Which centre did you get him from?'

'None, it was a private arrangement.'

'Someone take on too much did they?'

'Nah … they're just a shitty person.'

'Oh … well he's landed on his feet with you.'

Richard's Welsh Terrier steps forward sniffing at Buddy. Buddy freezes bent legged, and his hackles rise. Their noses touch once and as they are about to do so again Buddy bolts behind me taking the eight-metre extended cord to its limit. I brace my arm and Buddy jolts to a halt. I wind him in, and Richard steers his Terrier off the pavement and into the road. 'Nervous pup you got there; he's going to need some work to get him socialised. You have to be careful that a scared dog doesn't become a nasty dog.'

'It's early days, he'll come.'

After finishing the second lap I am as knackered as a third-world donkey and curtail the walk. I put down a bowl of milk for Buddy and make myself a late breakfast of baked beans and melted cheese on toast. The carb-heavy breakfast adds to the fatigue, and I go into the conservatory for a doze.

The phone ringing enters my dream and becomes a phone ringing in the report room of Sandfields Police Station. Although the dream is unique, the theme of it is the same as many I've had. I am trying to complete a task and going around in circles trying to accomplish it. In these dreams the people change, the situation changes and the task changes. This time I am back in the police hopelessly trying to put together a case. What I start gets undone, the facts I think I know alter, the items I have go missing, and people involved turn into people they are not supposed to be. I reach for the phone on the desk and awake with my hand fumbling for the ringing mobile on the drinks table.

With eyes out of focus, I swipe the green phone icon in the wrong direction, tick my forefinger through it again and answer, 'Will Cutter.'

'Are you the private investigator?' says a male voice with an accent someplace west of Swansea.

'That's what my business cards say,' I yawn.

'I think my wife is seeing someone behind my back. I've got a sick, gnawing feeling that she is shagging someone at the office, and I need to know. Is that something you can help me find out with surveillance and stuff?'

'Right … usually yes, but I'm not taking anything else on at the moment. Why don't you try Excalibur Investigations, they have a franchise in Swansea? Husband and wife team … Kay and Robert Mellor, they would be okay for what you're after.'

'I've already contacted them, and they charge fifty pounds an hour plus VAT, whereas you only cost a straight twenty-five. How come? They're not even ex-police.'

I pinch both my eyes with a forefinger and thumb and labour into an explanation. 'They are just charging the industry rate, which puts their services outside of what normal working-class people can afford. When I was in the police I served all communities, everybody, regardless of their income. I can't do that now because I have to live and the government isn't picking up the bill, but I try to keep my fees within the reach of most people.'

'And you undercut the competition … that must make you popular.'

'Outside of the schoolyard that is not a word that has ever held importance to me, and I don't trust people for who it does.'

'Okay. How long do you think it'll be until you're available? I mean, I could possibly wait a week … even though it is killing me.'

'I can't say, my future is … unclear.'

I abandon a game of sudoku and waste the afternoon channel hopping. I fancy going over the road to the Bagle Brook for a pint to rub the edges off the tiredness, but I can't, not while waiting for a tracker alert. Outside, night has drawn in and brought drizzle with it. I stick on my thigh-length, teak-coloured hunting smock, hook Buddy up to his lead and go out for another walk.

I keep the hood down and enjoy the sensation of the fine drops of rain lightly pricking my skin, and determined to push through the fatigue venture off the estate. I walk past the grandeur of Baglan Funeral home thinking there is money in the dead, and notice a clock that I hadn't noticed before set in the pitch of the front gable roof. It tickles me and absurdly I take it further. I imagine the bearded figure of Father Time wagging his hourglass, and pointing a bony finger at passers-by - your time is soon.

I cross the main road and before the hill becomes steep turn at St Catherine's church into Church Road. It is a pleasant and busy street of detached and semi-detached bay-windowed houses built sometime during the 1920s or 30s. A couple of old ladies are entering the church hall, one with an obvious bad hip and reliance on a cane, and the other sweetly holding an umbrella over the pair of them.

My eyes wander away to take interest in a solitary palm tree in a terraced front garden, and I am not cognizant of the van as it passes. Its back brake lights flare and the vehicle mounts the pavement in front of me and comes abruptly to a stop. My immediate thought is the person behind the wheel is a delivery driver falling behind schedule, then both front doors open like beetle wings, and I find out the urgent stop is for a different reason entirely.

Conrad Harris twists out of the passenger seat with a gleeful smirk on his chops, and the buoyant air of a man on the right side of a foregone conclusion. He is dressed in an urban-camouflage jacket worn open over black casual wear and ankle-high Nike Airs. Up on his toes with imaginary barrels under his arms he has blown himself up like a pufferfish. Dominic Jane pulls himself out of the driver's seat and suddenly several reasons appear for me to not be here. A tight, sleeveless red hoodie clings to his physique showcasing deltoids the size and density of cannonballs.

'That's the nosy fuck asking about you and the sly, thieving cunt that got my dog,' yells Conrad, his ratty eyes darting from Jane to me, and to a dog he cared enough about to coup up in a shed. Running is an option, albeit an undignified shit show of an option with a frightened lurcher, lead and road. It isn't my style and my feet stay firmly where they are.

In a bobbing motion, Conrad advances on the balls of his feet stopping four yards in front of me at my eleven o'clock. I shorten

Buddy's lead and he curls around the back of my legs. Jane moves unhurriedly, his thick, corded and sloped neck rocking his head slowly side to side, and presenting a face as happy as toothache. He has wide surprised eyes, so wide it is as though his eyebrows are about to seek refuge in his hairline. He stands slightly back from his friend and is dead in front of me on the pavement.

'I told this motherfucker I had mates and he said I'd better call them then. That's what he said Dom … well here is my mate … and you haven't got a fucking phone to hide behind,' antagonises Conrad, bristling on loaned machismo.

The alarming eyes continue to glare, and a question appears on a pair of scrunched lips that doesn't get asked. I suspect he doesn't want to hear the answer, nor Conrad to hear it either.

I say nothing. I am watching Jane's thick calloused hands and imagining them at work. Intent on getting a fire going Conrad pushes into the momentary silence, 'He wanted to know about you … and, and was spreading shit about me and fucking stinking my house out with rotten fish … and he stole my fucking dog!'

Conrad is agitated, is building a good head of steam and has a big enough grievance to keep it going. There is little to say when you've done what you said you would do, and are holding another man's dog, especially when you are not sorry, and are not under any circumstances going to give the dog back.

'You're going to hand that dog over to me now!' he shouts, tilting his head back and sneering, doing his best to impersonate an off-the-rails psycho.

'Nah, he's all right with me, he prefers not shivering in his own shit.'

'Huh, is that so? dog talks to you, does he? You mental fuck stick … you're going to get smashed now you old prick,' and he flashes his yellow teeth like he's sorry for me for not seeing it coming.

'You mean as much in this as a squirt of piss,' I say, my lip curling in a dismissive smile while thinking bugger it, this is only going to go one way anyhow.

Conrad looks to Jane and Jane shines the full beam of those crazy searchlight eyes into mine, and the edge of my resolve melts. 'Give him the dog,' he commands in a voice that belongs in the depths of a cave, a variation of his satanic whisper to intimidate a man in a street. For it is impossible now, when you know, to just see Jane as a thickset lad with creepy eyes. He is a depraved beast, and I imbue him with unnatural qualities on top of the ones he already has.

I decide that feigning compliance and testing that chin with a fully weighted right cross is how I'm going to get out of this jam. I give myself the go-ahead and I am about to offer the lead, when Conrad lunging like a squash player for a low ball makes a snatch at it; an upturned face full of daring, and the outstretched fingers of a right hand grasping at the cord of the lead.

Instinctively, I twist and drop, dynamically transferring weight from right to left and from high to low. The knuckles of a charged right fist intercept his moving head, and the collision is as terminal as if he had run into a wall. Conrad drops onto his back, his legs still bent in the lunge and his arm stretched out reaching, obliviously and comically giving a direction to nowhere in particular. The punch crushed the cartilage in his nose, flattening it out like a sausage whacked by a mallet, and busting the skin so that in places what is left of the bridge leaks blood.

Out of my peripheral vision, a hulking figure rushes toward me. I react but do not move quick enough to avoid a ginger-haired juggernaut slamming into me. I don't know what exactly hits my body, but I am shoved, shunted or otherwise propelled backwards with great energy. My backside hits the road first, followed by my back, shoulder and knee as the force rolls me over onto my front. The lead is knocked out of my hand, and I hear the skittering of its plastic casing on the road as Jane tears forward. I rise discombobulated and in pain.

Powerful hands grip the smock around the chest and collar. Spinning like a hammer thrower Jane swings me around in circles until my balance is broken and only my toes are touching the ground. I am launched a few feet away from a short garden wall and watch helplessly as I hurtle headlong towards it. The wall chucks me head over heels at the thighs, and my back thumps onto a muddy lawn a couple of feet lower than the level of the road.

I roll to my knees, see Jane hurdle the wall, spring off the top of it and come crashing down on me like King fucking Kong. I collapse onto my back, Jane climbs over my scrambling legs, and pushes aside resisting arms as if they are made of wet noodles. He straddles my stomach; I shield my face and he cuffs the side of my head with a chiding right hook. 'Why are you asking about me?' Jane growls.

'I'm not, Conrad is lying. I've been paid to harass him by the family of the man he killed in the car.'

'Bullshit! You wanted to know about Jemma Vinson as well.'

'Who the hell is she? Conrad's lying … to get you to do this to me!'

'Mmmm … whatever,' says Jane dispassionately in a way suggesting all roads lead to the same place.

Jane shows me his fist before he pounds my head with it. I grip the top of my head with both hands to make a roll cage. I block and weave side to side as his right and left fists set about redesigning my features. With every sinew of strength I form a bridge and try to buck Jane off to the left. He rises a few inches, sits down hard and then doesn't budge any further.

I feel my hair slide across the grass and mud, the still shuddering impact of partially blocked blows, the sharp pain of a lip splitting against teeth, the heat of a swelling cheek, the immovable weight of Jane, and the slow, steady slip into unconsciousness, and if not that, then to be switched off in an instant by a bomb of his landing right on the button. I'm finished unless I get nasty.

I crunch up and hug Jane in an S grip around his back. Burying my head between two slabs of muscle, I wiggle my mouth over to an erect nipple. I bite down on it as if it is a juicy apple and I really like them. Shrieks, hands grabbing hair and pushing my head away - his pain, my pain, his pain much worse as my teeth sever flesh. Frantically cocking his left leg Jane dismounts from the ground pin and pushes at my forehead. I release, roll the other way, and get to my feet. I taste his blood in my mouth mixed up with mine as I breathe and spit the visceral.

Jane's eyes look like they're going to pop as they take in the blood on his fingertips. His face contorts into the shape of a snarl and he charges forward with his right fist primed. Chin tucked and bending to the right I step into a spearing left jab. Jane's head compresses against the back of his neck as my sleek punch beats his slow winger. Jane takes a corrective step to restore his balance and a looping cross swipes the air. Before he can think of doing anything with the left hand, I double up the jab and put another in his grill, and this pushes Jane back on his heels.

A modest front garden is our arena - mud, walls, bushes, and plant pots to trip over and be trapped against. I risk turning away from him to sprint up the short concrete driveway to the street. A twinge in the left knee hinders an escape and by the time I reach the road, it is clear I won't outrun Jane. I spin around and Jane is closing in.

I tag his pissed-off face with another jab, this time off the back foot, and with my back near to a car shakily slide right away from his power hand. Emulating a rugby player Jane crouches with his arms wide, sidesteps to mirror my action and makes a grab for the smock. His meaty hand grips the zip, then he drops his weight like anchors into the road, and I am suddenly stuck in his hurtful orbit.

He yanks me towards his right fist, I shield my face behind the crook of a sharp elbow and jump on the ride. There is a double impact of stags locking horns which are felt and heard more than seen. Weight to the side of my head, bone against bone, the toppling of feet, the helter-skelter of near and far, up and down merging.

The world rights itself, though there is still a slight fuzz and a faulty line of communication between my brain and my legs. Jane has blood tears weeping out of a two-inch cut above his right eye and is wearing a look bullies get when a fight becomes tougher than expected.

Jane tries to lay another right hand on an already tenderised face; I drop my head and meet articulate knuckles with dense bone. I fire off a left hook and skim Jane's chin with it. Jane and I then trade concussive right hands before I get both hands unloading in combination to beat a blurry tattoo on his face. A couple are stinging shots and Jane lets go of the smock with a pained look of concern.

My initial thought is that he is a ponderous puncher and does not hit as hard as a layperson would think. Lifting heavy weights is one thing, throwing powerful punches another, and the two I have learned often don't go hand in hand. That being said, I don't want to take too many or one flush on the temple or chin.

The knee bitches as I backtrack on Bambi legs and the features of my face itch as they swell, but I draw comfort from the fact that Jane isn't winning any beauty contests either. Jane draws a deep breath, then another and advances warily. His arms are bent outwards with hands outstretched, warding against the danger of a highly qualified left hand.

I target the ripped eye with a stiff left jab and annoy him further with another. Jane licks a fattening lip, blinks away blood and rushes in. I shoot a jab which falls short followed by a straight right that Jane times and dives under, and I'm hit around the legs by a hard tackle. I go down on my arse a couple of feet from the side of a parked car. With his left arm still hooked around my legs Jane punches wildly with the other at my abdomen and groin. A pang emanating from below the belt line makes me wince and tense. Desperate for an out I turn my fingers into a claw and poke his eyes. Jane recoils and kicking out against his face I scoot my legs free.

I get up a collection of pains; Jane has the appearance of someone dragged through a thornbush doused in tear gas. Jane steps forward and I make him eat another ramrod jab, and I enjoy the sensation of adding thickness and colour to his face. His expression now is of someone being repeatedly zapped by a cattle prod. I land another discouraging jab, and the idea of another tackle is put out of his head by the feint of a waiting uppercut.

Blinking and breathing heavily Jane grunts angrily and kicks me as though I am a door that needs putting through. I make sure my elbow takes it instead of my ribs, nonetheless, it hurts and knocks me back against the pillar of a garden wall for a secondary impact.

Jane follows through with his fists flailing for my head. Employing a cross-arm guard I weave and roll with the punches and feel them weaken. I slip a right hook and dig a right uppercut into the pit of his stomach, then bring it round as a tight, perfectly leveraged hook against the hinge of his jaw. Jane wobbles and clips the top of my head with his own offering before gripping me by the shoulders. He thrusts a knee into my gut bashing it repeatedly into my body like a battering ram. Under the onslaught, my own strength drains and the ground welcomes me to crumble and become a part of it. His knees try to splinter my forearms, to breach the guard and smash my ribs.

I hear him guzzling air, gassing, losing the battle to provide oxygen for those big, thirsty, low-rep muscles. After blocking a knee, I stick him in the liver and gut with two short left hooks, and a spanner is thrown in the supply chain. Jane bends, grimaces and for precious seconds stops breathing. When he breathes again it is with gargantuan life grasping breaths, and it is then I know I have the beating of Jane, or more precisely he is being defeated by the huge demand placed on his heart and lungs.

I wrestle his under-fuelled arms off my shoulder and headbutt him in the cheek, his head jolts back and a solid left hook finds a home on the side of his jaw. My fist turns to an open hand, moves six inches, and clinches the back of Jane's neck. With the aid of fatigue I yank his head down to meet the first of several uppercuts. Short, savage punches driven by the hips brutalise his face. Jane tries to block, tries to straighten up out of my dirty hold, but I lean on him, and drag on him, change angles, and persist in the task of bludgeoning the consciousness out of him.

A shovel hook cracks the chin, legs sag, the hands drop, and the balance goes. Jane staggers back tipping over his heels and only crashing into a telephone pole keeps him standing. Rebounding off the pole he throws a Hail Mary, a sloppy right-hand swing that I step back and dodge. Just as I see Jane overextending and collapsing onto his knees my foot tilts off the edge of the kerb, and I trip into the road.

I save myself from a rough spill and the injured knee complains. Jane stands, chest heaving and waves of exhaustion rolling through him. I smile, see rain caught in headlights and the road engulfed by white light. I hear a screech of brakes, the sound of crumpling metal and experience the dislocation of sudden flight. For a second that seems to stretch smoky-grey clouds hang in front of an infinite black heaven. The harsh juddering reality of the road breaks the spell, and after flopping and rolling to a stop I am left with my face pressing against a cold, wet street - a captive of a coin spinning between life and death.

I hear a voice which becomes comprehensible. A man's voice, fraught, with an Indian accent, 'Shit, shit, are you all right?'
I can hear, I can understand, I can feel my legs and there is no blood erupting from my lungs. Tentatively I peel myself from the road and my right hip hurts like there's a nine-inch nail driven through it. I dab my earholes and my brain is not leaking cerebral fluid out of them.

Another male voice, 'Hey pal, are you okay?'
'Yeah, all things considered,' I say with pain modulating the reply.
'You should stay down in case there's something broken,' advises a third man.
'I'll phone an ambulance,' says one of the men.

I crawl to the bonnet of the black taxi, grit my teeth and gripping hold of the grill climb to my feet. Bathed in the headlights and the gentle patter of rain five men stand about me, wondering if at any moment I'll be heading back down. Four of them are dressed up young lads on the lash. The Indian man is a pudgy forty-year-old with an aquiline nose and rain-spattered spectacles. 'You just stepped out without looking,' he says, 'I braked but had no chance to stop in time … it's your fault, not mine.'

I take a bold, uncertain step away from the car and although I don't fall, it is as if an invisible hand is roughly twisting the nine-inch nail. Jane has gone, Conrad has gone, and Buddy has gone. I hear one of the men say, 'Mate, you've just been run over … I don't think you should be walking; you should sit down and wait for the ambulance.'

'I'll live … go onto the next pub … I need to find my dog.'

I know the meaning of struggle and I relearn it tonight hobbling on injured legs through the surrounding streets calling for Buddy. Rain and tears mix, pain and weariness collude and loss piles upon loss. Did Jane scoop up Buddy? Did he have time? Not with having to pick up Conrad as well, I hope. That word hope - the damage it does, like climbing to the top of a tree you fear is next for the axe.

I sink to my knees on a patch of grass next to a lamp post and a road, and surrendering myself to what will be, lie down. I'm unsure if I want to be absorbed into the bowels of the earth or float towards the light above – I'll have something transcendent tonight please - not on the menu, okay, serve up another slice of suffering then and I'll have that to go. I laugh and it hurts, but I laugh anyway. Just then I feel a warm, wet lick on my ear, then another reviving lick on my cold, wet cheek and Buddy is standing over me.

'You found me, you found me, boy!' I say, grabbing the fur around his neck and nuzzling my face to his. Relief eclipses pain and acts as a crutch to get me up on my feet, 'Come on, Buddy, let's go home and get out of the rain.'

CHAPTER 31

The text message is difficult to compose, more so as my fingers, knuckles, wrists, forearms and upper arms have been pummelled into an archipelago of soreness. The first draft is too wordy and the second is too blunt. Both are inadequate and a cowardly way for a father to let a daughter down. I bite the bullet and ring Annabel.

'Hello Dad.'

'Hello Bel ...'

'We're still on for lunch, aren't we?' she asks, accentuating *still* and framing the rest of the question in suspicion. 'Henry is really looking forward to meeting you.'

'No, I'm sorry we're not ... I fell over last night and hurt my hip and my knee.'

'What?' she snaps in equal parts concerned and annoyed, 'How badly? And how?'

I could lighten the load but that would lead to more questions and Annabel above all people deserves the truth, even though she won't appreciate it and make me regret telling it.

'It's the case I'm working on. I got jumped and stumbled off a kerb into the road in front of a taxi. It hit me at about ten miles an hour. I don't think anything is broken ... just badly bruised is all.'

'Have you been checked out at the hospital?'

'No, there's no need.'

'You're not a doctor, dad, you're not qualified to say.'

'I'm all right, Bel, I'm fine, just a bit banged up.'

There is an uncomfortable silence in which we both regroup.

'What kind of case is this? What are you mixed up in? No, don't answer, you at home?'

'Yes,' I answer, hesitantly.

'Right! I'm coming over.'

Jeez, all I need is Annabel on the warpath, she is going to have my guts for garters. I pop a couple of co-codamol and wait for Hurricane Annabel to arrive.

I take so long to get to the door that Annabel rings me thinking I'm avoiding her. I open it like a firefighter expecting a backdraft. She has had her hair feathered and subtle blonde highlights added. Her shoulder-length waves gather on a slim-fit burgundy leather motorcycle jacket, and the outfit continues with faded skinny-fit blue jeans and black spike-heeled ankle boots.

'Please, go easy on me, I have had more than my fill of aggravation lately.'

'Good God … fallen you said … out of an aeroplane without a parachute by the bloody state of you. Give me your arm you old fool.'

She leads me into the lounge, sits me down and makes me comfortable with cushions. Buddy pads over from the conservatory and regards her warily from a distance. Annabel squats into a crouch and offering her hand says kindly, 'Who is this handsome boy then?'

'His name is Buddy and he's a rescue.'

Buddy sniffs at her hand and tentatively permits Annabel to stroke his chin. 'You never mentioned that you were thinking of getting a dog,' she says, straightening up.

'No, it was one of those spontaneous, spur of the moment things … he needed a home, so I gave him one.'

'Well, it won't be a permanent home if you keep carrying on the way you are. Is this the same case you got beaten up on last week?'

'I didn't get beaten up and I didn't lose this one either.'

'You sure look like you lost. The other guy is in hospital hooked up on life support, is he?'

'No.'

'Well, there you are then,' she says, standing cross-armed in the middle of the room, looking down and frowning, applying heat like a paint stripper, making me proud and irritated at the same time.

'Same case, is it?'

'Yes … but it is not a grubby little job, it's not stupid or shady or any of those negatives … it has those things, but it is not them. It is serious and worthy and I'm oh so close to catching the creep.'

'Catching who? And for what?' Annabel asks, alarm creeping into her voice.

'A big fish in a big pond … the Port Talbot Slasher no less.'

Annabel's mouth drops open and her arms fall to her sides. 'Good grief no. I don't doubt what you say and because I don't … no! just no, dad, what the hell?' She looks either side, huffs and says, 'Pass whatever you have to the police and stay clear, do you hear me? You've done enough … enough!' and she brings her hands up to signal finito.

'I have, and they laughed me out of the station. Of all the people that could be running the investigation Sod's Law it has to be Alexander Pritchard-Hayes. I won't be humiliated like that again.'

'Go around him,' she suggests.

'No, I'll do it my way.'

'Damn your selfish pride. It's always been the same. Do you know what it was like growing up in this town with the surname Cutter? No fun let me tell you when your dad has arrested someone's brother, father, sister, or uncle. I remember the arguments mum had with you to move on, to get ahead, no! I want to police my town. I know it like the back of my hand, know the scroats and their crimes and habits,' she says in a sharp, deriding mimicry, drawing from a well of resentment hidden from me until now. 'Tell me, did it really matter? Are the streets any cleaner? No, it is still all there.'

I move my mouth to say words I haven't yet thought of. Annabel's bottom lip trembles and a corner gives out to emotion as she says, 'When you left the police, I was glad. I thought you were out of harm's way, and I would get to have my dad. It hasn't worked out that way, has it? Now, Ibiza I completely understand, Iceland too to a degree, you weren't yourself … this though is too far. I lost my mum … Nathan is in Germany … and you seem hell-bent on getting yourself sent back to prison or killed. Is that what you want … to die?'

'No, not now … though for a while after your mother died, I was indifferent about life, I won't deny that.'

My hip aches and adjusting my position in the seat doesn't do anything to alleviate it.

'Whatever you are planning on doing don't do it, because I know you and I know it will involve a truckload of risk. Please, dad, give what you have over to the police, get healed up, close the business, and go and work for Hannah.'

'I am sorry I couldn't meet Henry today … even if I could walk well enough I wouldn't have made a very good impression, would I?'

'As a football hooligan yes, as a respectable and responsible father … no.'

'A fair comment. There is the whiff of the gutter about me. I have shit on the soles of my shoes, grime under my fingernails and blood on my knuckles. But that being so, what you are forgetting is me wading through grief and unpleasantness all my working life paid the tuition fees for your law degree. You will do better than I, I want you to, but don't forget where and what you come from, and don't ever be embarrassed by it. Because whoop-de-do, Henry and his family import wine and live in a six-bedroom house in Langland. That doesn't matter either.'

Annabel makes a show of clapping silently and says, 'I'm grateful, nonetheless save me the martyr speech, you elevate self-pity to an artform.' Then cringing at her own cruelty says, 'I don't mean that, it was unduly harsh, I'm sorry.'

I give a sad smile, 'Accurate though, you've got a good aim girl.'

'No … I don't want you to get the wrong idea, I've always been proud of you, dad. It's just … I want you to stop now because eventually you are going to come unstuck, you'll get it wrong, and you won't be able to get out of what you've got yourself into … Ibiza was bad enough. So, for me, give it up, you know mum would want you to,' and balling her elegant hands into fists she presses them into her chest.

'You brought out the big guns. Right, you need to know this. The media call him the Port Talbot Slasher. Major Crime have dubbed him The Chair Rapist. If names are to be given, I prefer The Caterpillar Man, because he wants to turn beautiful, carefree butterflies into ugly, crippled caterpillars. That is his mentality, that is what makes him tick, it is what he says to his victims. And do you know who he selects … pretty women between the ages of twenty-five and thirty. Before you came to see me last week I had visited my client, Olivia Holland is her name. She is his last victim and apart from being more mixed-up than cement has the most horrendous, disfiguring scars. Words, Annabel, words just aren't up to the task of describing the horror of her face. And when we were speaking, I was thinking that you turn twenty-five later this month, and you would be the type of pretty, bright,successful woman that he'd like to rape and mutilate … and I envisaged it, transposed her ravaged face onto yours … and I made up my mind if I could do something about it I would.'

There is a ceasefire as we each weigh what was said and whether it is wise to say anything more. Annabel paces purposelessly and looks absently out of the window. I sit with my feet up wedged between my cushions watching her.

'Do you know who the Slasher is?' she asks, swivelling away from the window.

'I do, he's a carpet fitter named Dominic Jane. He used to work for Carpet Masters in Sandfields and now he has his own shop called Margam Carpets and Flooring. Be subtle but enquire if the girl you room with or the landlord has used either of those companies. It's unlikely with your flat being in Sketty, but you never know.'

'And you told the police this?'

'Yes, look here is a picture of him,' I say, showing her the powerlifting photograph on my phone that I keep at the ready.

'Eeuw,' is her comment and she makes a face.

'Not up to the standard of Henry, is he?'

'Definitely not. What are you planning on doing?'

'He has a victim lined up though I don't know who it is, but I have a GPS tracker on the car he is going to use. When that car moves, I'll get an alert and I'll phone 999. I'll pass all the details and while keeping an open line to the control room, I'll follow the car to where it and Jane is going. I'll guide the police in, and they'll intercept him.'

'That's it, follow and report from a distance?'

'Yes, that is all that is left to do, serve him up to the police and let them take it from there.'

'Promise?'

'Yes, scout's honour.'

'And when this is done you will go and work for Hannah as we agreed?'

'Yes, if you're sure that is what she wants?'

'You know it is. Hannah has made you the offer several times.'

'I just don't want her to feel obligated to help me.'

'Stop putting barriers in the way, it's not like that. It isn't obligation or charity; it is fondness and gratitude, and it comes from a good place.'

'It is no wonder that you are good at your job, you've argued the hell out of me. Okay, when this is over, I'll go and work for Hannah.'

'Okay, now that we've reached a compromise, shall I take you to the hospital?'

CHAPTER 32

Sleep is sporadic. Pain and the phone on the bedside table the saboteurs. The Picanto is stationary in the lair, as it was an hour ago and the hour before that and the hour before that. I get out of bed with the ease of a flipped-over turtle trying to right itself. The stairs are tackled swearing under my breath and with an iron grip on the banister.

I have co-codamol with my coffee and shuffle around the house to put some oil in my joints. After caffeine, opiates and blood flow work some life into me, I sit at the dining room table and expand my evidence to include the contents of the garage, and what Pritchard-Hayes did. I change a report into a statement, print four copies and sign each of them. I get four manilla envelopes from a sideboard drawer and place a statement in each. The first is addressed to the police, the second to Annabel, the third to Geraint Thomas and the fourth to Olivia Holland. I leave them in a line on the table.

The hands of the clock signal twenty-past-five - not tonight then, but soon I think. Although Jane had rag dolled me and beaten on me he wound up getting the worst of it - was getting the worst of it - until a black cab intervened and put him ahead on the scoreboard.

It is cold comfort though. Sure, the hurt stops and the man dishing it out gets hurt instead, but he'll know. He might make excuses and kid himself he could have turned the tide of the fight. It will be difficult for him though, to fully convince himself of this falsehood, to suppress the nagging, excoriating inner voice that we all have. He'll not want to hear it, but he will, and he'll want to do something to silence it.

This powerless boy made himself into a powerful man. He fashioned an armour of strength and muscle, won sporting titles, and set national records. Then in the night from terrified women, he exerts and extracts complete dominance. The cutting transforms, and the split face and scarred psyche are a form of ownership. Pillars of Power: physique, strength, dominance, transformation, and ownership. Our little street fight had shaken those pillars. He will go out again soon, he'll absolutely need to.

Getting dressed is a sweat-inducing ordeal. Eventually I manage to get on a pair of navy-blue chinos, Skechers deck shoes I can slip on, and a merino wool submariner jumper.

Mid-morning the Amazon Prime driver delivers the cane I ordered the day before. I try it out around the house, and it helps.

I check the van tracker and Jane is out laying carpets. The house is in Prince Street, Margam and the occupants have no idea what they've let into their home.

In the afternoon I order a taxi and swallow three codies with a coffee while I wait. I instruct the driver to take me to Pen-Y-Cae Road. When we get there, I point up the driveway of Olivia's house and he drops me off outside the door. I give a tip this time and ask if he'll collect me in half an hour.

The blackout curtains are drawn - a sign of a backward step. I press the doorbell and after the first ring Hector's barking takes over. Mr Holland answers the door smiling weakly, 'Mr Cutter, I don't think this is a good time, Olivia is feeling … tired,' he says softly.

As mild as milky tea is Mr Holland. I put some extra authority in my voice and say, 'Olivia, will really want to hear what I've got to say.'

'Oh, in that case, come this way,' he concedes, leading me through the hall. 'Had an accident, Mr Cutter?'

'No, Mr Holland, bad things tend to happen to me for a reason.'

'How unfortunate for you,' he says sympathetically.

'Just reaping what I sow,' I say without bitterness.

He chooses not to answer and instead knocks on the living room door. 'Olivia, Mr Cutter is here to see you.'

I hear a response of some kind, although with the music playing in the room, I can't make out what it is. Mr Holland opens the door and I limp through.

The room is lit subtly by its two lamps. Olivia is standing on the track of worn carpet in front of a dark hearth and marble mantelpiece. She has a lit cigarette angled upwards from her mouth like Popeye's pipe. In her right hand, she has a cut-glass tumbler half-filled with fortified lemonade. She is inside a voluminous man's shirt, red-checked flannel pyjamas and furry slipper socks. Her hair is tied away from her face and minus a scarf or cowl, all her scars are on display. The song she is listening to is *Show Me Everything* by *Tindersticks.*

'Will, I've been thinking about you ... oow, what have you done?' she says woozily, aiming her forefinger at my cane.

I brush off the question with a wave and say through a pained smile, 'I've good news to share.'

I collapse on the wing-backed chair with a loud sigh, and Olivia jumps on her fat leather chair like a child trying to be first to the seat. She must feel self-conscious because she makes a peak of her knees, clasps her shins, and hides her face behind her thighs. Smoke rises from behind her hide and the nail of one thumb spikes the fingertip of the other.

I look over to the mantelpiece and the tumbler is now empty. Olivia drops her knees to one side and taps the ash from her cigarette into a shallow glass ashtray resting on the arm of the chair. She peeks over the ridge of her knees and looks at me through misty, tired eyes and says with feeling, 'You're hurt.'

'If I'm getting hurt then I'm usually doing something right ... now, never mind about that. My news is I'm one hundred per cent certain Dominic Jane is your assailant, and if I play my cards right, I'll be able to prove it without a shadow of a doubt.'

Olivia takes a drag on the cigarette and whilst exhaling asks, 'How do you know ... I mean know, know?'

I fidget to find comfort in the chair and each position is pretty much the same level of discomfort. I eye the bottles on the drinks trolley and some vodka or gin on top of the codies would settle me nicely. I look back at Olivia before she asks, and I wind up saying I'll have a tall one.

'He's befriended an old drunk close to where he lives. He is using this drunk's garage to store all the equipment he needs to commit his crimes. Apart from all the sickening, incriminating items in his rape kit, two things are of particular interest. The first is a collection of door keys kept in a spectacle case and hidden in a can of paint. Each key is marked with a colour, yours is grey for Ash Grove. Another is green for Jodie Green and another purple for Jemma Vinson. The fourth key is red and is for his next victim.'

'He had a key for my house?' she says with an expression of astonishment.

'Yes, you didn't leave your front door open. On the day your carpets were being fitted he took the front door key and had it copied … probably at the kiosk in the Aberavon shopping centre. Then while you were still out on your bike, he put it back.'

'Sneaky fucker,' and her face takes on that mean piss and vinegar look that drinker's usually have before they glass someone. In the absence of a suitable face, she screws the cigarette into the ashtray with extreme prejudice.

 'The second is the car Jane is going to use. I have put a tracker on it. When it goes I go. I'll phone the police, lead them in and he'll be caught red-handed,' I rattle off, swinging my hand out and showing an open palm to signify a simple matter.

She needles her palm with her thumbnail and gives a lopsided smile, 'Wonderful, Will, that's wonderful, I'm so pleased. Have you any idea when he'll attack next?'

'Soon, I imagine, very soon.'

She nods and says, 'Good, I need this to end. I've been plucking up the courage to have surgery, Will … and with Dominic Jane rotting in prison I might. If only he could rot though in an Ecuadorian or Angolan hellhole, but he won't, will he? He'll have gym time, snooker and tv, have the opportunity to study, to have visitors, to find God. Doesn't seem right, does it? I'd like to brand him with a red-hot iron. A big sizzling R for rapist on his cheeks and forehead is what I would want to mark him with … and castrate him with a blunt, rusty scissors.'

'Like for like, cause suffering, experience suffering. I'm on board with that.'

Olivia's mouth moves as a thought plays out in her head. 'Do you know what I could do? What would be incredible is to phone Dominic Jane, pretend to be someone else interested in carpets and get him to come up to the house. He can then meet Hector who can chew his balls off. And while he's fighting for his life, I'll cave his head in with steam iron. Wouldn't that be better?'

'Maybe, if you have the strength and stomach for it, but a lot could go wrong, and then there is the aftermath, the consequences.'

'No jury would convict me.'

'Only if it is proved that he is the Port Talbot Slasher. Otherwise, he's a tradesman savaged to death by a dog and eh ...'

'Crazy woman,' she adds.

'Psychologically traumatised is what I wanted to say,' I salvage smiling.

She gets up and retrieves the glass from the mantelpiece. She laughs as she says, 'Fair point, I'll let you handle it. Would you like a drink?'

I envisage a vodka and orange slipping down my throat and ganging up with the codies for a sweet drift. Sink a couple, really meaning four of five and get stupid and abstract. Play some more *Tindersticks*, see if she likes *The Kills*, listen to somebody new. 'No, that's a door I'd better not open, not least until this is over ... then I'll have a proper drink with you.'

'I'd like that,' she says, 'And one day, when my face is fixed, I'd like to have a drink in the sun at a bar near a beach. Perhaps, you can come with me, and we'll have lunch outside with the sun on our faces?'

Her eyes become wistful, and it stirs feelings of pity in me, 'Sure, it's a date,' I say forcing a smile, as the pity reaches down to anger.

During the taxi ride back my work phone notifies me of a received message. It is from an unknown number. I open the message and it is a photograph of Annabel in a one-piece bathing suit standing next to a paddleboard on Three Cliffs beach. A caption underneath says:

'*Cute.*'

Fear and rage churn in my chest - it must be Jane. If he had searched for private investigators in the locality, he'd find my name amongst a dozen in the South and West Wales area. It would then be a process of elimination, checking names with images until he found the bloke he'd exchanged concussions with on Saturday night. From there a search on the name Cutter and affiliations with Port Talbot would turn up Annabel. The clincher tying us together is a photograph on Instagram of Annabel greeting me at Cardiff airport after my release from Algeciras Prison.

The message insinuates that Annabel will come to harm if I keep poking around Jane's business. I'm unsure how to respond. I type 'Fuck you Janet' before deciding against it. There are times to prod a bear, and this isn't one of them. Not replying to the message leaves my involvement and intentions unclear. Agreeing to back off acknowledges that I am indeed looking at him.

I receive a second message in case I'm not smart enough to work out the first. This one is a gif of a young cat sticking his head into an exposed electrical wall socket. The gif contains an apt caption of its own:

'*Curiosity is a bitch.*'

With my mind shooting in six directions, I nearly forget to pay the driver. When I come in Buddy makes a fuss of me, and not being able to take him for a walk I play a long game of tug and fetch in the living room. My movements are those of an automaton and I wonder briefly if the dog can sense this. I come to the conclusion that it doesn't matter to him, and a moving rope is a moving rope.

I check the trackers. The van is outside the shop and the crime car is stationary in Iris Close. What to do? Clear away the mental clutter and assess the threat. I trawl through Annabel's social media output and like a good copper's daughter, it is clean of useful information, well almost. You'd be able to find out that she practises commercial law but not for what firm, though with more digging on a search engine you could. There are no references to a home address. There are, however, too many photographs of cafes and bars in the Uplands to make a viewer think she is local.

I give it serious thought. A given is that Jane is more than capable of inflicting immense harm, in fact, has a pathological propensity to do so - he would snap her neck in a heartbeat. The question is could he find her? And if he did, would he step outside a tried and tested method and take the risk? It is a hard answer to accept and an even harder one to rely on, nonetheless, it is no. Jane has held onto his next target for months. He has every detail worked out. He has a red-spotted key to the front door, and he is going to use it. It is a calculated risk and one I'm going to take. After a little more thought I delete the two messages and phone Annabel.

'You all right?' I ask as casually as I can.

'Yeah, why?'

'You know, we had words … and I want to know that we're good.'

'We are, providing you hold up your end of the bargain and don't breach our contract,' she says with jollity.

'Verbal only, nothing signed …'

'Binding nonetheless in the court of a father daughter relationship.'

'Honestly, I wouldn't dare.'

'How is your hip?'

'I'm on the mend, I think. Co-codamol and a cane help. Did you ask Lacey about the carpets?'

'Yeah, and a local father and son team laid them.'

'Good.'

'Dad, I've got to go, I'm waiting on an important call.'

'Bel.'

'Yeah,'

'Take extra care of yourself, okay?'

'That's rich coming from you, but yeah, I will.'

Time crawls when it is made to carry apprehension. I deaden the minutes by picking locks, although anxiety enters all of them. Even a hearty appetite loses its heart but I make myself eat a peanut butter and banana bagel - if for nothing more than to line my stomach for the co-codamol to come.

The van is now at St Kitts and Jane is probably walking the dog around the estate, dropping off booze, and experiencing tingly feelings of anticipated pleasure outside ten Lupin Close. I stew in my own juices, try to distract myself with a documentary on the Falklands War, but it's the same as putting a sticky plaster on a profusely bleeding cut.

The van travels to Taibach and parks in the car park behind Filco supermarket. It stays there for two hours while Jane lifts incredibly heavy weights at his gym. I wonder what he told Ritchie Grange and the other lifters about my handiwork? Not the truth I suspect - the beast won, the beast destroyed.

The codies make it easier to change into a tracksuit. It is a no-frills, all blue Converse and I match it with the grey Skechers Go Walks. I hang my Trespass jacket on the head of the banister at the foot of the stairs. I put my phone on charge and check that the volume is set to maximum. I lay down on the living room sofa and scroll through films I've recorded. Down past *Goodfellas, Carlito's Way, Casino, Scarface, 8mm, Spartacus, The Shawshank Redemption, Thief, Donnie Brasco, Zulu, L.A. Confidential, Get Carter (original) to Dirty Harry*, where the highlight bar stays and the ok on the controller is pressed.

Sleep arrives late and is fitful. The type of sleep where you don't feel you're sleeping at all and are stuck between two states of consciousness.

I awake like a rabbit hearing a gunshot and the phone beside me is silent and still on the hardwood floor. The time on the lock screen reads 03:31. Distrusting the alert on the app I get into the phone and access the tracker. The Kia hasn't moved - it might not, or could it be that it is malfunctioning and providing a false reading? Another thought enters my head and this one gives me the chills. What if Jane has found the tracker, removed it, and left it in the garage? He knows I'm a private investigator and is playing me like a cheap three-stringed guitar.

My heart goes off in a gallop and I find myself over-breathing. Get a grip of yourself, it won't have occurred to him that you could pick a lock. I stand up and experience a fine giddiness and tingling of the fingers. The opiates have worn off and my aches are eager to tell me that they're still around.

The alert going off makes me jump. It's a siren effect like one you might hear in a nuclear facility when a reactor is melting. I pick up the phone and knock off the vibrating alarm. The app is still open, and a triangle is heading out of Iris Close.

I grab my coat, unlock the front door, and remove the car keys from the lock. I leave the door insecure and climb into the Hilux huffing and cursing. I click the phone into a cradle suction-cupped onto the windshield. The Kia is at the end of Southdown View. I reverse off the driveway and drive out of the close. The Picanto moves out of St Helier Drive, out of Sandfields and onto Seaway Parade - he's heading to Baglan or maybe Briton Ferry.

I pull into the side of the road and pick up the burner phone from the drink's holder. I ring 999 and within four rings I'm connected with the operator.

'South Wales Police. What is your emergency?'

'The Port Talbot Slasher is currently driving a green Kia Picanto registration lima, bravo, one, one, tango, November, kilo ... receive.'

'Yes, yes.'

He's heading along Seaway Parade in the general direction of Baglan, Port Talbot, and is on his way to claim his sixth victim ... receive.'

'Yes, yes, who is ...'

'Call an Operation Berlin and I'll direct you.'

'How ...'

'No questions, just listen.'

The triangle reaches Sunnycroft roundabout. I pull off and accelerate along the straight stretch of road, past the car park to the shops, and then turn right into the short section of road attaching the estate to the A48.

I stop at the junction and glancing at the tracker the Picanto has past the dual carriageway turn off to Briton Ferry, and is now passing the Sunny Mount junction for the westside of Baglan. It has to turn onto the road I'm on the junction of or the M4. I look left along the road and see the headlights of a car straighten as it enters the road - fuck he's coming this way. If I pull out, I am in front, but if I stay put and he turns into the estate he will clock me as our vehicles cross. The 999 operator is clamouring for more information, and I tell her he's just past the Bagle Brook and is on the A48.

The Picanto slows and its indicators propose a right turn. I slam my foot on the accelerator and shoot out ahead of the Picanto before it can make the turn. I look in the rear-view mirror and see the Picanto turn into my estate. I wheel the Hilux around in a U-turn mounting the pavement outside of the funeral parlour. The Picanto has turned right, then takes the first left into The Dell where it stops near the end house.

I drive back into the estate, turn left then throw the Hilux right over the pavement, and onto a wide concrete footpath that runs in a straight parallel to The Dell. I cut the acceleration and roll past the turning circles of Brookside Close and then Millbrook where the backs of the houses face one another. Going past, taking a gamble it is not a back door key because I can't cover all the bases. From where he is parked, he could go right into the Dell or left into a seven-house section of Heol Y Nant. The front of the Dell has ten bungalows occupied by elderly couples and white-haired widows. I'd walked a dog around there for years and never saw anyone who wasn't eligible for a bus pass. It is one of the seven.

I stop at the side of a house that is at the other end of the section. Jane one side and me the other and one of the seven our rendezvous. 'Destination Heol Y Nant, next to The Dell, silent approach,' I say, before switching off the phone and getting out of the Hilux.

With the hood over my head and snood up, I creep along a head-high hedge and low wall combo. To the left, there is a ring-metal fence shutting off a flood defence for the brook, that separates the houses from the rest of Heol Y Nant. Across the road in front is a high wooden fence blocking off the motorway, and behind the fence is a line of trees, languid tonight in a layer of mist. In these life-changing seconds no sound, silence, except for the internal workings of a body amplified. The smell of dew on the grass, and the night air fresh and virgin.

I take a chance and peek a part of my head around the corner. Nothing, the pavement in front of the houses is clear. Is he already inside? There is a Transit van parked outside the end house. I lurch across the pavement to the cover of its back, the pain from the hip and knee stealing my breath. I cling to the side of the van as if it is a ledge on the ninth floor of a building. Furtively, I edge my head to the corner of the passenger window looking through it, and the windshield at the length of pavement.

The call should have already been transferred to a dispatcher, who would immediately put it out over the radio as an Operation Berlin. On hearing that broadcast every available unit would respond and flood the area. But the nearest unit could be ten minutes away or more - For now I'm on my own.

Then I see it come around the corner. An ominous, hulking black presence, black boiler suit, black hood, black gauze face and blue surgical gloves looking like a nightmare made flesh. It strides past a house with a child's trampoline in the front garden. I stay still and watch. After the malevolent figure passes the fourth house, it puts its left hand in the boiler suit pocket and stops outside the garden gate of the fifth house. It looks over the houses, glances behind and goes through the little latch gate.

The house has grey-framed windows and UPVC door with small diamond windows arranged in a crescent. The garden has an ornamental fountain set in a bed of stone chippings, and a grey metal bench placed beneath the front living room window. A young woman had made aesthetic choices and personalized a space. Chippings or pebbles? What bench? Which water feature? are the decisions of an animal without a predator. What would happen would make them and nearly everything else irrelevant.

I remove my hands from my coat pockets and dragging reluctant legs cover the distance to the chosen house. Supercharging on adrenaline the air crackles and pain becomes muted. It pauses midway on the garden path, and momentarily examines the closed blinds of the front window before continuing to the door. I step up to the open gate and stretch my hands apart. I am about ten yards behind The Caterpillar Man as I watch him insert the key into the lock. A dark band appears as the door opens. I shout, 'Oi!'

The black figure spins around and I see the compressed and distorted facial features through the forks of the Titan. The dimple of the top fork already where I want it to be, I release the .47 calibre lead ball. The band flaps and falls about the forks with a thwap. Then a split second later there is a sharp knock of lead butting bone. The black figure nods as if acknowledging a friend, and then falls back into the door frame.

I take another ball bearing out of my coat pocket and without taking my eyes off the creature reload the catapult. For a few seconds it stays awkwardly propped against the frame. The key drops out of its hand and clinks against the concrete path. The hood slips off as a latex covered hand claws ineffectually at the stocking. A thumb hooks under the elastic hitching it halfway up its face, creating a division of pale and dark from the left eyelid to the right corner of the mouth. It is Jane.

Jane totters forward as if walking on uneven lead feet. He stops and sways from the back of his heels to the tips of his toes. He emits a long inhuman groan sounding how I imagine a cow would sound if it had vocal cords. His motor difficulties and inability to speak are easily explained by the .47-inch cavity in the centre of his forehead, which is busy oozing a stream of blood into and out of the stocking.

Jane's right hand fumbles in the boiler suit pocket and I maintain aim on his head. A bit more action from him and I'll unleash a finisher. He stares at me vacantly and so does the dense, black, and unblinking third eye. The left corner of his bottom lip seems dragged down by an invisible fishhook. The hand keeps rummaging. Another bovine groan. My thumb and forefinger twitch. The hand about the pocket flops to his side and Jane tilts over.

He veers off the path, his feet crunching the chippings in quickening steps vainly trying to keep him vertical. Jane runs blindly into the waist-high garden wall, and with the slap of flesh against brick it bends him in two and rocks him to a stop. Blood drops patter on the pavement and instead of moans, there is deep agonal breathing. The partly concealed face is pressed to the wall. The tips of latex encased fingers dangle an inch from the pavement. A pool of blood forms and expands.

Hung over the wall like this he reminds me of an outlaw slung over the saddle of a horse. I shouldn't leave him in this position because with all that weight on his stomach he could asphyxiate. Shouldn't in the medical sense, morally though, with a torture pack strapped to his back - he can hang there and suffocate.

I put the Titan back in the left pocket and the ball in the other. I survey the house and the ones on either side for a camera - wall-mounted and doorbell. Not seeing any, I cautiously search the pocket he was keen to extract something from. Inside, in a locked open position is the Hawkbill knife. I take it out and place it on top of the wall several feet away from a dying Dominic Jane.

It is justifiable shooting, nonetheless, there is no point dealing in narrow margins when you don't have to. The way I'll be telling it is that he already had the knife in his hand and dropped it near to where he is now. My defence arranged, and whilst keeping an eye on the prize, I get out my phone and ring Olivia. She picks up immediately.

'Will.'

'Olivia, I caught him, caught him in the act.'

'Yes!' she cries, 'Yes!' in savage sounding joy. 'Do the police have him?'

'No, I have him,' I state with naked pride.

'Captured him ... killed him?'

'In between ... he has a ball bearing the size of a Malteser lodged inside his skull. He'll die or be left with the brain activity of a turnip. The police are on their way.'

'I knew I could count on you to do ... what was right, what was necessary,' she says with an elated sense of seriousness.

'To kill a man, to put him a decreasing inch from death, is that what you mean you could count on?'

'Yes, if I'm honest that was always there in my mind ... that if you found him, you'd kill him.'

'Olivia ... I'm not a ...'

'Oh Will, you are, in the best possible sense of the word, you are. My father loves me dearly, but he has a soft heart and just couldn't. You and Jay killed those sex traffickers in Ibiza because you had to, you could, and they deserved it. It's a good thing, Will, a vastly under-valued ability that most people don't have ... because the truth is ... it takes a killer to slay a monster.'

'Olivia ...' and I stop reaching for denial or explanation. No one had made me do anything. I steered my own course to a destination I had been before, am at now, and perhaps could even be again. Olivia, simply saw me for what I am and gave me a job to do, hoping I would do it the way I have. If the shoe fits, I suppose. I smile at that and the smile breaks into a chuckle - there is another upside - Alexander Pritchard-Hayes is going to have an apoplectic fit when he finds out. When it becomes known what he did, what he ignored, the ignominy and sanction rained down on him is going to be devastating.

'Will, thank you, thank you ... I may now finally be able to sleep, and not be constantly awake at the time of when it happened,' she says, and her relief is palpable.

I hear car engines being pushed hard and know that in seconds I'm going to be thrust into a circus.

'You're a good boy,' she says affectionately.

'Pardon?'

'The dog … I was saying he's a good boy.'

'Thank you for reading a book in the William Cutter Hardboiled Crime Series. Gaining traction as an independent author requires visibility and validation. So, if you have the time and inclination please consider leaving a rating or review. It really does help.'